They shared unusual black eyes. Other than that, he must look like the birth father of whom he'd found no trace. Averting his face from the fifty-six-year-old woman he'd driven six hundred miles to see, he tossed around conversation starters.

"Just wondering why you gave me away when I was hours old." Or "Thought you might have changed your mind about having a son." Neither would do.

No one knew his feelings about his adoption. His parents would have been upset, and he'd been a little ashamed that his own mother had given him away. As an adult, he'd lost any concern for his past in his focus on his family.

His children remained his first concern, but now that he saw Eliza Calvert dancing up the walkway in her husband's arms, Sam longed to know someone else who shared the blood that ran in his veins.

If Eliza accepted them, his daughters would never be alone again.

Another woman climbed out of the car. Taller than Eliza, she was slender but curvy. She must be Molly Calvert.

Sam opened the car door with trepidation. Eliza had adopted Molly when she was fifteen. Would she resent him and the girls if Eliza accepted them?

Dear Reader,

Molly Calvert has one priority: family.

Her first family—her birth family—abandoned her, but
then the Calverts took her in. It's from them that she
learned about love and family. And it's to them that
she feels she owes everything. And that sense of debt
is what makes her different from her Calvert "cousins."

When Sam Lockwood comes to town, he's the last man
Molly should fall for. A widower with two daughters, he's
searched for his birth mother so that his children will
always have family. But his birth mother is Eliza Calvert,
the same woman who adopted Molly and delivered her
from danger into a safe life.

Eliza envisions them all together, one big happy family.
Molly can't see Sam the way her mother does. He's a
devoted father, a compassionate man and the lover who
makes her believe in a husband and children of her own.
Yet accepting him might destroy her mother's dream.

Thanks for joining me in Bardill's Ridge. If you enjoyed
Molly's story, you might want to visit her cousins— Zach
in *The Secret Father* and Sophie in *The Bride Ran Away*. Let
me know what you think of THE CALVERT COUSINS at
anna@annaadams.com.

All the best,

*Anna*

# The Prodigal Cousin
## Anna Adams

TORONTO • NEW YORK • LONDON
AMSTERDAM • PARIS • SYDNEY • HAMBURG
STOCKHOLM • ATHENS • TOKYO • MILAN • MADRID
PRAGUE • WARSAW • BUDAPEST • AUCKLAND

If you purchased this book without a cover you should be aware that this book is stolen property. It was reported as "unsold and destroyed" to the publisher, and neither the author nor the publisher has received any payment for this "stripped book."

ISBN 0-373-71188-3

THE PRODIGAL COUSIN

Copyright © 2004 by Anna Adams.

All rights reserved. Except for use in any review, the reproduction or utilization of this work in whole or in part in any form by any electronic, mechanical or other means, now known or hereafter invented, including xerography, photocopying and recording, or in any information storage or retrieval system, is forbidden without the written permission of the publisher, Harlequin Enterprises Limited, 225 Duncan Mill Road, Don Mills, Ontario, Canada M3B 3K9.

All characters in this book have no existence outside the imagination of the author and have no relation whatsoever to anyone bearing the same name or names. They are not even distantly inspired by any individual known or unknown to the author, and all incidents are pure invention.

This edition published by arrangement with Harlequin Books S.A.

® and TM are trademarks of the publisher. Trademarks indicated with ® are registered in the United States Patent and Trademark Office, the Canadian Trade Marks Office and in other countries.

Visit us at www.eHarlequin.com

Printed in U.S.A.

To Laura Shin

Thank you for suggesting that the Calverts might make good cousins. But deepest thanks also for your patience, your creativity, your clarity when mine fails and— most of all—for making the books better.

**Books by Anna Adams**

**HARLEQUIN SUPERROMANCE**
896—HER DAUGHTER'S FATHER
959—THE MARRIAGE CONTRACT
997—UNEXPECTED BABIES*
1023—UNEXPECTED MARRIAGE*
1082—MAGGIE'S GUARDIAN
1154—THE SECRET FATHER**
1168—THE BRIDE RAN AWAY**

*The Talbot Twins
**The Calvert Cousins

Don't miss any of our special offers. Write to us at the following address for information on our newest releases.

Harlequin Reader Service
U.S.: 3010 Walden Ave., P.O. Box 1325, Buffalo, NY 14269
Canadian: P.O. Box 609, Fort Erie, Ont. L2A 5X3

# CHAPTER ONE

IT WAS THE KIND OF DAY Molly Calvert loved best. One filled with family celebration. Her cousin Sophie's new baby, Chloe, had been christened that morning. Around six the whole family had converged on the Bardill's Ridge Country Club to celebrate.

Her cousin Zach's young son, Evan, and daughter, Lily, raced among the knots of relatives catching up. Her grandparents were dancing their feet off. Her widowed Aunt Beth, Zach's mom, seemed to welcome the romantic intentions of Zach's father-in-law, James Kendall. Her own parents, who ran a bed-and-breakfast, had taken responsibility for supplying ample food and drink, which they'd been too busy arranging to eat.

But something was wrong with Molly. Instead of wrapping herself in the cloak of family affection, she felt as if she were hanging around on the edges of love.

Surrounded by everyone who mattered most to her, she peered from baby Chloe in Sophie's arms to pregnant Olivia, Zach's wife. A strange emptiness yawned inside her. She'd never have a child of her own. Her two cousins, who'd been more like brother and sister to her, had reached a stage in life that she couldn't share.

An inner voice, refusing to be silenced, whispered that she wasn't even a real Calvert. That she was adopted.

Loneliness prodded her as Sophie passed Chloe to her husband, Ian. Behind him, Zach and Olivia each caught one of their children for a hug. Evan and Lily wriggled away, far too excited to stand still for affection.

Molly watched as if from a far place. She loved her parents, enjoyed her job, couldn't imagine living anywhere except on Bardill's Ridge in Tennessee's Smoky Mountains. But at twenty-five, she envied her cousins and hid a secret longing for a husband and family of her own—a husband who could love her despite the holes in her soul.

But what kind of man could love her after he heard the truth? She'd controlled her self-destructive impulses in the ten years since she'd survived a catastrophic miscarriage, but no amount of understanding could change the fact that she was damaged goods. Every man in this town knew her past. They didn't come looking for her. She invited none of them into her life.

Loving her cousins, resenting her own envy, Molly eased through the throng in the wood-smoke-scented dining room. At the doorway, she braced her hand on one of the wide posts that ran from ceiling to floor and searched for her mother's loving, lovable face. Her mom smiled back, and Molly felt a little better.

Since the age of eight, when Eliza and Patrick Calvert had accepted her as their foster child, she'd known no other mother. She owed her parents everything. They'd saved her life and then forgiven her for all the increasingly bad things she'd done. Owing them made her different.

None of her cousins were obliged to their parents for love. None of her cousins hungered for a child and someone—a lover or husband—to call her own.

"Have some wine for me." Sophie, still nursing Chloe, pushed a glass into Molly's hand.

Molly fastened a smile on her face. "Thanks. Chloe's lovely in the dress." Made of white lawn, lacy and yellowed with age, it had been Calvert christening attire even before their grandparents had been thought of.

"You're falling behind," Sophie teased. Molly thought she meant everyone else was putting away the commemorative vino. "You'd better have a baby of your own before one of our kids kicks a hole in the family gown."

A swallow of wine and a harsh breath bit the back of Molly's throat at the same time, choking her. Only her parents knew about her miscarriage and its resulting effects. Full of shame, she'd hidden the truth from the rest of the family and she'd made her mom and dad promise never to tell.

She glanced at Sophie, who waited with a sweet smile, wanting only to share her happiness. Molly harnessed her shaky resources and pretended nothing was wrong.

"Can you imagine Grandpa in the gown?" She nudged her cousin, pointing as Seth Calvert once again led his wife, Greta, onto the small dance floor.

Sophie grinned. "They were just waiting for someone to put Glenn Miller back on. And no, I can't picture tall, white-haired Grandpa in that fragile gown—or his father before him." She leaned closer. "You feel left out today?"

Molly blinked back disgraceful tears, wishing she were a better actress. "It shows?"

"Maybe I'm a little more sensitive since I almost gave up Ian to do motherhood *my* way." Sophie rested her gaze on Molly's latest cousin-by-marriage, a relationship as strong as blood in the Tennessee mountains. "The right guy will show up, Molly. Maybe you already know him."

"I'm not looking for a guy." Unconsciously, she raised her voice enough to draw curious attention from Aunt Beth.

Sophie touched her arm. "There's no shame. You've finished college. You have a good job. You wouldn't be a Calvert if your mind didn't turn to multiplying."

Fine for an OB-GYN to say, but Molly clenched her teeth, forcing herself to keep smiling. Just in time, Ian beckoned Sophie to consult on the state of their daughter's diaper. Expelling a held breath, Molly set her glass on the nearest table and made for the doorway.

In the foyer, she negotiated a path through the after-work golfers who were sending impatient glances toward the Calverts hogging the dining room for their party. Molly answered the reluctant hellos the guys offered. Half of them had kids in her class.

As she fought a gust of wind to force open the door, she felt as if she were breaking through the delicate barriers of a bubble. She sucked crisp, early October air into her lungs.

"Molly? Honey, what's wrong?"

She spun. "Mom?" Her mother faced her from the club's doorway. "I thought I saw you in line to hold Chloe."

"Until you ran for your life." Eliza Calvert, a perfect lady in palest pink chiffon, floated across the redbrick porch. "You aren't—" She stopped, ambivalent about broaching a subject they both considered put to bed. "It's not a panic attack?"

Molly still had them, but she'd learned to control them until she could reach privacy. "Nope. It was hot in there."

"Not that you're twenty-five? The youngest of your generation—the last to remain unmarried?"

Her mother reached for her hands. Molly couldn't step back, didn't know how to reject her mother in any way. "You don't have to hurry for the sake of the family."

Usually, Molly chose to appreciate the happiness life and her parents had given her. Ashamed of wanting more when she had so much, she tried to make light of her mom's concern. "I'm not man-hunting. I'm fine—I just couldn't breathe in the heat." She shivered in the cool breeze, betrayed by her own body.

Her mother held her tighter. "I was twenty-nine when I married your father. You have so much time."

Molly saw no point in arguing. Once her mom got the bit between her teeth, she didn't stop for miles.

"You know lots of young men, and I wish you wouldn't hold back because of…"

"I am reluctant with men because I can't have children. I don't know when to talk about it. But maybe I hold back because no one's made me want to get that close."

"You don't give anyone a chance. You stop seeing them after two weeks, maximum."

Because no man waited longer than two weeks for sex these days, but she wasn't about to enlighten her mom.

Eliza turned toward the highly polished doors. "Why don't we go home?" Her hair fanned around her head. "I'll find your dad, and we'll make dinner out of whatever's in the fridge. None of the guests plan to be in tonight." She tugged Molly's braid. The familiar pressure remained the most poignant gesture of affection in Molly's life. "You stay out here and breathe," her mom said.

"Thanks, but I'll say goodbye to everyone." She hugged her mother. "Meet you back out here."

As she ducked inside, Eliza dragged her dad off the dance floor. He'd indulged in liberal helpings of the wine Ian's former-ambassador father had provided, so Molly asked for his keys at the car.

"You can drive," her dad said, "but remember, a good chauffeur doesn't peek into the back seat." Feeling like a deer in headlights, Molly watched her parents get in the back, noisy with their joy in each other. She faced firmly forward in her seat. As she pulled away from the curb, her parents began a duet of their favorite song, "I Only Have Eyes for You."

For the past eleven years, they'd also sung to her. After a long time with eyes only for each other, they'd seen Molly and made room to love her.

SAM LOCKWOOD HATED feeling like a stalker. He waited in the gathering dark outside the Dogwood, a Victorian bed-and-breakfast. His heart pounded like the percussion in a horror movie. The B and B belonged to his birth mother.

Not his real mother. Jane Lockwood had taken him home as a newborn, raised him and fed him and taught him to be a man. Eliza Calvert had given birth to him and then given him up for adoption.

Sixteen at the time, she'd probably seen no other alternative. Babies cost money. Children cost more. He understood the fiscal reasons, but he couldn't deny the resentment he'd felt since his investigator had reported that she'd later adopted another child.

Forty years old and resentful. Nice start.

He glanced back at his own daughters. Nina, five, had finally fallen asleep in her booster seat, a peacefulness he hadn't seen since the car accident that had taken her mom and his parents. Tamsin, fifteen, had kept her nose buried in a book for most of the nine-hour drive from Savannah.

Nine hours for him to cement a year-long decision. And, oddly, nine hours that had taught his girls to relax in a car again.

Tamsin's book rested in her lap now, caught between her elbow and her chest. Mostly asleep, she twisted to put her arm around Nina, who burrowed into her.

Sam smiled. Tamsin had been a normal, occasionally sullen teenage girl sixteen months ago. She'd dressed in jeans and shirts that often made him nervous with their tightness and a tendency to expose skin, but he longed for that kind of scary clothing rather than the unrelieved black she wore now. A wardrobe that often matched her makeup.

Tamsin's resentment made his appear amateurish. She seemed to take exception to the fact that he'd lived while her mother had died. Since he often shared the thought, he couldn't blame her.

Sam's throat tightened as an image of his wife, Fiona, invaded his thoughts. Delicate as she had been alive, her smile filled with love and understanding, the memory reminded him how long forever was going to last without her. Fiona would have known how to comfort their daughter. Tamsin had rejected his every effort, as well as the grief counseling that helped Nina.

He looked over the seat again, love for his girls swelling his chest. He'd promise to keep them safe always, but he'd made that same promise to Fiona and then he'd lost her, anyway. He couldn't remember when he'd decided to become a doctor, but cardiology had been his only path after Fiona had told him about her incurable heart disease. He'd met and loved her at the age of ten, but he'd based his career on decisions that might help him save his wife.

Fate had snatched her out of his and their daughter's lives despite his plans. Now he had to make sure his girls would have someone else if fate came back to his door.

Sam turned on the dome light and checked his watch. Seven-thirty. Half an hour had passed since he'd opened the Dogwood's front door but received no answer to his greeting.

He pressed the back of his head against the seat rest, resisting guilt about the mess he might be making of the Calverts' lives. As his grief for Fiona and his parents had begun to ebb, he'd realized his daughters would be alone if something happened to him.

Fiona had grown up in an orphanage, unwanted by adoptive parents because of her disease. His first conversation with her had been about her life in the orphanage. Convinced his adoptive parents had barely saved him in time from a similar institution, he'd felt empathy for Fiona, which had resulted in several fistfights with his best boyhood friends and her lifelong love.

He refused to think of their girls feeling as alone as she had. He owed Fiona security for Nina and Tamsin, so he prayed his birth mother had suffered a few second thoughts. Especially after Tamsin had found the investigator's paperwork and shown her first spark of interest in sixteen months.

Lights flashed in his rearview mirror and a car parked in the gravel lot beside the house. Sam gripped the steering wheel. A man and woman, laughing, spilled out of the other car's back seat.

His investigator had taken plenty of photos and he recognized Eliza. Her salt-and-pepper hair lessened the resemblance, but they shared unusual black eyes. Other than that, he must look like the birth father of whom he'd found no trace. Averting his face from the fifty-six-year-old woman he'd driven six hundred miles to see, he tossed around conversation starters.

"Just wondering why you gave me away when I was hours old." Or "Thought you might have changed your mind about having a son." Both approaches involved whining on his part and hurting her. Neither would do.

No one except Fiona had ever known his feelings about being adopted. His parents would have been upset, and he'd been a little ashamed that his own mother had given him away. As an adult, he'd lost any concern for his past in his focus on making sure Fiona survived for their daughters—and for him.

Tamsin and Nina remained his first concern, but now that he saw Eliza Calvert dancing up the pansy-bordered walkway in her husband's protective arms, Sam longed to know someone else on the face of the earth who shared the blood that ran in his and his children's veins.

If Eliza accepted them, his daughters would never be alone again.

Another woman climbed out of the car. Taller than Eliza, she was slender but curvy. Her thick, dark red braid slid over her shoulder as she shut the door. She glanced at his car and lifted her hand in a brief wave. With a glance at Eliza and the man disappearing inside, she started toward Sam. Her silky dress outlined her body with each step she took.

She must be Molly Calvert.

Sam opened the car door and stood with trepidation. Eliza had adopted Molly when she was fifteen. Sam's investigator had picked up rumors of juvenile misconduct, nonspecific because the court had sealed her records and the townspeople avoided talking about her.

Her own parents had abandoned Molly. Again, he knew only the bare bones. Would she resent him and the girls if her mother accepted them?

"The door was open." Her voice flowed, as smooth as her dress. "You didn't have to wait out here."

"We haven't checked in." He shut his door and opened the back. Tamsin blinked, stretching a little, smiling before she remembered where she was—who he was.

"We're here." He squeezed her hand, still draped around Nina's shoulder. She drew back, rejecting tenderness—as if she couldn't bear to be comforted since Fiona's death. "Wake up, sweetie," he said anyway.

"Dad." She instantly donned her armor.

He kissed her little sister's forehead. "Nina, girl, time to wake up."

Nina kicked at his hand in her sleep as he took

her out of the booster seat and straightened to face Molly.

"We didn't make a reservation. Do you have two rooms?"

She nodded, smiling at the sleepy girls. "We have something with bunk beds if your daughters prefer—or two adjoining rooms, one with a dressing room that's been converted to hold a child's bed."

Her friendly reception heightened his guilt. He hadn't considered Molly's feelings.

"We'll take the second combination." He elbowed the car door shut as Nina peered into the growing darkness. "Nina can take the dressing room attached to mine."

"Daddy, where are we?"

"Bardill's Ridge, Tennessee." Love of home deepened Molly's voice. "Let me get your bags."

"No, I'll come back."

"I'll get them, Dad." Tamsin surprised him, but maybe she hoped to avoid the possible debacle inside.

"I'll help." Molly grinned at Nina. "Your little girl may want her pajamas in a hurry."

"Who are you?" Nina demanded.

"Molly Calvert." She offered a hand on which a couple of rings glittered in the streetlights.

Nina giggled, because people rarely shook hands with her. "Do you have food?"

"All kinds." Molly's mouth trembled with an infectious urge to laugh. "What do you like?"

"Ice cream."

Sam chuckled, pulling his daughter closer. "Good try, but no go. This is Nina, Molly." He backed around the trunk and dropped his hand on his older girl's shoulder. "This is Tamsin. I'm Sam Lockwood. We'd all love a sandwich."

"Peanut butter and strawberry," Nina said.

"Or whatever you have." Sam had worried about Nina and Tamsin for so long he hadn't noticed Nina's manners slipping. She might be a little spoiled.

"How about you, Tamsin?"

The teenager smiled, her manners in better shape. "Whatever you have."

"Me, too. Whatever." Nina kicked against his side. "Lemme walk, Daddy."

He let her down and then opened the trunk and reached for the large canvas rolling bag that held most of his and Nina's clothes. Tamsin grabbed her own suitcase. Molly took Nina's backpack full of stuffed animals and the smaller suitcase that held the rest of the child's stuff.

"Thanks," he said. A quick search for his younger child revealed her tugging at the B and B's heavy front door. "Nina!"

"She's fine. I'm sure my mom saw you, and she'll catch her." Molly slid the backpack over her shoulder. Cool air wrapped her skirt around Nina's suitcase, exposing her slender calf. Sam forced his gaze back to her face. "We came from a family christening," she added.

Eliza and her husband had clearly celebrated. "We can find our own dinner if you'll point us at the kitchen."

"Seriously, we were just about to loot the fridge and we always share meals." With a friendly smile, Molly waited for Tamsin to move along the sidewalk in front of her. "We want our guests to feel like family."

It was the perfect opening. Much as he hated spying, Sam needed to see Eliza Calvert with his girls. To see if she'd be as open as Molly. If Eliza was uncomfortable, he and Nina could drag Tamsin through the Smoky Mountains for a few days and then head home.

They caught up with his youngest, still doing battle with the door.

"I—can't—open it."

Sam reached over her head with a rueful glance at Molly, who smothered her laughter in a cough. Over her shoulder, Tamsin looked revolted. Sam cleared his throat and held the door for all of them.

Inside, Patrick Calvert waited behind a dark pine registration desk. Molly started toward the stairs with Nina's things.

"Dad, they want rooms three and four. I'll take these up."

"Thanks, honey." With a smile at Tamsin, Patrick spun a ledger toward Sam. "Glad to have you. If you'll sign in? Have you eaten?"

"That big girl said she had food," Nina said.

Laughing, Patrick leaned way over the desk to see her. "Driving makes you hungry, Miss—" he glanced at Sam's signature "—Lockwood?"

"Daddy hates to stop," she said. Tamsin actually laughed, which made Sam's public humiliation more than worthwhile.

"I packed snacks," he said in self-defense.

Patrick's bark of laughter nearly burst his eardrum. "A kindred spirit. That's what I always say, too. You wouldn't know it to look at my daughter, but she's an eating machine."

"Dad." The startled protest burst from Molly.

Sam grinned at Tamsin, who promptly dropped her gaze. He glanced at Patrick. "Need anything else?"

After a swift perusal, Patrick shook his head. "Be sure to come back down. My wife is putting dinner together."

Sam nodded, uneasy again, because Eliza's husband, welcoming now, might come to view him as the enemy. Sam didn't enjoy invading Patrick's home under false pretenses.

With Nina clinging to his free hand and Tamsin back on her side of the great generational divide, he carried his bag upstairs behind Molly. At the top, she took a right, her footsteps whispering on a thick burgundy rug. Soft lighting increased warm tones in the paneled hall. Had this place belonged to the Calvert family since it was built? Sam couldn't imagine that kind of continuity.

Molly opened the third door. She set Nina's bags on a chest in front of a surprisingly plain four-poster, and his younger daughter bolted across the room. Sam had expected frills and lace. Instead, the early American primitive paintings and a fire laid on the hearth offered hospitality.

"Daddy, come look!" Nina swung on a door frame, summoning him to her room. Tamsin leaned over her shoulder and forgot to move when Sam joined them.

Frills abounded in here, from the lace-trimmed duvet on the child-size sleigh bed to the skirt on a miniature dressing table. "It's like a playhouse," he said. "Only no spaces between the walls." Nina's stuffed animals would be at home at the tiny table set for high tea.

"Wow," Tamsin finally said. Sam suspected the word had escaped her.

Molly's smile reached all the way to her hazel eyes. "I like it, too. I wish we'd had it when I was a little girl."

"How will I talk Nina into going home?" Sam asked.

The little girl grabbed her backpack, snatching a tattered blue elephant and a threadbare green lizard from its zippered opening. She seated them on the small white chairs, chattering about tea.

"Tamsin, come." Nina patted the one open setting.

Tamsin glanced at Molly, adolescent reluctance all over her face. Sam fought a fond smile. She showed inordinate patience with her little sister, but what teenager wanted to take tea with a green lizard in front of a stranger?

"Would you like to see your room?" Molly asked her.

"No—after tea," Nina said.

"I'll come back, Nina." Tamsin turned toward their hostess.

Molly edged around Sam, trailing a whiff of spice and woman that disturbed him. She crossed his room to open another door. "Here you go."

Tamsin hauled her bag behind her. At the door, she glanced from her assigned quarters to Molly, and her bright smile made Sam glad he'd dragged her here.

"It's great," Tamsin said.

He was dying to see it, but she didn't invite him in, and experience had taught him to wait for her to make the first move.

Molly clasped her hands as if to say "My work here is done," and backed out, pausing at Sam's hallway door.

"Dinner will be waiting. I'm sure Mom will find something fun for Nina." She already knew Tamsin wouldn't want to be classified with her sister. "When you come out of your rooms, turn left and go past the stairs. Mom and Dad use that end of the house, and the hall ends in a door to the kitchen stairs.''

Hearing her call his birth mother ''Mom'' shocked Sam. He nodded, trying to look as if he felt nothing, but her gaze narrowed as she caught his response, anyway. After a moment, she continued through the door.

She left it open, so he had to close it, but he couldn't help watching her stroll toward the family side of the house. Her slender back and the gentle sway of her hips drew his gaze, inappropriate as that was. For God's sake, she couldn't be more than twenty-five.

''What's wrong, Daddy?'' Nina had entered his room again. ''You look sad.''

''Sad?'' He shut the door and scooped her into his arms. ''Why would I be sad when you and Tamsin and I are going hiking tomorrow, and you've got this great room to sleep in tonight?''

She planted a sloppy kiss on his cheek. ''I like this place. It's cool.''

Astounding him, tears stuck in his throat. Nothing had been cool for her since she'd lost her mom. In fact, he didn't believe his baby had ever used that word before. ''Where did you learn 'cool,' Nina?''

''Tamsin says lots of stuff is cool. Daddy—'' she pointed her toes toward the floor ''—lemme down. Judy wants tea with Lizzie and Norm.''

Out of her pack came Judy, a doll with short blond hair that stood on end and bright blue eyes nearly kissed off her painted face. Fiona had named Judy before Nina could even turn over.

"Settle Judy and the gang and then wash your hands and face, and we'll go downstairs."

He couldn't say if it was the long drive or his daughters' excitement at their temporary rooms, but like Tamsin and Nina, he was suddenly interested in his surroundings.

Until he remembered he had to find a way to tell Eliza Calvert who he was.

MAYBE AN HOUR AGO she'd assured Sophie she wasn't looking for a man, but Molly was an honest woman and she couldn't restrain herself from listening for the least little sound from above. Inappropriate. A man who loved his daughters the way Sam Lockwood clearly worshipped Nina and the reluctant Tamsin, probably also loved his absent wife.

Sam's reasons for traveling alone with his daughters made her curious, but she didn't sense a divorce. Molly had dealt with plenty of children in the past four years. Usually, the extroverts like Nina, who believed even the adults around her were waiting for her conversation, came from a loving home. Tamsin was too quiet, but under all that Goth makeup, she was a young woman enduring the torture of her teenage years.

"They're nice girls?" her mom asked.

Molly looked up from the beans she'd been staring at instead of snapping. "Nina's chatty." She broke a couple of beans at once. "She loves the room. Tamsin, the older girl, seems…"

The more Molly thought about it, the more she realized Tamsin seemed unusually quiet. She wore the unnerving yet familiar air of the walking wounded.

"I knew Nina'd like the dressing room." Molly's dad came in from the pantry behind the kitchen, brandishing several freshly cleaned trout. "Think they'll enjoy these?"

"You're going all out." Tamsin was none of her business. Molly tried to put the girl out of her mind—or relegate her to the position she should occupy, that of a guest. "I thought we were doing leftovers."

Her dad grinned. "I liked the way Nina called you the 'big girl.' And her sister looks as if she could use a treat."

"The father sounded tired even from here," Eliza said. "We might as well start their visit with a special dinner."

"You're staying, Molly?" her dad asked. "I cleaned one for you."

Molly pried her gaze away from her mother's face. She hadn't imagined Sam Lockwood's fatigue if her mother had sensed it, too, but Molly's interest in the little family felt inappropriate. She'd resisted rash acts for ten years. No need to ruin her record and let herself feel involved because something about Tamsin spoke to her past. "I have stuff to do for a science project at school tomorrow."

"You have to eat," her mother said. "Stay."

Upstairs, the door squeaked and Sam's voice floated down. "Hold my hand, Nina. Don't run. Hold on to the rail."

"He's overprotective." Eliza looked upward. "Those stairs are perfectly safe."

"Sh." Patrick clearly felt the Lockwood family deserved privacy.

Her mom returned to the stove. Molly snapped the last of the beans and carried them to the sink as Nina's sneakers slapped across the black-and-white-tile floor.

"We're *back,*" she said.

Molly searched their faces for some hint about Tamsin's restlessness and pain. Sam looked away, but not before she caught the trace of an old injury in his eyes. Something was wrong.

"I tried to bring Judy, but Daddy said she needed a bath before she sat at a strange guy's table."

"Stranger," Sam said. His discomfited silence stretched. "That sounds pretty bad, too."

"Not at all." Molly's mom took over. "I'm Eliza Calvert. Welcome to our home."

Sam remained too quiet for too long. Molly turned to find her mother holding out her hand, while their guest stared at her with blank black eyes that reminded Molly of Eliza when she was annoyed and trying to hide it. At last he took her hand.

"Mrs. Calvert." He quickly let go, still staring at her.

Molly turned completely to face him. His distracted glance barely brushed her face, but then he started as if he realized his response wasn't entirely normal.

"Thanks for the great rooms." He reached for his older daughter, who avoided his hand, stepping off the stairs in front of him. "This is Tamsin. I'm Sam Lockwood. The little one's Nina."

She marched across the room to peer into the sink. "I don't like beans."

"Nina."

"But I'll eat 'em." Her forced enthusiasm drew laughter from everyone except Sam and Tamsin.

"I stir-fry them," Eliza told her. "You'll love them. They taste sweet."

"I liked *my* mom's."

Sam offered an apologetic grimace. Tamsin turned to inspect the tile backsplash over the dark granite counter. With a troubled expression, Sam dropped his hand on Nina's head. "My wife... passed away...sixteen months ago."

Molly forgot about not getting involved. His control made his grief more palpable, and the loss of her mother explained Tamsin's pain. Molly's parents closed ranks with her, offering silent, united support.

Sam rounded up his girls, clearly unable to handle one more nuance of sympathy. "Why don't we go outside and clean your snack stuff out of the car before we eat?"

Nina skipped ahead of him. Again, Tamsin evaded comfort. Sam glanced over his shoulder at Eliza.

Molly's heart thudded. He stared at her mom as if he knew her. His inexplicable concentration seemed to include her dad and Molly, too.

She barely waited for the door to close. "Have you met him before, Mom?"

Her dad looked surprised. "How would your mom know Sam Lockwood?"

"Actually, he seems familiar, and I can tell he thinks I do, too." Eliza took the beans. "I'm trying to think where I might have met him."

"You couldn't have," Patrick said. "He's driven a long way today and he's tired. The little girl's a sweetie, but she keeps him hopping, and he's obviously concerned about the older one. You two are reading more into that."

"Maybe," Eliza said.

Molly couldn't agree. Her parents were such innocents. Sam had definitely looked at her mother as if he knew her. Later, Molly eyed him as they all sat down to dinner.

Sam checked Nina's trout for bones before he

started his own meal. Suddenly, he looked up, his knife in midair. "I thought you mentioned sandwiches, Molly. I hope you haven't gone to all this trouble for us."

"I caught these earlier today." Molly's dad chewed with enjoyment. "We planned to have them for breakfast."

Sam set his fork on the table. Tamsin did likewise. "Will you have enough?" he asked.

"We can supplement with bacon and eggs." Eliza flicked Molly a glance. "What my daughter calls a breakfast platter."

"A breakfast platter?" Sam trained his dark eyes on Molly.

Heat climbed her throat. Annoyed, she answered without thinking. "I spent a lot of time in diners before—" This stranger had no need to know about her homeless days at the age of eight. "Before," she finished.

He nodded, compassion softening his eyes. Molly placed her own utensils on the table as a chill fingered her spine. He knew about her. He wouldn't feel sorry for a woman who'd just happened to eat in a few diners.

This man didn't deserve their trust. "Mom," she said, "I'm too tired to drive home tonight. I'll stay here."

# CHAPTER TWO

THAT NIGHT NINA WAS SO exhausted, she slumped against the bathroom cabinet as Sam washed her hands and face and then helped her brush her teeth. She was asleep before he tucked her and Judy into the little bed. He turned off the light and closed her door except for a thin wedge of space. Bad dreams woke her most nights, and he wanted to make sure he heard if she called.

It was still early. Barely nine o'clock, according to the art deco clock on the mantel. Glancing at Tamsin's closed door, he crossed to his open window and looked out on the verdant garden Eliza and Molly had discussed during dinner. According to her proud daughter, Eliza had a green thumb. Apparently, she could nurture anything except a son.

He shook his head, ashamed of being unfair. There was more to her story than his investigator had uncovered. Sam had the facts, but Eliza's motivation remained a mystery. Not that it mattered anymore. Finding out why she'd given him up had once been a priority, but now he just needed her to be a loving grandmother to his daughters.

Movement near a lamp below drew his gaze. It was Molly, sitting on a stone wall. As if she felt him staring, she glanced up. He nearly backed out of sight, but he was tired of hiding. Tomorrow, when the B and B was quiet, he'd tell Eliza the truth. She could decide what came next, but he looked forward to being honest.

Not that his act had succeeded. Molly's silences had grown more speculative as trout and vegetables progressed to fruit and cheese for the adults and Tamsin, and a dish of homemade chocolate ice cream for Nina. More streetwise than her parents, Molly had recognized his interest in Eliza—and in her.

She'd decided to stay here tonight because of him, and he didn't blame her. He'd gone to dramatic lengths to find protection for his family.

Sam turned his back on her and the compelling view of moon and darkness over the courthouse square, and knocked on Tamsin's door.

"Yeah?"

Close enough to "Come in." With her knees up beneath the fluffy comforter, she was reading. Her face devoid of makeup, her dark hair in a ponytail, she looked so much like his little girl that she filled an ache in his heart.

"How are you?" he asked.

"Tired." She set down her book and reached for the nightstand lamp.

"Wait. I'm serious." He'd almost said "concerned." That would have been a mistake. "You didn't say much at dinner."

"Who can get in a word with Nina babbling?" A soft tone betrayed love for her sister, despite her harsh question.

"I know you're unsure about being here."

"Because you're about to spring us on a woman who didn't want you?"

He refused to back down. He should have come alone, but since the accident, he'd feared losing his girls every time they left his sight. Besides, once Tamsin had snooped through his papers, she'd known the worst.

"Honey, I have no other family. If something happened to me—" He broke off, and Tamsin swallowed hard. They'd both learned death arrived in an unsuspecting second. "If something happened to me, you and Nina would be put in state care. If Eliza regrets a decision she made at sixteen, you'll gain more family than either of us could imagine."

"We have friends in Savannah, Dad."

Wrong. He'd cultivated colleagues. Fiona had made friends. He'd been so intent on perfecting procedures to keep a sick heart alive, he'd managed to forget that humans needed less tangible sustenance, too.

"I don't know anyone well enough to trust them with your future."

She twisted her sweet young face into a scowl of contempt. "But you figure we'll be able to trust strangers who suddenly find out we exist?"

"I trust blood," he said, unable to explain that his adoptive mother had loved him but had held back, still longing for a child of her own. He'd only known such ties with Tamsin and Nina, and nothing short of death could ever part him from them. "You're predisposed to love the people who share your blood."

"No, *you* are. Other adopted kids get along just fine without launching a sneak attack on the people who didn't want them."

"You're talking out of pride, which I can't afford. I need to give you and Nina someone else to depend on."

"These people treat strangers like family. They deserve better."

"I'm not too proud of myself right now, but nothing changes our situation." His smile hurt. "If Eliza doesn't want us, we'll go home, and I'll pray we stumble across friends who'd make good substitute parents."

"Only you would look at it that way. We might as well take out personal ads."

"What do you know about personal ads?" He kissed her head. Stubbornly, she slid away. She wanted her mom. No one else would do.

"I'm no kid, you know."

Since her mother's death she'd tried to separate herself, as if she could lose him or Nina with less grief if she stopped caring about them. Sam figured that if he kept proving he'd love her no matter what, she'd eventually realize that loving was still safe. He started toward his room, and she turned off the light before he reached their adjoining door.

"'Night, Tamsin. I love you."

"Uh-huh."

He left her door open about an inch, too, and she didn't shut it.

The next morning he woke the girls in time for a late breakfast. Tamsin claimed she wasn't hungry. To her disgust, he checked her for a temperature, but let her go back to sleep.

After a quick bath, he wrestled Nina's long blond hair into a sad-looking braid. Fortunately, she was still too young to care that his surgeon's hands were useless for styling hair. Unless she was too grown-up at five to hurt his feelings. He kissed her cheek.

"Hungry?"

She nodded, head-butting him, and he stood, eyes watering as he rubbed his nose.

"Tamsin, we'll bring ya something." Nina tore out of the room and down the hall ahead of him. He caught her before she reached the stairs.

"The dining room, today," he said. "We have to be invited to use the kitchen."

"Okay, Daddy."

At the bottom, they found Eliza carrying a heavy tray from the kitchen. Sam took it.

"Thanks." She inspected them, clearly looking for his older daughter. "Where's Tamsin?"

"She chose sleep over breakfast."

"Molly was the same at her age. Trout or the breakfast platter for you two?" She beamed at Nina. "We have plenty."

"Two slices of bacon and a scrambled egg for Nina," Sam said, "and I'd like the trout again."

"Great." She pointed at a couple just inside the room. A baby lay in a stroller next to the blond woman. "The tray goes to them. Sophie, Ian, this is Sam Lockwood and his daughter Nina."

The man stood, reaching for the tray as he nodded a greeting. Sophie shook Sam's hand and then patted Nina's shoulder.

"Good morning," she said. "Aunt Eliza mentioned you'd checked in yesterday evening. First time in the Smokies?"

"Yeah, so we're going for a long walk if my sister wakes up." Nina had a future as a society page columnist. "Can I look at your baby?"

"Sure. Her name is Chloe." Sophie pulled back the blankets so Nina could examine the infant.

"What brings you here?" Ian asked. "We're out of the way."

"A brochure." A lie this late seemed pointless, but Eliza might need the cover if she sent them home. "One of my patients had it, and I thought my daughters might enjoy the mountains."

"You're a doctor?" Ian glanced at Sophie, who was completely absorbed in Nina and the pink-swathed baby. "So is my wife. An OB-GYN."

"I'm a cardiologist," Sam said.

Sophie looked up with interest. "You wouldn't be looking for a change of pace?"

He smiled blandly, not understanding.

"She's always thinking of work." Ian grimaced. "Sophie and a few other physicians from the surrounding area are opening a clinic in town and they're still scouting for staff."

His wife looked regretful. "I don't suppose we'd have the facilities you're used to."

Sam didn't suppose Tamsin would survive even talk of a permanent move. She'd made him promise not to think of it, and Nina, coming in on the tail end of that battle, had chimed in, though she'd really had no clue what they were arguing about. "I'm settled in Savannah."

"I love Savannah." Eliza stopped herself before she said more, but Sam pressed his advantage.

"You've been there often?"

Her blush was as good as a confession. "I grew up there, but when I graduated from college in Knoxville, I answered an ad for a teacher's position here. In fact, I used to teach kindergarten and first grade in our little school, just like Molly. Then

I met Patrick, and he made me an offer I couldn't refuse.''

Sam tried to laugh with the others, but her light-hearted recovery hurt a little. He hadn't tempted her to keep him. His children might not tempt her to want them, either.

"What's the big girl doing out there?" Nina pointed at Molly, who was out in the garden with her back to the window, leaning over a tall, gray tank.

"Blowing up balloons." Eliza smoothed Nina's braid with her palm, unconsciously trying to tidy it. "She needs them for school today."

Nina latched on to Sam's hand. "I want to go to school, Daddy." She turned to Sophie. "I can write my name, and I can make numbers up to ten.''

Sam let her swing from his arms. "She's been badgering me to let her go to 'big kid' school for the past year. You can't go today, Nina. We're hiking, remember?''

"I wanna do balloons with the big girl!''

Heading off her tantrum, Sam smiled an apology at Sophie, Ian and Eliza, and guided his suddenly weeping daughter toward a back table. As he settled her in a chair, Eliza appeared at his elbow, offering a small square whiteboard and a couple of markers.

"I thought she might like these.''

"Thanks." He took them, searching her gaze. A

thoughtful woman planned ahead for young cus-
tomers—a kind woman gave them markers that
could destroy her furniture. He handed the board
and markers to Nina. "Thank Mrs. Calvert."

"Thank you," Nina said through a haze of tears.
She grabbed her napkin and wiped her nose, and
Sam stared, appalled. Fiona had instilled a deeper
respect for linen in her daughters.

Eliza misunderstood his dismay. "Don't worry.
I'll get her a clean one. And then bacon and eggs.
Do you like cheese with your eggs, Nina?"

Up and down went her head. A wisp of hair fell
out of her braid and poked her eye. Sam hooked it
away with his little finger. With a fortifying smile
at both of them, Eliza hugged Nina and hurried
back to the kitchen.

"No more crying, Nina, okay?" He sat across
from her, and she nodded, sniffing back the last of
her tears.

"But I wanna go to school. I like balloons."

"You don't have to go to school to play with
balloons. We'll find one in town."

"The big girl has better ones."

"Her name is Miss Calvert."

"I thought that was her mommy's name."

He gave up. "Just try calling her Miss Calvert
when you see her."

As they waited for their breakfast, Nina taught
him to write her name and then speedily learned
how to write his. Every so often, he followed his

daughter's glance to the garden, where Molly was stuffing filled balloons into large white plastic bags.

Strands of dark red curls slipped over Molly's shoulder, lifting with the same breeze that wrapped her long, feminine skirt around her legs. Sam returned his attention to his child.

Eliza brought their breakfast about the time Sophie went out to the garden and distracted Molly from the balloons. Ian took their baby out to join them, and Nina finally lost interest enough to eat. At least until Sophie and Ian left and Molly returned to her work.

"Can I go out, Daddy?"

"I'll come with you." She might try to climb into one of the bags. Holding her hand, he led her through the garden door.

Outside, Molly looked up, flustered, her skin pink from battling the slippery balloons.

He liked her happy smile for Nina. He couldn't look away from the faint sheen of moisture on her cheekbones and throat. Sixteen months alone, and his mother's daughter had to be the one woman who reminded him he was a man.

"Hi, Nina." Finally, Molly looked at Sam, who wished he could backpedal to the house. "Children can't resist these things." She tied a knot in a bright yellow one. "The machine broke two balloons ago, and I still have to blow up a few more."

"I'll help."

"I'll manage." She peered through the window at his full plate. He hadn't finished a meal since the day he'd become a single parent. "Eat," Molly said. "If Nina blows one of these up, she can keep it."

Nina clapped her hands. "Daddy?"

He stared, speechless with guilt. If Molly looked after Nina, he'd be free to explain everything to Eliza. The plan might stink for Molly, but it helped him.

"She's fine." Molly's too-neutral tone betrayed her wish that he leave. He didn't have time to diagnose her motives. She'd offered him a better opportunity to talk to Eliza than he could have hoped for. No one else ever had to know anything if Eliza rejected him.

"Thanks." He knelt beside Nina on the damp grass. "Don't get in Miss Calvert's way, and if she leaves, come back inside." With a lick of his finger, he rubbed a smudge of cheese off his daughter's nose while she wrestled for freedom.

"I'm *all right*, Daddy."

He hoped she would be—that Eliza and her family would accept Nina and Tamsin even if they resented him. His own parents had loved him, but they hadn't been good at the expansive, arms-wide affection the Calverts offered even to guests.

Standing, he brushed grass off his knees. "Thanks again, Molly." Emotion unexpectedly deepened his voice, making her curious and him uncomfortable.

"Go ahead," she said.

He found Eliza alone in the dining room, standing beside his plate. "You're not hungry?"

"I am." He couldn't choke down even a swallow of coffee, but he sat, hoping to make her stay. She eased around the table to watch the woman and girl outside.

"Nina's a lovely child. You're obviously doing a good job with her."

Neither of them mentioned Tamsin, his greater worry.

He filled up his coffee cup from the carafe on his table. "She's latched on to Molly. She might be a nuisance."

Eliza shook her head. "Molly's wonderful with children." How could she remain blind to his rising tension? "She's a patient teacher, creative, eager to get involved. Her students feel how much she cares for them." Eliza broke off with a nervous laugh. "I'm proud of her."

"Naturally." He left the table to stand beside her at the window. "You have no other children?"

"No." Her lack of hesitation slashed like a knife.

A nice, clean wound. It would heal.

"I'm afraid I have to disagree with you, Mrs. Calvert."

She didn't answer. Her silence lasted so long

Sam finally checked to see if she'd fainted. She was rooted at his side on the patterned rug of her cozy dining room.

He would remember this moment for the rest of his life—the smell of fried bacon and rich coffee, the tick of a grandfather clock that guarded the far corner, the slight tang of a fire that had burned to ashes the night before.

And Eliza Calvert, trapped in stillness like a photo of herself. His wound might take a little longer to heal than he'd estimated.

"Who are you?" She closed her eyes for the briefest moment. "Don't answer. I know. Since last night, I've tried to remember who you remind me of, but now I know. I've wondered about you for so long—wondered if you'd show up, if you hated me, if you were happy." She jerked her head toward the window, and he followed her gaze, watching Molly hand Nina a fat green balloon. "I wondered if you had children of your own."

"I don't know what to say." He couldn't tell from her delicate, frozen features what she felt. "I couldn't locate my birth father."

She took a deep breath. "Neither could I. He told me he wanted to help, that he wanted you even if he couldn't marry me. He came along to my first doctor's appointment—the day before he and his family left town in the middle of the night. He wanted to be a lawyer—kind of ironic when you consider I eventually married a judge. His mother wanted a good career for him and his father refused to let him pay for my sins. I guess they didn't think I was the proper appendage for him…. But I shouldn't tell you this.'' She looked horrified. ''You don't want to know about—''

''I want the truth.'' He pivoted toward the window, ashamed that his birth father had discarded her. Nina and Molly were drawing on the green balloon with a dark blue marker. ''I came because of the girls.'' He took a deep breath, hiding grief that still squeezed his heart. ''When my wife and parents died, I realized Tamsin and Nina would have no one else if I…weren't around.''

''So you want me to…''

She stopped, and Sam turned his head to look at her, tempted to take the trembling hand she'd raised to her mouth the way he would comfort a patient to whom he'd given bad news. But she wasn't a patient.

He dropped his hands. He was a stranger. He couldn't comfort her. She felt no attachment to him.

''I won't ask for anything. I'm offering you the chance to know Nina and Tamsin.''

''And you.'' Joy flashed in her eyes, giving him a second's astounding relief. In the time it took him to feel disloyal to his adoptive parents, Eliza's joy changed to panic. ''Do the girls know?''

He lifted one eyebrow. ''Does it matter?'' At her

openmouthed groan, he relented. "Tamsin knows. She found the file."

"I don't want to hurt her." She pressed her hand to her throat, staring over his shoulder. "Or my husband. Molly…"

He empathized, though sudden anger shook him. Even at his age he wanted Tamsin and Nina and him to matter most. But he was no child. Eliza's concern for her present family meant she was a loving woman. She had the right to turn him away. She'd arranged for him to have a healthy, happy life. She'd done all a sixteen-year-old girl could do.

"Were you happy?" she asked.

Meeting her tumultuous gaze, he considered lying. He couldn't. He'd lied enough to last a lifetime. "Happy, yes, but my parents had tried to have their own child for years. My mother told me once that she'd heard a lot of people had babies after they adopted. She expected to get pregnant as soon as they took me. Naturally, she was disappointed when she didn't, but I think they were afraid to give everything to me. They wanted something left over for their real child."

Eliza frowned. "Adoption is a strange fertility treatment."

He wasn't capable of saying anything else against his adoptive mother. "Being infertile wasn't just a medical condition for her." Her restraint had colored his father's feelings for him.

Sam couldn't help wondering why they hadn't been as grateful as most adoptive parents to have a baby.

He nodded toward the garden. "You must have wanted a child, too."

"You know we adopted her?"

"I hired a detective."

"I don't expect you to understand."

Not the wholehearted effort to help that he'd hoped for. If he was going to stay in touch with this family for the sake of his daughters, he had to know they could love Tamsin and Nina with a generosity his adoptive parents had never achieved.

Eliza's mouth quivered, apprehension obviously chipping away at any joy. "I can't explain about Molly until I talk to her." She backed away from him. "And to my husband. I never told Patrick...."

With a muffled cry, she turned and left the room. Sam didn't try to stop her. He just listened to her low heels thudding up the stairs.

As they faded, Tamsin appeared in the doorway. "Well?" she said. "Are you happy now?"

"Where were you?"

"I bumped into her. I guess she wants us."

He wasn't so sure. "Are you angry?"

As she shook her head, tears filled her eyes, terrifying him. She'd cried for weeks after Fiona's death, but her silence ever since had been harder to take. He steeled himself to tackle whatever Tamsin needed him to handle.

"Honey, we don't have to stay." He reached for her, and she didn't fight for once. "If you want to leave, we'll go."

"I want my mom. I want my grandpa and grandma and my mom."

She fell on him, and her sobs broke his heart. No fifteen-year-old girl should ever have to learn the true meaning of forever. His own loss lodged in his throat. No one should have to feel this way.

He stroked Tamsin's head and held her, praying Nina wouldn't walk in. Tamsin's grief unsettled her sister almost more than their mother's death. To Nina, Fiona's absence was as confusing as it was painful, but her longing came in nightmares that worsened when she was afraid for her sister.

"Tamsin, I've been trying to make things better for you."

"You think these people can take Mom's place?"

"No one will ever replace your mom. Not for you and Nina. Not for me. I just wanted to give you family, but if you don't want that, we'll go. You and Nina matter most."

"Then why did you drag us here?"

"If I'd realized you thought I was trying to replace your mother and grandparents, I wouldn't have."

"Daddy." She wrapped her arms around his

shoulders the way she had when she was Nina's age. "Sometimes I think I'm falling apart."

Sometimes he feared he was, too. "You're fine, Tamsin. You've had to face too much for a girl your age, and I've made you remember it again."

IN HER ROOM, Eliza ran to the window on thick carpet that dragged at her feet. She bumped her head against a pane of wavy glass that distorted her view of Molly and Nina. Finally, another figure joined them. Sam.

He leaned down to speak to his daughter. His parents had taught him to be a good father. Forty years of living without her son filled Eliza's eyes with hot tears of resentment toward that couple who hadn't loved him the way they'd promised to.

She should have been the one to teach him everything. She should have changed his diapers and walked the floor with him when he was sick at night, and listened to his stories of school days and sports and whatever else boys shared with their mothers.

A sob threatened to escape. She'd never know those things—unless she found a way to include her son now. How many times had she daydreamed about contacting his adoptive parents, begging for news of him?

But she'd chained herself into a corner. Her parents had ousted her from their home when she'd asked for help with her pregnancy. She'd finished her GED while she was in a home for unwed mothers, waiting for Sam's birth. From there, she'd worked her way through the University of Tennessee.

After she'd started teaching in Bardill's Ridge, she'd met Patrick, an ambitious attorney on his way to being a judge, like his father. She'd believed he couldn't love a woman like her, so she'd never told him about her past.

How could she tell Patrick the truth now? He valued his position, the respect people here held him in, the mornings he spent ''jawing'' with his friends about how to improve county government. She couldn't admit she'd come here to pay penance in a needy school.

How could she explain to Molly, who'd worshipped her as though she were a saint?

Eliza pressed her fists to the chilled glass. She could not abandon her son—even grown—a second time.

She'd made the right decision for Sam. But what would her husband say when she told him she'd regretted letting someone else care for her baby? What she'd done had been right for Sam but wrong for her. She'd wanted him back every day since she'd placed him in a sweet-smelling nurse's starchy-stiff arms.

She needed him far more than he needed her. She wanted to be his mother, to try to ease the pain that drove a young man to believe he needed backup in case his daughters lost him.

She had to tell Patrick first, and then Molly. Sam needed her, too, and she wasn't capable of putting him out of her heart again.

For the first time since they'd opened the bed and breakfast, Eliza left dishes in the sink and snuck out the kitchen door.

She found her husband in his usual late-morning spot on the bench across the square from the courthouse. From there, he and Homer Tinsdale got a clear view of every miscreant—both the members of the legal profession and their clients—who set foot inside the building.

Patrick stood, alarmed the second he saw her. She'd never been good at hiding her emotions. He grabbed her by both arms, his fingers biting into her skin. "What's wrong?"

She wanted to blurt "My son found me," but she loved her husband and couldn't bludgeon him with the truth in front of his friend.

# CHAPTER THREE

ELIZA PUSHED ASIDE the orange-leafed branch of a maple.

"I need to talk to you." She glanced at her husband's friend, who'd also risen. "Alone, if you don't mind, Homer."

"Let's get a coffee," Patrick said.

He was still holding her too tightly, almost hurting her, but she said nothing. This might be the last time he would touch her. Grass whipped around their ankles like grasping fingers until they stepped onto the sidewalk. Dimly, she noted cars and people and the chirping of a few hardy birds that hadn't fled with the approach of cool weather.

At the crosswalk she stepped in front of a slow-moving vehicle whose driver hit his horn and his brakes, shouting insults she couldn't hear.

"Damn out-of-towner." Patrick yanked her closer. "What's wrong with you, Eliza?"

She memorized every beloved line on his face, the concern in his warm green eyes. "I'll tell you when we sit." Even God couldn't begrudge her a few more moments of her husband's love.

Patrick stared. "You're worrying me. Are you ill?"

"No—nothing like that. I'm... Let me tell you inside."

He waited for her to precede him through the doors of the Train Depot Café. Over the years, they'd divided the work at the B and B so that she did most of the morning shift and Patrick manned the evening desk. Patrick spent the cold mornings of winter at the café with Homer and sometimes with his father, Seth. Eliza often joined them for a late breakfast. The café's owner waved at them now as a signal that she'd bring their usual orders.

"Just coffee," Patrick said, and Becky Waters nodded.

Patrick pulled a vinyl-upholstered chair away from one of the Formica tables. Eliza sat, avoiding her husband's gaze until Becky brought their coffee.

"Tell me," Patrick said.

The truth trembled on the tip of her tongue, astounding her with the promise of unexpected relief. Sam had been a hard secret to keep for forty years. She looked at her husband, but his wary eyes made her hesitate. "You won't like it."

"After twenty-seven years of marriage, what are you afraid to tell me?"

"You're an honest man, Patrick, a blunt man." Another of his friends strolled past, clapping him on the shoulder and greeting Eliza. The second he saw her face, he cut his welcome short and sped to his own table. She leaned across the Formica, lowering her voice. If she didn't get this out now, she'd never say it. "I haven't been honest."

As if Patrick sensed the dangerous secret she was about to disclose, he leaned back, adding several inches of distance between them. The morning grew cooler. Desperate to keep her old life even as she forced her way into a new one, Eliza peered around at the walls. She cataloged the familiar menus and feed store advertisements, calendars that featured Jesus praying in the garden and others with scantily clad women sprawled on tractors.

This town had become her home. She'd have to leave if Patrick couldn't accept her and Sam. She took a deep breath. How could she doubt her husband? Gary Masters, Sam's birth father, had abandoned her to deal with consequences alone, but Patrick had always stood at her side.

"I did something I'm not proud of. Before I met you, when I was sixteen, I gave birth to a child." That wasn't what she meant. She wasn't ashamed of Sam—though she had been ashamed, the smart young girl who'd gotten in trouble with a boy who'd almost immediately left her.

Patrick's mouth opened on a sigh that might have been a groan. Eliza couldn't stop.

"A son," she said, "whom I gave up for adoption. My parents refused to help me. I went to a home for unwed mothers, but it wasn't like what your mother and Sophie do for the girls at the Mom's Place. I can't tell you how awful—''

"What are you saying?"

"You have to listen to me." He'd heard, but a blank expression betrayed his shock. She tried again. "I have a son. I gave him up—''

"I can't believe what you're saying.''

"You have to.''

He wiped sweat off his upper lip. "That's why you always slip Mom money.''

"You knew?" Her donations were supposed to have been her secret.

"Molly noticed. She thinks you do it because she was one of those girls. She gives her grandmother what she can as well.''

Eliza covered her face. "What will Molly think of me? What will this do to her? Me, falling off my pedestal.''

Patrick eyed her with the neutral expression he offered defendants in unwieldy court cases. "I was going to ask if you'd told her.''

"Not before I told you." How could he think that?

"You're so close I thought you might have…. What made you speak up after all this time? Certainly not an obligation to come clean.''

His unexpected taunt nearly strangled her. She left it hanging, poisonous in the air between them until she managed to gasp a short breath. "I wanted to tell you many times, but I've been afraid.'"

"After lying to me all these years, you should fear the truth." He sipped his coffee as they stopped being a couple and turned into two separate people.

"*Sam* is my son." Best to tear the Band-Aid off in one quick motion. Screaming inside, she allowed herself no outward reaction to her husband's hand falling limply from the table or to his eyes dulling in shock. "Nina and Tamsin are my granddaughters. Sam brought them because he was afraid they'd have no one else if something happened to him. I want to know them, Patrick."

His Adam's apple bobbed. "Sam?"

"Sam is my son."

"Sam at the Dogwood, with the two little girls?"

"Patrick, are you all right?" Had she caused him to have a stroke or something?

"I'm lost. You had a baby, and the baby grew up to be Sam?"

"I need him. He thinks he wants something from me, but I'm getting a second chance I can't turn down."

"Even if it costs you Molly and me?"

"Patrick, Tamsin knows—and she needs us. Sam and his girls could have all of us."

"I'm sorry about Tamsin, but I don't see us as one big happy family." As he straightened, he looked like a stranger. Patrick had never been a man who could withhold love for the sake of revenge, but his anger felt like hatred.

Her world splintered. She closed her eyes for the briefest moment, but she had no time for fear. She'd been afraid and given up Sam. Look where that had brought them.

"I can't stand to lose you, but I can't turn my back on my son again," she stated. "Think of Tamsin. She troubled you, too. She needs a family's love."

"My family's? How can I accept them? How can I even accept that you've hidden Sam's existence?"

"Try to understand. I've missed Sam every day of his life, but I could never tell anyone." Her eyes filled with tears. "You admired me because I came up here to the middle of nowhere to teach. You thought I was someone better than I've ever felt. How could I tell you?"

Her fear brought life back to Patrick's eyes, but not forgiveness.

"I won't speak for Molly." Standing abruptly, he threw money on the table. "But I can't fall in with this little change you're making in our lives. You're not the woman I married."

"Where are you going?"

"You have no right to ask." His cold gaze pronounced her guilty. "You never trusted me."

Patrick rushed to the door of the café, stumbling

against a table edge, bumping a rack of property rental magazines. Her heart broke. She pressed both hands to her chest as if she could catch the pieces.

Cast off again.

It hadn't happened in such a long time, she didn't know what to do. Cry or run after Patrick? Go to her son?

She couldn't do either. She had to talk to Molly. The world spun crazily. How could she face disillusionment in her daughter's eyes?

THE BALLOONS LAY in pieces on the floor. Molly swept them up, spreading a cloud of dust that smelled of wet children and dirty shoes and musty books.

A big splash of green balloon reminded her of Nina. The children in her class had written the letters they knew on their balloons. Earlier that morning Nina had written her name, and Sam's and Tamsin's with only a little help. She'd added Molly's name, remembering it well enough to write it again after Molly had spelled it for her only once.

Moments like that reminded Molly why she loved to teach. Children who were eager to learn made the mind-dulling business sessions and the fight for funding, even in such a small school, worthwhile.

Her thoughts returned to Sam's girls. Nina's curiosity charmed the daylights out of her, but Tamsin's Goth clothing and makeup alarmed her. In Nina's big sister, Molly sensed the quiet desperation that had once been her constant companion.

Molly often wondered if her colleagues worried about their students' home lives, but she never asked. Asking would expose one of those traits she wasn't sure every woman shared. Where "normal" people assumed their friends, their families, even the children they taught lived in safety, Molly prepared herself for...not the worst, but not the best, either.

Eliza and Patrick had taken her into foster care after Eliza discovered that the dirty-haired, unkempt girl who'd once inhabited a corner of her classroom was "living" in an empty house on the edge of town. Molly had been alone for seven months by the time Eliza realized her so-called parents had abandoned her to live their separate lives in Knoxville.

After several inconvenient visits from Child Protective Services, Bonnie, Molly's birth mother, and Mitch, her father, had been more than willing to give up their daughter. Eliza had made Molly feel special when the girl had wanted to hide in humiliation.

Molly had assumed no one could love her. Patrick and Eliza Calvert's home had been paradise— a most unreliable situation so far in Molly's short life. She'd tested her foster parents with behavior that horrified her in retrospect. But they'd kept loving her.

After the miscarriage, Patrick and Eliza had adopted her. In return for their kindness—and as penance for her own unforgivable mistakes—Molly had finally learned to consider every possible consequence before she made a move.

"Molly?"

She straightened, immediately alarmed. Tears had marked her mother's cheeks. "Mom." Aware only of an urge to fix whatever was bothering her mom, she crossed the room, taking her hands. "You're crying."

Eliza touched a lace hanky to one eye, smearing mascara. "A little. May I come in?"

"Why would you ask?" She forced a smile, but the floor seemed to tilt. She hated anything that hurt her mother.

Eliza floated into the classroom. She was still wearing the soft green dress she'd worn at breakfast, but a grease stain formed a circle just above her belted waist. Molly frowned. Her mom believed in the Southern tradition of chiffon and pearls for outside the house. She never wore grease.

"What's wrong?"

Eliza sniffed the air, showing a sweet profile that only became more lovable to Molly with each passing day. "No more chalk dust. I miss it."

Molly pointed at the long, shiny surface that had

taken the chalkboard's place. "Whiteboard. Smell the markers?"

"Not the same," she declared, avoiding the real subject she'd come to talk about. She was starting to shake.

Molly negotiated a path through the wooden desks and helped her to a chair. "I'll get you some water. What have you been doing?"

"I hardly know. I've walked and thought, and now I need to talk. I don't want water." With a sudden return of strength, Eliza pushed her into the closest seat. "Let me tell you about myself."

"What?" Adrenaline lifted Molly's voice several decibels. Something bad was coming. She gripped her mom's hands again, reminding herself not to crush the delicate bones. "You're scaring me."

"Your father's furious."

"Daddy?" She was eight years old again. In the way. Totally expendable. "What's happened?" For some reason, she thought of Sophie's mother. Aunt Nita's affair had nearly destroyed Sophie and Uncle Ethan, but Molly's mother would never have an affair. Not this mother, anyway. The one who'd cut all ties with her would have considered an affair small potatoes.

"It's Sam," her mom said. "And me—and something I did when I was a young girl."

"Sam?" Molly's mind went blank. "What does Sam have to do with you?

"I've kept the truth from you and your father."
She licked her dry lips. Molly wanted to get her
that water, but she couldn't make her feet move.

"What did you ever do that you'd have to
hide?" Suddenly, Sam's eyes, dark, watchful and
worried looking, swam in Molly's mind. He'd reminded her of her mom. That fast, Molly knew.
She'd also been pregnant too young. If any woman
on earth had lived a life that prepared her to accept
her mother's confession, Molly had.

But her image of Eliza left no room for such a
mistake, and shock blunted her good intentions. "I
can't...I can't believe you, of all people—"

"He's my son." Despair filled her mother's
voice instead of joy.

To Molly, Eliza had been the fairy godmother
who'd spirited her out of life's wreckage. Eliza
Calvert had abandoned a child? Never.

A hint of distaste must have shown on Molly's
face, but she'd been an abandoned child herself.
She couldn't contain her feelings or stop herself
from showing them.

Even as her mother pushed back from her, Molly
found restraint. Whatever Eliza had done, Molly
owed her for the only happiness she'd ever known.
She had to let her mother explain.

Eliza's cold hands felt devoid of life. Molly
chafed them, dropping to her knees. "I'm sorry,
Mom."

"You looked as if you hated me."

Molly swallowed tears. "I'm scared." Who knew what came next?

"I didn't want to give him up. He's my child—just as you are. But I didn't know how to give him a life. Please understand."

"I do." She couldn't imagine being able to make the same decision, but this was her turn to give back a little of the support she counted on from her mom. "But why are you sad? I'd give anything to have a second chance with the child I lost."

Hope entered her mother's eyes as Molly fought the innate dread of what Sam's prodigal homecoming meant for her. He was her mom's real son, born of her body. Her natural child, as Molly never could be. And he'd brought her Tamsin and Nina. Molly would never give her parents grandchildren.

"Can you forgive me this easily?" With a quiver in her voice, Eliza sounded as frightened as Molly had ever been. "Or are you turning yourself into the family protector again?"

"Do you know what I owe you?" Molly continued rubbing her mom's hands. "I carry my past like a lead weight. I'll never have anything to forgive you for."

Her mother's astonishment surprised Molly. "I don't want you to forgive me because of some imaginary debt," Eliza said. "And I thought we didn't worry about your past anymore."

Molly shrugged. "I don't talk about it because

you want me to forget, but some of my decisions don't seem forgivable.''

"Is that how you see me?"

She shook her head, loyalty adding emphasis to her denial. The somewhat terrifying news that Sam belonged to her mom didn't make Eliza any less of a good and loving mother. "What happened?" Molly asked.

"I wish your father had waited for an explanation." She pulled one hand free to cover her mouth. Over her fingers and her wedding ring, her eyes looked blacker than ever.

"Last night Sam's eyes reminded me of yours." Molly patted her mother's other hand and let her go. "Don't worry, Mom. Dad's probably stunned."

"I have to tell you—he walked out on me."

The room began a slow whirl. It was the one possibility she couldn't bear. "No." She searched in frightening darkness for comforting words. "You know Dad. He has to deliberate, but he loves you. He'll walk right back in, ready to listen."

Tears glittered in her mother's eyes, brighter than the burnished gold of her wedding band. "A woman who can hold such harmful grudges against herself shouldn't be able to believe the best of someone else."

"I haven't lived with you and Dad for seventeen years without getting to know you."

"You can't say that about me now."

"I am surprised." She pictured Sam, tall and lean and dark. The widowed father of two children. No one's idea of a brand-new son. "What does he want? Why did he come?" Then she remembered what he'd said about his wife and parents. "He's worried about Tamsin and Nina," she said. "He wants us to be their family."

Her mother scooted the small chair back and stood. "How did you guess?"

Molly returned to gathering balloon detritus. "I'd feel the same." She shuddered, thinking of Tamsin and Nina being alone as she had been until Eliza Calvert had discovered the truth about her. "Was he adopted at birth?"

"Yes. I agreed not to get in touch with his family and I never learned their names." Her mother plucked a ragged blue strip of balloon off the floor and passed it to Molly with an absent smile. "Can you be his sister? I think he needs us, Molly. He needs our normality."

His sister? The idea repelled her. "I'm twenty-five—too old for a brother." She'd never think of Sam as a brother.

"I don't see why."

Then Eliza hadn't taken a good look at Sam last night. Molly gnawed the inside of her lower lip. She hadn't noticed Sam for his fraternal qualities, and she couldn't look at him that way now. Not even for her mom. "I'll do my part."

"I don't like the sound of that." Her mother

knelt to pull a tangle of balloon bits from under a group of four desks pushed together. "You want to hold back, but our new family won't work unless you accept him and the girls."

"I don't even have to think about accepting them." She'd welcome Jack the Ripper if her mother asked her to. "But one big happy family? Sam, as a brother, seems odd to me."

Eliza curved her hands around Molly's wrists. "I need you to try. You are his sister now."

Desperation in her mother's tone and fingers made Molly smile without responding to her demands. "What about Dad?"

"I don't know." Eliza sank onto one of the desks. "He said he doesn't know me, and I got the feeling he might not want to."

"After he understands, he'll bend over backward." Molly dropped the balloon bits into the garbage can. "He already learned to love me because of you. He knows how this works."

"Are you crazy?" Eliza snorted, the only unladylike sound she'd ever made, and Molly couldn't help laughing. Her mom took Molly's shoulders in her hands. "No one learned to love you. Your father and I couldn't love you more if we'd brought you home from the hospital the day you were born, as I wish I could have done with both my children."

Staring into her mother's eyes, Molly longed to believe, without doubt, just once in her life. Words were so easy to say. Bonnie, who'd abandoned her in every way a human being could abandon her child, had said words like that. But now, as then, words weren't enough.

Molly's inability to trust gave her sympathy for her adoptive father. A firm defender of justice, he might not know how to stop feeling betrayed.

But she hugged her mom. "Why don't we ask the girls and Sam to come apple-picking this weekend?" Honestly, it was the last thing she wanted. Apple-picking at Gran's was her favorite family gathering, and she was childishly unwilling to share.

Her dad and Zach always fired up the deep fryer for apple fritters. Her mom and Aunt Beth and Grandpa led the smaller children in a pagan march of gratitude among the fruit-laden trees. Best of all, everyone shouted gossip and news between the heavy branches and then ate potluck lunch until they slumped to the ground, overfull of good food and family feeling.

Three more pickers would lose themselves among the teeming Calverts. Sam and Tamsin and Nina couldn't ask for a less stressful introduction to their new family.

Eliza's grateful tears made Molly both proud and guilty. Her mom hugged her again—a quick squeeze that reminded Molly that Sam might have a place in her mother's heart, but she owned a corner already.

"Thanks, honey. I knew I could count on you."

Smiling hurt, but for her mom's sake Molly had to welcome Sam into her territory.

"Dad, I think Mr. Calvert's leaving."

As Tamsin opened the door, Sam looked up, and the ball he and Nina had been tossing hit him in the knees. Nina collapsed in giggles.

"Why do you say that?"

"I was reading on a bench in the square, and I saw him pack his car and drive off."

Sam stared at her. First, she hadn't asked if she could leave the Dogwood. Second, she should have told him about Patrick before he'd driven away. Last, Sam had managed to ruin Eliza's marriage, the last thing he'd meant to do. "I hoped it wouldn't come to this. He's really gone?" Sam asked.

"Yeah."

"Have you seen Eliza?"

"No. I was surprised she wasn't with him."

"Where's Mr. Patrick going?" Nina asked.

"I don't know, sweetie. Tamsin, why didn't you tell me when you saw him packing?"

"I'm not his keeper." Tamsin looked blank.

Annoying, but she was right. Keeping up with Patrick Calvert after her own father had ruined the man's life wasn't her responsibility. "Will you look after Nina?"

"If I don't have to drink fake tea with that lizard and Judy."

"Ooh, tea." Nina danced toward her sister. "Let's play tea party. I'll go get everyone."

"Yeah," Tamsin said, meaning the opposite. She scooped the ball off the ground and tossed it at her sister. "Let's play with this."

"Nina, play catch with Tamsin, or maybe try out the swings over in the side yard." Sam withstood a wave of guilt. He couldn't take back the truth now, but he hadn't meant to hurt Eliza or her family. A vision of Molly flashed in his mind. His guilt doubled. "I won't be gone long, Tamsin. I just want to find Eliza."

"All right, but she may want to be alone."

Naturally, his daughter considered him to be the most inept human being ever called upon to offer comfort. He'd done her little good over the past year and a half.

He punched a small, silver bell on the reception desk. No one came. He called Eliza's name. Tapping the scarred, polished wood, he waited a minute or so.

Finally, he circled the desk and opened the door behind it. The dark hall was empty. He'd almost hoped Eliza would be hiding there, reluctant to talk.

"Eliza?" The hall emptied into the wide kitchen, which didn't feel half as welcoming without his birth mother and his daughters there. And

Molly, but he could hardly bear to think of what he'd done to her.

Molly might try to look hard, but she hadn't been able to conceal her tenderness with Nina or her concern for Tamsin last night.

He turned toward the stairs. Somewhere up there lay his birth mother's room, but he had no right to climb those stairs uninvited.

He'd caused the havoc in this home, and he should try to fix it if he could. Forcing himself up the stairs, he wondered what to say if he found Eliza.

He knocked on the first two doors. Silence met him.

At the third door, he knocked again and Eliza immediately opened it.

"He's my son. I have nothing else to say, Pat—" She backed up, her eyes red from crying. She pushed her fingers beneath each eye and looked away. "Oh. I thought you were my husband."

"He left you?"

"Wouldn't you if you found out your wife had lied to you the whole time you'd known her?"

"What do you mean?"

"I never told him about you."

He understood. Fiona had lied at first. She'd thought he wouldn't want to date her if he knew about the condition that had prompted so many prospective parents to leave her at the orphanage. But he'd fallen in love with her.

He managed a hesitant smile. "I'd forgive her once she explained."

Eliza turned, covering her eyes again. "I'm sorry. This isn't your problem."

"It is. I came hoping Tamsin and Nina might be part of a family, but if I've already ruined yours, I'll leave."

"You won't." Eliza turned. "Now that I know about you, you aren't going anywhere and you aren't taking my granddaughters." He must have looked startled, because she laughed at his expression. "I don't make the same mistake twice, Sam."

"I have a conscience."

"So do I."

Her conscience made his decision harder. "I don't want to stay because you feel you should make up for the past." He straightened. "I had a good life."

"You don't understand." She grasped his hand, and he stared at the prominent veins on the back of hers. They'd lost a lot of years already. "Sam, look at me."

"Even if you want to know my daughters, Tamsin couldn't stand being part of the reason your husband left you. She's been through enough. We'll pack and get out of here. You find Patrick and tell him to come home."

Eliza shook her head, her gaze directed inward. "You can't turn back the clock by leaving now. Do you think Patrick can forget any more than I could?"

Sam pulled his hand free, rubbing his face as an excuse. The truth was he'd never known so much ready affection. It unsettled him, especially when he'd caused a rift between Eliza and her husband.

"Maybe I could talk to Patrick," he suggested. "I honestly don't want to stay if your family can't accept us."

"You're staying." She shrugged. "Patrick does love me. He'll find his way home. Until then, I've finished my crying. I'll come down and start some supper."

"I can't stay in this bed and breakfast after Patrick's moved out."

"I say you can. Bardill's Ridge might as well get used to the idea of you, and Patrick should, too. I know my husband. He won't ask me to give up my son." Her smile looked more broken than bright. "Besides, staying here will be best for the girls."

She might be right, and she certainly looked determined, bracing as if for a tempest. If she truly wanted a relationship with him and his daughters, staying under her roof would be best for Tamsin and Nina, who both missed having a maternal figure around.

"Please don't go." Eliza touched his arm

briefly. "You're my family, too." Tears filled her eyes, but she struggled to continue. "I won't lose any more time with you or my grandchildren. Now, let me clean my face, and I'll come downstairs."

He accepted her dismissal, knowing he hadn't eased her distress. He hurried down the hall and the stairs to make sure Tamsin was okay.

The garden was empty, but somewhere Nina laughed. Sam strode through leaves, sparse on the ground as yet, to the side yard, where Tamsin was pushing Nina on a swing.

"Higher," Nina said, queen of all she observed.

"This is high enough." Tamsin sounded maternal.

Sam breathed a sigh of relief. Maybe she'd only pretended her detachment from her sister.

"Daddy!" Nina flung her head back, and her braid scraped the scuffed ground. "Look how high I go."

"We have to teach you to pump."

"I can do that." She flailed her feet and he tried not to laugh.

He joined Tamsin behind her, taking over as Nina's locomotion.

"I found Eliza," he said under cover of Nina's enthusiastic "wees."

Tamsin searched his features. "Is she sorry we came?"

What a relief. His daughter cared. He felt like

crying and hugging her at the same time, but she wouldn't welcome either. "No." He tried to make it seem like no big deal. "I told her we were leaving and she asked us to stay. She doesn't want to lose any more time with you and Nina."

Biting her lip, Tamsin turned away. The breeze blew her hair around her face, offering extra cover. Sam waited, wanting with all his heart to hug his daughter and explain that Eliza was smart to want her in her life.

Tamsin cleared her throat. "That doesn't mean Mr. Calvert will like us."

It was his turn to look away. If Eliza was willing to choose a son and grandchildren over her husband, he should be grateful, but he didn't want to destroy anyone else's happiness.

"You can't fix everything just the way you want it, Dad. You can't make Mr. Calvert glad to know us, and you can't make a family."

"If we all want a family, we'll be one. You and Nina will have other people who care about you."

"I want my mom back. You can't fix that and it's all I want."

She started to move away from him, but he caught her. She stared at his hand, willing it away. Maybe he and Tamsin had both lost too much to make themselves vulnerable again.

"I love you, Tamsin. No matter how hard you push Nina and me away, we're still your father and sister. We aren't going anywhere, and you don't have to be afraid to love us.''

''Yeah?'' She pulled back. ''You're afraid or we wouldn't be here.''

She sped across the grass. He stared after her, his heart aching for her lost childhood. Fiona's death had made Tamsin a lot older than fifteen.

# CHAPTER FOUR

SATURDAY MORNING WAS cool enough to make Molly hunt down her favorite faded University of Tennessee sweatshirt. It'd taken her three years to wash the bright orange into a shade that didn't blind all comers. She dressed quickly, having promised her mother a ride up to Gran and Grandpa's orchard. She was weaving her hair into a braid when the doorbell rang.

Racing down the stairs, she expected to find her mother. Instead, her dad faced her warily. He hadn't been home in four days, ever since her mother had dropped her bombshell.

"Have you seen them?" he asked.

"Not since Mom told me." Visiting the Dogwood would have felt like disloyalty to him.

"Me, either. I feel he's displaced me."

"You're wrong, but you could talk to Mom about living in the place you're supposed to." Her heart beating hard for her father's pain, Molly stood aside to allow him in. "Sam is Mom's son. You're her husband, and she misses you."

"I've called her. I always hear Nina chattering

in the background." He closed the door. "You're wondering why I haven't called you."

She nodded, finishing her braid. She'd wondered if he'd decided she was another encumbrance her mom had forced on him.

"You and your mother are so close, and I knew you must be disappointed in me. This is the first time I've felt capable of seeing you."

"Dad." She hugged him, hating his unhappiness. "You're crazy if you think I can do without you."

He laughed, hugging her back. "Thanks. I needed that."

"Have you made up your mind? What are you going to do?"

He stepped away, obviously still stunned by all that had happened. "Your mother lied to me from the day we met." Molly started to speak, but he held up his hands. "You don't have to tell me it was more an omission of truth. When you're on the receiving end, there's no difference."

"I see why she might have been afraid to tell you."

"We're adults, Molly."

"Imagine how much harder her choices were as time passed."

"I've lived a lie. My family is a lie."

"I can't let you say that! You have a right to feel betrayed. I'm scared, and I feel sorry for both of us, but our family is real." She was trying to reassure herself as much as him. "And Mom needs us to include Sam and Nina and Tamsin. You already gave one stranger a home, and you can do it again."

"You were never a stranger." He kissed her temple. "We assumed the stork dropped you off at the wrong house."

A rush of gratitude filled Molly. "That's what I needed to hear, Dad, but Tamsin and Nina need love, too. And Sam must or he wouldn't have come this far to find his birth mother."

"I don't trust Sam."

Molly blinked, startled to find she wasn't the only suspicious Calvert on the mountain. "I don't know how he could have been more honest, but I'd like to be certain he understands what he's brought on himself."

Her father let her go. "What do you mean?"

"He's here now—and he's told Mom who he is. He's come between you and her, so he must be vital to her happiness. He'd better not suddenly get cold feet and sneak out of town at midnight."

Grinning, her father nudged her arm. "You're the most territorial little cuss. I don't want to find you've body-slammed Dr. Lockwood."

She grimaced, unashamed to admit she had a protective streak. She'd once tackled a fellow high school sophomore for tripping her best friend, hampered by a cast at the time, on the stairs. "A loving father wouldn't refer to such a humiliating episode. And Tommy Redburn deserved it." Her friend had been the class scapegoat—the kid the others picked on. She'd never stood bullies well, but she'd gotten in awful trouble for handling Tommy Redburn "her way."

"Just keep your mitts off Sam."

"I'll make you a deal. Sam leaves the orchard whole in body if you'll offer Mom a ride today."

He stiffened as his smile faded. Her father enjoyed being pushed around about as much as she did.

"Eliza and I have to talk before we put on a front for the family. I'm not going today."

"You just changed your mind—to keep me out of trouble." Molly gave her watch a pointed glance. "If you leave now, you'll find Mom on the curb with a picnic basket."

"I'm not ready to see your mother."

"Come on, Dad. The longer you wait, the easier you'll find not speaking to her." She urged him toward the door. "I'll bet she's hoping you'll show up. She'll have cooked all your favorites. Deviled eggs and fried chicken, Patrick Calvert style. And you know Aunt Beth's made her coleslaw. A cordon bleu chef would kill for a crack at that recipe."

"Coleslaw is hardly ever cordon bleu fare." But he turned the doorknob and started down her walkway, still grumbling.

His compliance surprised her. He must be eager to heal the break with her mother. "Tell Mom she can count on us to be on our most hospitable behavior.''

''You're as bossy as she is.'' He tossed the cranky accusation over his shoulder as he opened his car door.

Maybe she should have gone along to act as a buffer between her parents.

No. Privacy carried stronger healing properties than having a buffer would.

She hurried back to the kitchen to finish her own packing. She layered her picnic basket with fresh fruit and rolls she'd bought early that morning. Fortunately, her mom had only delegated her foodstuffs she didn't have to cook. Capable chefs didn't run in Molly's generation of Calverts.

She grabbed a short jacket in case it got cool and ran to her rust-stricken MG. She had to scrunch a little to fit in the driver's seat, but she'd loved the car since the day she'd talked a Nashville-bound mandolin player into trading it for a bus ticket and five hundred dollars.

At sixteen, she'd been afraid to drive her new prize home because her parents kept hoping she'd be like other girls instead of working car deals with guys at the café. But her dad had congratulated her on the transaction and let her keep the car.

She downshifted up the mountain road to the orchard. A fence provided nominal privacy around her grandparents' property. Only a dust cloud lin-

gered from the previous car to pass as she got out
to open the gate. She must be late.

Not quite late enough. She saw Sam the second
she reached the square of mown field they all
parked on. He straightened from taking something
out of his trunk, and she owned up to her real
reason for staying away from the B and B.

She'd wanted to see Sam. She'd sensed his deep
wounds that first night, and something about his
pain touched a chord in her.

She ignored her racing pulse as she nosed her
MG into a space at the orchard's edge. Sam was
looking for family who'd care for his daughters
and accept him. Like her mother, he might consider her his sister.

The moment he saw her, his body went still. He
waited, lean and too male in faded jeans and an
oat-colored sweater. She searched his sharp features for signs of her mother's face, but only his
eyes were like Eliza's.

Releasing a long, slow breath, Molly opened her
car door and then popped the trunk lid. Sam joined
her, reaching for the picnic basket.

''You don't have to.'' She broke off, coming
face-to-face with the warp-and-weave of his
sweater. She'd hardly ever known a man tall
enough to make her look up.

She started at the center of his broad chest and
followed the strong column of his throat—which
worked as he tried to swallow. His confident mouth

presented a masculine challenge she refused to accept. Those kinds of challenges were best left in her past.

Sam's nose was slightly too large and just a touch crooked. Maybe he'd also had to tackle an enemy. Molly pulled herself together. Sam was a handsome man and she'd noticed. She knew the danger signs well enough to avoid them.

But then she saw black eyes filled with too much emotion.

Sam had known the kind of loneliness that often licked at her heels. Whether he knew it or not, he wanted family because he was alone, too.

"Let me carry the basket." His husky tone scared her. Time to think of Sam as her mother's son. He held out his own basket, clearly bought from a store, the goodies inside wrapped in cellophane. "You can stack yours on top."

"I'm fine." With a death grip on the handles, she searched for other company among the parked cars and trucks. But the two of them were alone. She took a deep breath. "My mother told me who you are."

His eyes widened minutely. "I've wanted to talk to you and your father. I tried to find him, but even Homer didn't know where he'd gone."

"How do you know Homer?" What she meant was "How are you so familiar with my hometown and my family's friends?"

"I shared a bench with him for two hours yesterday morning."

"Dad doesn't trust you."

"Neither do you."

"You catch on fast." Her basket was growing heavier by the second so she got to the point. "I trust my mom. I'll do what she wants, but I hope you're committed to the long haul."

Startled laughter lightened those dark, familiar eyes. "The long what?"

"I mean, don't leave now that Mom knows who you are." That wasn't right. She could hardly expect him to squat in the nearest empty house. "I mean, don't dump her."

Anger tightened his mouth, but Molly wasn't intimidated. She balanced her basket under her arm and flexed her fingers.

Sam muttered a word she rarely heard these days. "Give me that and stop trying to prove how tough you are. I'm not looking for a fight." He put his own basket on the ground and then took hers. His was smaller, so he motioned for her to place it on top. "I told Eliza the truth. I came for Nina's and Tamsin's sake. I've been curious about your mother all my life, and I'll be glad if we eventually come to care about each other, but my daughters have lost their mother and their grandparents. I want to know someone will love them if they lose me, too."

Touched by the pain in his voice, Molly forgot

to keep her distance as they walked. "Family's a hell of a thing, isn't it?" They had that in common, too—the unwieldy branches of a "not normal" family tree.

"But worth any indignity." A smile started in his eyes and fanned out in lines that ran from his nose to the corners of his mouth.

She liked those lines too much. They reflected hours of concern and caring. Molly added space between herself and her mother's son. Males had fooled her before.

Laughter from the orchard gave her an excuse to look away from him, but she had to finish her speech before they reached the others. "You'll break Mom's heart if you leave now." She donned the expression that had kept her safe on the streets when she was eight and alone. "Don't even think about hurting her."

"Why would I want to hurt Eliza?"

"I don't mean to be cruel, but how do we know we aren't your rebound family? You might be trying to replace your adoptive parents with my mom, but that wouldn't be fair to her or to your daughters."

His scowl suggested she didn't know what she was saying. "I hired detectives to find Eliza, so I know you were alone when you were little. Your past is none of my business, but wouldn't you do anything to keep a child of yours from feeling the way you did when you had no one?"

His question was a punch in the stomach. She'd lost the only child she'd ever have, pregnant so young her body hadn't been able to carry a child to term. Right or wrong, she felt guilty and responsible for her baby's death in utero.

Molly sped up, pushing the past out of her mind. She searched for her father's car. He and her mom must not have arrived yet, but the rest of her family, laughing and chatting in the orchard, reassured her. She stopped to face Sam. "Do your girls and my other relatives know what's going on?"

"Tamsin knows. Nina doesn't, and Eliza hasn't told anyone except you and your dad."

Molly's misgivings flooded back. "You're still taking a wait-and-see attitude?"

"I have to feel sure Eliza wants to be a grandmother for the rest of her life."

"Oh. What if Nina and Tamsin get attached to her?" Molly's world, so safe and secure for so long, seemed to rock on an unsteady axis.

Sam nodded, his eyes still hard. "We'll all explain soon," he said. "I haven't left any of us a lot of choice."

Molly shook her head. "What choice did you have? I can understand what you've done, but you'd better know I'll do anything to protect her."

Amusement tightened his smile. "I don't think a woman's ever threatened me before."

"I don't make threats." She shrugged. "Not since high school, anyway. But I can feel how hurt you are, and I'm afraid you're reacting on instinct.''

''I'm not.'' If he wasn't honest, he gave the best performance she'd ever seen, looking straight into her eyes with an earnest gaze. His small smile chipped at the tension. ''You and your threats may be an unfortunate example for Tamsin and Nina, but if Eliza can inspire so much love she's going to be great for them.''

''I owe her,'' she confessed, before she realized she'd spoken the words out loud. Unwilling to expose so much of herself this soon, she turned toward the orchard. Let her mother's basket-toting gentleman son keep pace if he could.

He managed with no effort. ''Where is your mom?''

''She and my dad aren't here yet. At least I don't see his car.'' She made a big production of looking for it. ''Where are Tamsin and Nina?''

''Your aunt—Beth, I think—was with a man who really looks like James Kendall. She showed the girls to one of the tables, and they were sampling snacks when I came back for our stuff.''

''It is James Kendall. His daughter married one of my cousins.''

''I remember the stories about that. About a year ago. I didn't connect the families.''

Molly nodded. The media mogul's increasingly obvious feelings for Aunt Beth probably meant the families were going to be even more connected one day soon.

"Molly?"

She didn't like looking at Sam. She couldn't avoid his grief. He needed her mom, and she hated fearing her mother would find her true child more lovable than the daughter she'd saved from homelessness.

"Did you say your dad and Eliza are coming together?"

"I hope so."

"Good. I didn't want to break them up."

It would be easier to think Sam had stormed into town, not caring what he did to her family.

A whiff of barbecue drifted past, and Molly sniffed. Any excuse to end such a personal conversation. "I'm starving, too. I'll see what the girls found to eat."

This time she escaped Sam. He would have had to run to keep up.

LUGGING BOTH BASKETS, Sam gave Molly plenty of room to reach her family before him. He felt conspicuous with his gift-store basket full of cookies and fruit. Everyone else had brought food they'd prepared in their kitchens. He and the girls had decided not to come empty-handed, but now the store-bought goods felt inappropriate.

A shout rose ahead of him from the clearing where the Calvert family had set up buffet tables.

He arrived to find Molly the recipient of hugs and happy greetings. Her smile, tender with love for the people surrounding her, made him a little envious. He couldn't wait to see Tamsin and Nina smile like that.

Molly broke away from her cousin Sophie. "I'm starving," she said again, and headed to the table where Tamsin was dangling a pickle above Nina's head.

"I want it." Stretching up on tiptoes, Nina grabbed.

"My mom made those." Casually, as if she weren't helping Nina at all, Molly plucked another pickle from the jar and handed it to Sam's younger daughter.

Sam stared at his basket again.

"Your mom makes pickles?" Nina sounded as if she hadn't known people could. "My mom didn't know how to make pickles."

"Mom did other things." Tamsin rose to Fiona's defense.

"She raised a couple of pretty good girls," Molly said, earning Tamsin's obvious disgust.

"I'm not a kid. Don't say stuff just to make me feel better."

Sam set his and Molly's baskets on the end of the table with a thud that got his older daughter's attention. Tamsin blushed.

"We're guests," he said.

"I know. Sorry." She grimaced in Molly's direction.

"No. You were right. Have you seen the cupcakes on the dessert table?" She pointed. "My cousin's wife makes them, and I never can wait to try them. We could break one into three if you want." Clearly assailed by a second thought, she looked to Sam for permission.

He shrugged and she herded the girls in front of herself. He unstacked their baskets and then followed, interested in anyone who could patch up a tiff with Tamsin in short order.

Molly chose a cupcake and broke it in half, passing the pieces to Tamsin and Nina. Then she picked up another and broke it, too, but she surprised Sam by turning to offer him half. He hadn't realized she knew he was behind her.

"Thanks." He took it but didn't try it.

Molly bit into her piece, grinning. "They're the best. Go on."

Nina ate the chocolate bottom of hers and passed the vanilla frosting back to Molly. "I don't like this part."

"Oh." Before Molly could dispose of it, Tamsin scraped what she could off Molly's fingers and shook it into a garbage can.

"Napkins?" she asked.

Molly found a pile on the end of a table and passed one, two-fingered, to Tamsin before she got another and cleaned her own hand.

"Can I have more?" Nina asked.

"She won't eat dinner, Dad."

"That's just what I was going to say, Tamsin."

Behind them, more shouts rose. They all turned to find Patrick and Eliza entering the clearing. They were walking a good distance apart, and Sam couldn't help recalling how happy they'd been the night he'd met them, dancing up their walkway.

He glanced at Molly. She lifted both shoulders, but her eyes revealed no emotion. She edged closer so that no one else could hear. "They're together. That's good enough for today."

After running the gauntlet of hugs, Patrick started toward Molly, and Eliza seemed startled to find herself at the other side of the crowd of Calverts.

Patrick hugged his daughter, eyeing Sam with something almost akin to dislike. "I did it," he said to Molly. "Do I get a gold star, teacher?"

"I don't bring them to picnics," she said. "Everything okay?"

"Yeah." He offered his hand to Sam. "Good to see you."

Taken completely off guard by Patrick's change, Sam shook hands with the other man. "Thanks."

"Tamsin. Nina." Patrick patted Nina's shoulder. "I'm glad you two came. We'll start picking apples soon."

Another little girl, blond and sweet-looking, barreled up to the table to stop directly in front of Nina without a word.

Nina stared at her, twisting one foot on the trampled grass. "Hi," she finally said and then giggled.

"This is Lily, Nina." Patrick hugged the girl against his side. "Lily, this is Nina. She's about a year younger than you."

"Are you in Aunt Molly's class at school?"

"I don't live here," Nina said.

"What are you doing here?"

Tamsin laughed, as if she were wondering the same thing. Teenage angst, or was she already fed up with the family picnic?

"We're on bacation," Nina said.

"I have a brother." Losing interest in the "whys," Lily pointed toward the crowd of Calverts. "Wanna see him?"

"Can I, Daddy?" Nina reached for her sister's hand, ready to drag Tamsin along to view this brother of Lily's.

"Go ahead," Sam said. "But you'll be fine on your own. I can see you from here, and Tamsin looks as if she's dying for another cupcake."

"Don't ruin your tights, Tamsin." Nina started off, and Lily grabbed her arm to lead her in the right direction.

Tamsin blushed again, glancing at Molly. "She means my appetite." She smoothed her baggy black jeans.

Patrick leaned behind her to filch a pre-lunch

cupcake of his own. "Sometimes you need a trans-
lator for little kid talk, don't you?"

"I'm used to her." Tamsin looked at Sam as he
glanced distractedly over her shoulder at Eliza ap-
proaching. "Dad, I left my book in the car. Can I
go get it?"

"You don't want to read on a day like today,"
Eliza said, overhearing. She grasped Tamsin's
shoulders. "Come see the orchard. We'll take the
rest of the children."

Molly eyed Tamsin, anxious to let her off the
hook if her mom's plan didn't appeal. "Maybe
Tamsin doesn't want to…"

At Eliza's hopeful expression, Tamsin softened.
"I'm fine," she said. "Besides, Nina won't go
without Dad or me."

"I'll come, too, Mom. Lily's showing Evan to
Nina." Molly smiled at Tamsin. "He's the
brother."

Tamsin observed the three small children across
the clearing. The boy was clinging to his pregnant
mother's leg.

"Olivia looks as if she could use a break, too,"
Molly murmured.

"Yeah." Tamsin's grin seemed to forge a connection between her and Molly. His daughter was
hardly ever so willing to be friends.

"Let's go, then." Eliza prodded her daughter
and Tamsin with a gentle hand on their waists.

"We'll choose the best trees before anyone else starts."

"Tamsin…" Sam glanced at the ladders. "Nina's too small to climb."

"Dad!" She managed to convey impatience and condescension at the same time. She didn't even have to add, "I know." That was more like his Tamsin.

Eliza sent her husband an anxious smile, and he returned it, but Sam had a feeling the other man hadn't recovered from his anger.

"I wanted to talk to you," Sam said.

"You don't have to. My wife explained."

"I didn't mean to cause problems for you and Eliza."

"What did you think would happen?"

Sam contemplated the blunt question. "I guess I assumed she'd have told you about me already."

Patrick didn't answer. Sam saw that as a good sign. He might not be willing to defend Eliza's actions yet, but he wasn't about to condemn her, either.

"I hoped to find someone else Tamsin and Nina could count on, but I didn't mean to hurt your family."

Patrick watched his wife gather up the small children and Tamsin. With Molly at the end of the line, they headed into the trees, a pagan parade, greeting the harvest.

"I see how much you love your daughters," Patrick said.

"I do, sir."

"I'm not old enough to be 'sir' to you."

"Sorry." His adoptive parents had brought him up with manners, and he tended to forget his mother had been barely more than a child when she'd given birth to him. Patrick couldn't be much older than Eliza's fifty-six.

"I apologize," Patrick said. "I'm eager to find fault with you because I want my wife and family back the way we were. I didn't ask you and the girls to come into our life." He shook his head, his regret apparent. "That sounds harsh. Tamsin and Nina are lovable, and Eliza's perfect for them. Probably because of you, she has a soft spot for children in need."

Sam almost resented the inference that he couldn't love his daughters enough, but Patrick was right. Why else would he have barged into Eliza's life? "You don't think you can accept us?"

"I will in time, but right now you're a constant reminder of how long Eliza kept a secret from me."

"You're a relentlessly frank family."

"It's the only way," Patrick said. "My daughter forced me to see Eliza today. She's right about not waiting to patch up this situation. Eliza isn't giving me a choice and I might as well face what's to come."

"It's my fault. There were probably a million better ways to handle this situation."

Patrick remained silent, considering. "I can't think of even one, but I still need time." Tension built until a kid's marching song drew them both toward the trees. Eliza had her gang walking circles beneath the apple-laden limbs. Even Tamsin.

Sam brushed his thumb across his forehead. "Eliza's a miracle worker."

"Molly probably worked the miracle."

"Molly?" Even to himself, Sam sounded too intrigued. He continued, avoiding Patrick's eyes. "Tamsin refuses to have fun with her old friends. I can't believe what I'm seeing."

The women and children paraded their way. Patrick performed a military turn toward the loaded tables and the frosty coolers. "I do love my wife, but I thought all women had nice singing voices until the first time Eliza burst into song." He checked his watch. "It's early, but I think this performance calls for a beer."

# CHAPTER FIVE

NO SOONER DID PATRICK leave in search of an early beer or maybe less stressful company than Olivia Kendall Calvert strode purposefully to Sam's side.

"Morning," she said.

He nodded. "How are you?"

"I hear you're a guest at the Dogwood."

Should he engage in the Calvert habit for bluntness and disclose that he knew she was a journalist? Her magazine, *Relevance,* might not be cutthroat news, but it wasn't all frills and entertainment, either. He held out his hand. "Sam Lockwood."

"*Dr.* Sam Lockwood, according to Sophie. Have you come to help her and the other physicians at the community health center?"

A surprisingly cool breeze kicked up, brushing the back of Sam's neck. He couldn't lie and say he'd come strictly on vacation, but he and the girls remained Eliza's secret to tell.

"I've heard about the community center. Sounds like a good idea. This area seems fairly remote."

"How did you find us?"

Her phrasing made him cautious. "I asked around when my daughters and I decided we wanted to see the Smokies." True enough. He'd been asking about Eliza for sixteen months.

"I didn't realize the Dogwood was so renowned. You spoke to a former guest?"

Sam had to laugh. "Why are you interrogating me?"

Olivia smiled, too. "I'm new to this family, but they are mine, and I watch out for my own. I noticed the strain between you and Molly, and Patrick and Eliza don't usually invite their guests to family events. There's something different about you, and 'something different' usually indicates a situation I should investigate."

"You've lost me," he said. "Why should you investigate?"

"Molly's instincts are reliable. She doesn't trust you."

It shouldn't matter. But he turned to look for Molly, grimacing as he realized Olivia would know her comment had gotten under his skin. "Did she discuss my family with you?" he asked.

"No. Should she?"

He shook his head, half his mind on that beer Patrick had mentioned. "I don't see why. Excuse me. I think I'll talk to Sophie about the community center."

"I wonder why you'd do that."

"I love my work." He concentrated on her motivation. This family was hers now. These people looked after each other. Soon Tamsin and Nina would have an equal claim to all this security.

He traversed the clearing to the brick barbecue, which had already been pressed into service. Sophie and an older man, probably Seth Calvert, were hard at work cooking. Or so Sam thought till he reached them.

"Sophie, listen to my advice," the man said. "Or you know you're liable to ruin everyone's meal."

With a wave of her hand, Sophie ignored his assessment of her cooking skills. "Grandpa, Ian's been teaching me."

"About brisket." He pointed to a large, square, foil-wrapped package on the top level of the barbecue. "And that'll be fine in an hour or so. Leave everything else alone."

"I've been nursing this brisket along since six this morning without causing a disaster. You can trust me with a hot dog."

"Not one I'm eating." Laughing at her wordless frustration, her grandfather planted a kiss on her forehead.

"All right, all right." She pulled away when she noticed Sam. "Hey. Have you met my grandfather?"

The older man transferred a long-handled fork

from his right hand to his left and offered to shake. "Seth Calvert."

"Sam Lockwood. My daughters are…" Searching for them, Sam spied Molly's red sweater. Her body sweetly curved, she was leaning over to help Nina choose apples. Her perfect heart-shaped behind, in worn jeans, distracted Sam, and he had to clear his throat.

Too young. Eliza's daughter. Out of bounds, even for wayward, lascivious thoughts.

"My daughters, Tamsin and Nina, are down there with Eliza and Molly."

"We're glad you all joined us." Seth reached into his back pocket and pulled out a handkerchief. He wiped sweat off his forehead, perspiration that seemed out of proportion to the barbecue's meager heat, especially on a cool fall day. His skin seemed pale despite his tan.

Sam glanced at Sophie. She'd been as close to the fire as her grandfather, and she was dressed more warmly, in a fleece vest as well as a sweater, but her skin seemed normal and dry.

Sam tried to turn off his work ethic. He knew nothing about Seth Calvert. After a week away from his office, he must feel the urge to diagnose someone.

"Sophie, I wondered if we could talk about your health center. I might know people who'd like to contribute if you still need funding."

"Not here you don't talk about it." Seth nudged

his granddaughter. "Get the man something to drink. I hear enough about the clinic at home. You notice your grandmother hasn't arrived yet, Sophie?"

"She won't be long." Sophie took Sam's arm, towing him away with a stealthy glance at Seth. "My grandmother hopes to work with us part-time, but her schedule annoys Grandpa. She's at the baby farm this morning, in fact."

"The what?"

"The Mom's Place."

Sam shook his head, confused.

"It's a spa for pregnant women who want some time off and a little pampering before their babies come. My gran opened it years ago, and we both run it now. We're training a new doctor who's joined us, so Gran's been working extra hours."

"And your grandfather resents the overtime?"

Sophie glanced at Seth as they reached a deep cooler full of ice and cans and glass bottles. "She's supposed to retire any minute now, but she keeps finding excuses to work." Sophie seemed to remember he wasn't one of the family. "Not that you want to inspect the dirty laundry."

"I'm glad you told me. I noticed your grandfather was perspiring just this side of profusely, but if he's annoyed with your grandmother that would explain it."

Sophie narrowed her gaze. "I've noticed the sweating, and a couple of months ago, when my husband had an accident, Grandpa came to tell me, and I didn't like his color.''

"You work too hard, too," Sam said.

"Goes with the territory, or you wouldn't have noticed."

Here in the midst of laughter and fluttering leaves and a sky full of puffy clouds, he had to agree. "But anxiety for your husband and anger with his wife could explain both symptoms—if they were symptoms."

"Yes…" She drew out the word. "But maybe I'll ask him to arrange a physical. No—I'll ask Gran. She'll give him a strong push." Sophie waved a hand toward the cooler. "Have something to drink and tell me about your funding sources."

"I have friends in Savannah—"

Before he finished, a giggle followed by a warning shout distracted him. The giggle he recognized. The shout filled him with paternal panic, and he spun around.

He could just make out Molly's jeans, an expanse of bare skin peeking from beneath her sweater, and Nina's flailing sneakers about level with Molly's head. Nina dangled by her arms from a branch, and Molly had climbed to the very top of a ladder to support her in safety.

He swore and ran down the path, reaching them before anyone else seemed to notice. The other children were playing in trees farther along, except for Tamsin, who'd disappeared.

"Nina!" he snapped, terrified to lose anyone else he loved.

"Sam, can you give us a hand?" Molly managed to sound unconcerned, supporting Nina's rump with both hands as his baby girl clung to the branch.

"Hi, Daddy." She peered down at him. "I'm stronger than the big girl."

"Not really." Laughter lit Molly's eyes. "I'm just reluctant to dislocate her little arms, yanking her off there."

"Nina, I told you to stay off the ladders." He climbed up behind Molly, crowding her. Too aware of her curves against his chest, he tried to hold himself away, but it was impossible. "Sorry," he said.

"That's okay." Molly wasn't laughing anymore. Could she tell that being so close to her disturbed him? "Back down a bit, and I'll pass her to you. I had to climb so high to reach her I wound up stranded."

When Molly had made the transaction, Sam scooped his daughter into one arm, ignoring her giggles. "I've got her."

"Daddy, you tickle."

He shifted Nina higher, glaring at her with disapproval that instantly made her clamor for escape. "Lemme down, Daddy."

"When we're on the ground. Say thanks to Molly."

"What for?"

He glowered again. "Little girl, I told you to stay on the ground, and you agreed."

"I was fine, Dad."

She sounded endearingly like Tamsin, but the world seemed to darken in front of Sam's eyes as he imagined her falling. "We'll talk about this in a minute."

"Can't, Dad. *Miss Eliza!*" Nina let out a wild shriek for assistance.

"Yes?" Eliza appeared from beneath the branches, where she'd apparently been passing warm cider to Molly's cousin Zach. She held out her hand, and the second Sam set Nina on the grass, his daughter scurried toward her.

"Mom won't let her climb."

"She already outfoxed your mom once."

Molly looked over his shoulder. "Mom?"

Eliza looked up again, a tender, questioning smile on her face.

"Don't let her out of your sight," Molly said.

She nodded and went back the way she'd come, leading Nina by the hand.

Sam dropped to the ground, then turned to help Molly down, as well. He caught her hips, too aware of the thrust of her bones, her body heat that could be felt through a thin layer of denim. She stared at him in surprise. Before he could stop himself, he ran his thumbs over the flesh above her low-slung waistband. Molly's gasp reminded him what the hell he was doing. Her quick glance around the orchard reminded him where they were.

Her troubled eyes reproached him as her muscles jumped beneath his thumbs.

"I'm sorry." He slid his hands down, accidentally following the curve of her bottom as he did so. She gasped again, but he couldn't let go. She might fall, now that she'd leaned into his palms. And frankly, her moment of weakness made him want to go on holding her.

"Sam."

Her voice revealed only half of the emotion in her gaze. Too much hunger, too much pain and so much doubt his heart broke for her.

He ached to slide his fingertips beneath the hem of her sweater again. The angular sharpness of her bones, the incredible tension in her muscles, the coolness of the fall air and his own need all stimulated his senses, making him feel as if he'd just woken up after being asleep for the past sixteen months.

He managed to pry his hands away from her, holding them up as if she'd pulled a weapon on him.

"I can make it down on my own steam." Her voice was hoarse, her eyes hollow.

"I don't know what I was—"

"What you were doing seems fairly obvious." At last she looked away, and he checked to see if anyone had seen him manhandle her.

The Calverts had gathered to pick apples, and his girls, even Tamsin—now hanging from a branch to show Nina not everyone was a baby— were having their own fun. He must be the only guest who'd climbed this ridge to maul a woman.

He couldn't explain what he'd done, except that he liked being near her. Her spirit both surprised and intrigued him.

Molly still possessed the indifference of youth. She hadn't even worried about Nina as she'd held his daughter in the tree. He'd lost his sense of immortality, living with Fiona's heart disease, and he longed for a taste of Molly's faith in life.

She jumped off the ladder, avoiding the last several rungs. Breathing through his mouth, he couldn't take in enough oxygen.

Molly tugged at the hem of her sweater, as if she could erase his touch. His fingers tingled with the memory of her firm, forbidden flesh. Right now he suspected the urge to touch her would linger in his mind for the rest of his life.

"I actually meant I don't know what I was thinking." Except that her youth had dragged him back to life.

"Fortunately, I'm pretty clear on your thoughts."

"Fortunately?" Her wry tone made him feel like one in a long line of perverts. Of course, he couldn't claim not to be, since he'd acted that way.

"Don't think about me like that."

"No." At his ambiguous reply, her gaze widened. "I don't even know what you mean," he said, stunned.

"Sex, Sam." She pulled her sweater down as far as it would go again. "Don't feel too bad. Something must be wrong with both of us if a minor incident matters." She walked past him on the dirt lane between the trees, also heading for the safety of Eliza's side.

He'd screwed up royally. Sam clenched his jaw, feeling riddled with guilt. He and his girls didn't stand a chance with Eliza if he made her daughter too uncomfortable to spend time near him.

He ran his hands down his own jeans, but he couldn't help following Molly's long-limbed stride with his eyes.

TOO UNSETTLED TO BE sensible about her intense awareness of Sam, Molly glanced back at him as she reached her mom. His eyes looked too serious for her safety.

She'd wanted him the instant he'd touched her. The feel of his body heat blended with an ache of unquenched desire. For ten years she'd controlled her slightest sensual response, but this was different. Not just sex, but need. Irrational and powerful, and almost beyond her control.

Eliza looked up from redoing the braid Nina had caught on a tree branch. "What happened?"

Molly tried to hide all signs of feelings her

mother might recognize after ten years. "Nina got away from me. She climbs faster than a cat."

"Yup, I'm good." Nina nodded her head.

"Sam's not annoyed?" Eliza seemed worried. Behind her, Tamsin dropped off the branch she'd been swinging on.

"I don't see why he would be." Who wanted to think about Sam? While her heart skittered, trying to find an even beat, Molly sucked in her stomach, remembering his touch.

She was hungry. Really hungry. "When do we eat, Mom?"

"Soon."

"I'm ready now." Nina clasped Molly's hand. "Maybe we could have another pickle?"

Molly's constant state of starvation during the past week was another warning. After her birth parents had disappeared and even after she'd gone to the Calverts as a foster child, she'd translated insecurities into a craving for food, and thought she might never be satisfied. The feeling had finally waned after her adoption, but ever since Sam's arrival, she'd been famished again.

"Pickle, Miss Molly."

"Okay, Nina." Taking her new niece's hand, Molly led Nina toward the table. As much as she wanted to avoid him, she couldn't resist a glance in Sam's direction.

What had he felt? He clearly grieved for his wife. Had he let himself imagine she was Fiona?

That would explain the desire in his gaze, but not her own response.

Her stomach growled. "Let's hurry, Nina."

As NIGHT FELL, Greta called from home. She hadn't made it to the orchard picnic, but she wanted to lure everyone to her house with promises of hot cocoa to take the edge off the chill.

Seth relayed Greta's offer to the rest of the family. To Eliza's dismay, Sam strolled up just then, looking as if he was about to say good-night. Nina was drowsing on his shoulder. At his side, Tamsin balanced a heaping, covered plate Eliza's sister-in-law, Beth, had given her.

"We're going back to the B and B." Sam pressed his cheek against Nina's forehead, eliciting a weary half smile. "Tamsin's cold and Nina's nearly asleep."

Eliza smiled at Tamsin. "Come with us, honey. You don't have to go because your sister's sleepy."

Tamsin looked surprised, but pleased. Still, she shook her head. "Thanks, but I'll go with my dad."

Eliza wished she dared hug the young teen, who remained so terribly self-contained. "You can stick with Molly and me. You'll have a good time."

"Thanks, anyway." But Tamsin sounded reluctant, and Eliza took that as a good sign.

"It's fine." Sam gave his older daughter a warm smile. "Go have some fun."

"Nah, Dad."

He studied her as if he was trying to read her mind, but he finally nodded. His patience touched Eliza. Tamsin's grief for her mother had made her touchier than most adolescent girls would be, and Eliza admired her son for being so anxious to understand his injured child.

"Okay." Sam smiled at Eliza, and again the strange realization that this was her son sent an incredible sweeping joy through her. "We'll see you later. Maybe in the morning."

If he were Molly, she'd ask him to wait up. But though she was overjoyed for each second she spent with him, she felt as if she had no right to ask for extra time. Besides, he was a father, with a father's duties.

On impulse, she raised herself on tiptoe to kiss his cheek and then squeezed Tamsin's shoulder. "I'd rather keep you all with me, but I'll see you later."

As they walked away, Patrick joined her. "They're going home?"

"To the B and B." Nothing with Patrick felt normal. She longed to lean into his embrace. In the cool climate of their fledgling truce, she wasn't even sure he'd welcome her hand on his.

"Are you ready?" he asked. "I've packed the car."

"Sure. Have you seen Molly?"

"She and Zach carried the drinks cooler to her car. She's already on her way to Mom's."

"We might as well be, too." Eliza dared a lowered glance at him. "You're coming?"

"Yes. Let's go." Side by side, but a foot apart, they retraced their way to the clearing where they'd parked. Patrick unlocked her door first and waited while she slid onto the cold, hard leather seat. He started the car and they followed Zach and Olivia and their children down the ridge.

"Why haven't you explained to the family about Sam and the girls?" he asked eventually.

Thankful for the darkness, Eliza pressed her hands to her warm cheeks. "Don't you know?"

"If I did, would I ask?"

His tone stung. "I've never known you to be so brusque."

"I've never dealt with something like this." He looked at her for a long moment. "I was a judge. I had to read people. It was my job to see guilt and innocence—to recognize a lie."

"I'm sorry," she said, for maybe the thousandth time. "I don't know how to make you understand."

"I get it, Eliza." Pain lowered his voice. "But the facts make our old life a lie."

"No two people can live together for twenty-seven years in a lie. You know me. I was capable of giving Sam up, but I never wanted to do it."

She clenched her fists. "I tried to make sure he had a better life than I could offer him. I'm still your wife and Molly's mother, but I also belong to Sam. I can't give up a second chance to be his mom, or Tamsin and Nina's grandmother."

Patrick nodded, and a hint of their old love warmed his eyes. "I don't resent Sam and the girls. I resent not knowing about them."

"That's the one thing I can't change."

He took a deep breath, then released it. "I'll learn to accept the truth, but I repeat, when are you going to tell the others?"

Feeling like a coward, she forged on. He wouldn't like the truth. She didn't want to admit how weak she still was. "I wanted to tell them before today so we could make it a welcome party, but I lost my nerve because I didn't know how you felt."

He hit the brakes. "How I felt? What do I have to do with it?"

"What are you talking about? You're Molly's father. Sam and the girls know what you mean to me." How could such a smart man be so obtuse?

"How much do I mean to you? I'm the one you're willing to let go."

As if being apart from him was easy. "Please don't make me choose. I don't know how to give up Sam again—but I also don't know how to live without you. When you're not in the house, I feel as if I'm living half a life."

Patrick's sense of honor ran deep. He wouldn't throw away their life together no matter how big the lie she'd told. But he wasn't one to make some spur-of-the-moment declaration he couldn't live with later.

At last, he sat straighter and hit the gas. "Tonight's a good time to tell the family," he said. "Sam and the girls won't have to sit through their reaction, and everyone can troop·over to brunch tomorrow to welcome them."

Tears welled in Eliza's eyes, hot and painful and altogether too familiar lately. "I'm not sure I deserve you, Patrick Calvert."

Laughing, he sounded more like his old self than she'd dared to dream. "I'm not positive you do, either." He turned to her swiftly. "Don't be surprised by the occasional backslide. I'm only human, and I feel threatened for the first time in my life."

THE NEXT MORNING Sam woke and got Nina ready for breakfast. Coloring on sheets from her pad of scratch paper, she waited with him for Tamsin, but finally, the clock struck eight and Nina sighed as only a spoiled baby sister could. Together, they knocked on Tamsin's door. No one answered.

Alarm crept up his spine. He coped badly with unexpected absences. "Tamsin? I'm coming in." He opened the door to an empty room and, thank

God, an unmade bed. Wherever she'd gone this morning, she'd slept here last night.

"Where is she, Daddy?" Nina grabbed his hand, fear in her voice. "She's not gone like Mommy? Where's my sister?"

He tried to sound calm. "She probably went for a walk." He lifted Nina and headed for the hallway. "Maybe you can stay with Miss Eliza while I look around for Tamsin. You know she likes to read on the square."

"No. I have to come." Nina gripped him around the neck as if she couldn't let him out of her sight.

Looking her straight in the eye, he reached for the doorknob. "I'll always come back, Nina."

"You promise?" She cupped his face in both her small hands, tearing his heart out.

"I promise." It might be a lie. Fate had taught him that disaster could strike when you least expected it, but his daughter needed certainty.

"You might forget me. What if Mommy's really alive somewhere but she just forgot where we live?"

"Is that what you think, Nina?"

She buried her head on his shoulder. "It could be."

He closed his mouth. Even his teeth ached with the pain of having to tell her again. "Mommy died, Nina. I wish she hadn't, but she's gone."

"So you won't go anywhere without me."

True panic fueled two urges—one to run, the

other to stand and rail at the loss they'd suffered, the effects of which kept changing. What on earth had come over Nina? He'd left her with baby-sitters in the past sixteen months. She'd returned to her day care a few weeks after Fiona died.

Then he understood. She liked Eliza already, but he'd always been within sight. He'd never left her alone with someone she didn't know.

"Sweetie, I can look for Tamsin faster if I'm not carrying you."

"You need me. I know Tamsin better."

Her claim hit pretty hard, but she probably did know her sister best. All Sam's adult life he'd tried to cure everyone who came to his office, in some crazy, unspoken bid to keep Fiona alive. She'd cared for the children and he'd never noticed the distance between him and his daughters.

Since her mother's death, Tamsin had retired even further into her own world. Nina was the only one who could bring her sister back to her old self.

It might be time to break his habit of assuming he had something important to do that meant his children could wait. "All right. Let's find her."

They hurried down the stairs, startling Patrick, who stood behind the registration desk, as well as Eliza, who was crossing the room with a tray of breakfast plates.

"Have you seen Tamsin?" Sam asked.

"We can't find her," Nina said.

Eliza shoved the tray onto the desk. "You can't find your sister?"

"I've been down here for over an hour," Patrick said with obvious concern. "She hasn't passed me."

The lump of panic in Sam's throat grew. "I'll check the square." He patted his pocket for his ever-present cell phone. "Then we call the police."

"I'll come with you." Eliza sent Patrick an anxious look. "Could we close up and both go? The square's pretty big. We can't see through the trees, and the stalls from the farmers' market are up."

"I'll put up the sign."

"Thanks." Sam felt as if he'd already waited too long. Holding Nina close, he plunged through the doorway, hurried down the path and sprinted for the square.

Tamsin's favorite bench was empty. His heartbeat thudding in some crazy version of Morse code, Sam started a circuit of the sidewalk outside the square's wrought-iron fence, hoping she'd chosen a different bench. He questioned the stall owners, already setting out pumpkins and squash and bouquets of Indian corn. No one had seen any sign of a teenage girl in Goth getup.

Why he'd ever cared what the hell she wore, he couldn't say, but he longed for a single glimpse of her baggy black clothes.

"Tamsin!" Nina jumped in his arms, pointing with emphasis toward a small shop across the street. Antique glassware? What would Tamsin want there? But she was peering through the shop window, her clothing and face painted with glinting sunlight reflecting off cobalt-blue and ruby-red glass.

She turned as if thunderstruck.

"There she is, Daddy."

He released a breath and felt as if he'd held it for hours. His relief turned to anger, and yet he'd never been so damn happy in all his life.

"We're lucky you saw her, Nina." Hugging his younger daughter, he ran across the road. Nina bounced in his arms, making funny noises to emphasize the jostling his flat-out speed caused her. Tamsin stayed where she was.

"Tamsin." It was Eliza's voice. She and Patrick must be somewhere behind him, but Sam didn't stop to look. When he reached his older girl, he wrapped his arm around her and yanked her close. Let her wrestle free if she wanted. He didn't know whether to strangle her or shout his gratitude to the sky.

"Don't ever do that again," he said.

"Dad, I can't breathe."

"Me, neither." Even Nina wriggled to get out of his arms. "You're choking us, Daddy."

"You scared the…you scared me half to death, Tamsin."

"I just looked around in the shops. I would have

told you, but you were all asleep and I was awake.''

"You know better.'' This point they wouldn't argue about. "We have rules.''

Tamsin pushed away from him with both hands. "Mom had rules. I didn't even know you'd heard them.'' Sharp as a knife, the resentment in her eyes stabbed at him.

It was time they had this out. "I may have been a lousy father when your mother was alive, but I'm trying my hardest now.''

"And you're probably planning to dump us, since you've found—''

Before she could finish, before Sam could even make sure she was serious, Eliza caught her in a near headlock. "I was so scared. Where have you been?''

Tamsin remained stiff in Eliza's arms. She jabbed her thumb toward the store. "In there. I don't know what the big deal is. You all act as if I was abducted by aliens.''

"This is a small town,'' Eliza said, "but someone could have grabbed you—some stranger who could then disappear in these mountains. Don't you ever do this again, Tamsin Lockwood. I won't lose you now.''

Tamsin's mouth dropped open.

"I thought Daddy and me lost Tamsin, Miss Eliza.'' Nina sounded comically doubtful.

Eliza released Tamsin to kneel beside Nina for

a fierce hug. Sam read her next move in her desperate gaze. He stared, dumbfounded, but unable to speak. Events were moving way too fast. Once Nina knew, they couldn't turn back. It was bad enough that Tamsin had this lunatic idea he'd been searching for his birth mother so he could abandon his daughters with her.

"Eliza, wait."

"Dad?" Tamsin sounded worried.

Eliza peered from Tamsin to Nina to him. "What's wrong?"

"Don't do it this way."

Huffing, Patrick hurried up to them. "Thank God you found her. I went around the other side of the square, and you know, Tamsin, a band you might like is playing at the theater this weekend."

"Patrick, Sam doesn't want me to say anything." Eliza reached for her husband's hand.

"About what?" Patrick seemed to be the least concerned among them. Maybe the most normal?

"I'm glad you showed up," Tamsin said with a scared glance at Eliza. "Everyone else is treating me like I'm a criminal. I'm going to look at the theater. Why do you think I'd enjoy the group?"

"They dress like you." Patrick patted her shoulder and then stared at his hand as if he wasn't sure he should have made the overture.

Meanwhile Sam tried to control an adrenaline rush that had his fight-or-flight response in overdrive. He wanted to shove both his girls into the

car and head back to Savannah. They had to tell
Nina about her grandmother eventually, but he
suddenly needed more time.

"Don't be frightened, Tamsin. And, Eliza, think
about what you're doing—why you're doing it."
She had to commit for good or not at all.

Tamsin ignored them. "Let's go, Mr. Patrick.
I'm not hungry, and I'd like to see who's playing."

"No." Eliza grabbed her arm and held on to
Patrick, too. "Let's go into the square and talk."

"Not now." Sam couldn't risk it. "You think
everything over, and we'll talk when you're
calm."

Patrick moved to Eliza's side. "She's sure."

Sam stared at him. "What are you saying?"

"We told the rest of the family last night. It's
about time we talked to Nina." He offered Tamsin
an encouraging smile.

"And you're okay with it?" Sam doubted the
older man. He'd recovered too suddenly.

"My problems aren't with you and our granddaughters."

"Huh?" Nina finally spoke up. She'd been listening to the grown-ups as hard as she could.
Maybe she didn't grasp the whole situation, but she
seemed to know she played a part.

"Come sit with me," Eliza said. She tugged
Tamsin's arm again gently, begging with her eyes.
"Please?"

"Dad?" Tamsin reached for him, and he lifted

his hand. She took it, confusion and fear on her face.

"I don't know why you'd think I want to be rid of you."

She tilted her head back in surprise. They'd hardly ever talked about their feelings, much less in front of strangers. He'd taken too much for granted, thinking that saying "I love you" every night before she went to bed was enough.

"You and Nina are my daughters. I'm your father. We're family no matter what happens with anyone else."

"But can't you let Patrick and Molly and me be part of your family, too?" Eliza stroked Tamsin's ponytail. "I already love you as if I'd always known all of you, and we have plenty of room in our lives if you can make a little in yours."

Tamsin edged closer to Sam. She'd known, but maybe she hadn't fully understood what was going to happen.

Nina whimpered and wrapped her hand in the loose material of Tamsin's pants. "What's wrong?"

"Nothing." Tamsin leaned down, but Sam scooped Nina up.

The last thing he wanted was for Tamsin to feel responsible for her little sister. He'd like to salvage what was left of their childhoods.

"I'm okay, Nina," Tamsin said.

"Are you scared of Miss Eliza?"

His older daughter shook her head, but sought Sam's gaze with her eyes.

"Are you sure?" he asked.

"If I'm scared? I'm not." She eyed her grandmother. "I'm not, but I had one family, and now we have a new one."

"Daddy, who's Tamsin's new family?"

"Miss Eliza has a surprise." Sam spoke quickly, though his mind was blank. "She knew me a long time ago. It's hard to explain, Nina, but Miss Eliza was my mom when I was a baby."

Nina considered for a second and then shook her head. "I thought Grandma was your mommy."

"She picked me when I was little, but Miss Eliza had me like your mommy had you."

"Then why don't you live with her?"

To Sam's total surprise, Tamsin leaned against his shoulder. "Is this really happening?"

He glanced at Eliza and Patrick, who were watching Sam and his daughters with apprehensive expressions. "If you and Nina want it to happen, Tamsin, I think we can make it work."

"Can you want us?" Eliza asked.

"Are you a grandma, too?" Nina asked. "Like my real grandma?"

Tears filled Eliza's eyes and Sam felt sorry for her. Who knew what she'd gone through forty years ago, alone and frightened, a child herself?

"I'd like to be a real grandma." Eliza ran her hand down Tamsin's sleeve. "And to you, sweetheart. But only if I'm not going to drive you to run away to glass shops for a little respite.''

"I didn't run away," Tamsin said with typical teenage annoyance. Her earnest expression reminded Sam of how she'd sometimes looked before the accident.

"Just tell me when you want to go out." He tried to smile, but his face felt as if it might crack. "And I'll try not to make a big deal out of every move you make."

"Thanks." She breathed a heartfelt sigh and looked at Eliza and Patrick. "I guess we're in if Nina wants to be, too."

"I don't get it." Nina playfully smacked Eliza's shoulder. "But I like ya."

# CHAPTER SIX

MOLLY TOOK HER TIME preparing for Sunday's welcome-to-the-family visit at the Dogwood. She couldn't face Sam again when every thought brought back the wrenching sensuality she'd felt with his hands on her skin.

She would overcome those feelings. She might be more attracted to him than she'd been to anyone in the past ten years, but her mother believed they could will themselves into being a big, happy family.

Anything Eliza wanted, Molly would try to do, but Sam was starting to matter to her in ways she couldn't admit. Molly wanted to know more about him than what he'd been doing since his adoption.

Clearly, he'd built a career. Sophie had praised his reputation last night. Sophie and Greta, both doctors themselves, had discussed the strains of maintaining a family and such a high-powered career at the same time.

Sam's family obviously came first. In fact, she'd better keep his commitment in mind. If anyone had seen them together yesterday, today wouldn't be a celebration. The Calverts would be gathering to talk about Molly seducing the wrong man—again.

Shaking her head, she stared through her bedroom window at the familiar stand of pine and maple and oak, the stream that trickled down the hill behind her house and then veered to the side, following her driveway to the main road. This was her haven.

She wouldn't compromise it for anyone. She'd long since realized she was too much trouble for most men. She laughed without feeling the least bit happy. Sam had only touched her bare stomach for a few misguided moments. It didn't have to be a tragedy.

This was just vintage Molly. The girl who made all the wrong choices.

From the day Patrick and Eliza Calvert had taken her in as a foster child, she'd feared they would decide they didn't want her, either.

She'd tested them with drugs, drinking and bad, bad boys. She'd expected Patrick and Eliza to hand her back to the state, until the day they'd shared her grief over her lost baby.

When they'd adopted her, she'd known they loved her and she'd learned in therapy how her birth family had damaged her.

Her new knowledge had fueled a direction change. She'd buckled down at school and became a good teacher, a respectable citizen of Bardill's Ridge who never shamed her mother and father.

But she couldn't evade the memory of Sam's touch. It scattered all her careful intentions. All the knowledge she'd gathered hadn't yet made her smart.

"MY FAMILY LACKS perception." Greta Calvert, Eliza's mother-in-law and the apparent matriarch of the Calvert clan, eyed the rest of her kin with doubt, then turned to Sam. "I can't believe you fooled anyone. Looking you in the eye is just like looking at Eliza. Genes don't lie."

"I was glad no one noticed." Sam kept his voice low. "If she'd wanted me to go away, I would have gone. Family means everything to Eliza, and I know you're shocked."

"We're not big-city sophisticated, but we have all the vices and blessings one sees in any town. What you need to understand, Sam Lockwood, is that Eliza's a conscientious, loving mother. I'm not surprised she'd make a choice that must have tortured her all these years, if it kept you safe."

He felt funny hearing what a good mom his mother had been to Molly, who had yet to show up. How angry was she now that everyone else knew the truth about him?

"Sam? You understand about Eliza?"

He couldn't lie to this woman. "She wants to love my girls and me, so I'll learn to live with the facts."

"You're upset?"

He shrugged. "Greta, I know she decided what was best for me, and that was all she could do at sixteen. I loved my adoptive parents, and they would have been hurt if I'd looked for Eliza, but I did feel abandoned. I always wanted to know what kind of people my birth parents were. I still want to know."

"And you're a physician. You're accustomed to sorting facts and coming up with a reasonable diagnosis." She nodded. "Well, you're right about one thing—no, two. First, now that you've found Eliza, your girls will have a family. Second, you have time to find out Eliza will never let you down or disappoint you. Ask Molly."

His complicated feelings for Molly made her the one person he couldn't ask. Ironically, he was far less certain about the future now that he'd found Eliza.

"I'll leave the interrogation to you all."

His irritable response seemed to amuse Greta. "How does a family treat a long-lost son? Nothing will make you more comfortable than answering tactless questions that give us too much information about you."

"It's a theory," he said. "But I'm starting to feel cornered."

Her smile widened, but he liked her anyway. "How are your girls accepting the changes?" Greta searched for them among the dining room crowd.

"Tamsin's taking a wait-and-see attitude. I'm not sure she trusts as easily as she did before my wife and parents died. Nina doesn't understand, but I think she loved Eliza instinctively."

Greta's gaze found Tamsin, dressed in her distinctive black—a featureless dress and boots over black socks today. "Maybe you should bring Tamsin up to the Mom's Place."

"Why?" Was Tamsin in more trouble than he knew? He studied her slight body.

"Because of the paying guests, we're able to help girls who've made mistakes." Greta's smile asked forgiveness even as she spoke. "I'm not suggesting Tamsin's headed that way, but talking to other girls might help her."

"I'm not sure...."

"And, of course, you might enjoy a tour of the facility. I hear you're a cardiologist." Her eyes narrowed. She looked a little sly, and Sam had to stop himself from laughing as she prepared an attack. "You might want to hear about the community health center," she said, all innocence.

"I am interested." His attention wavered as Molly entered the dining room. In a straight khaki skirt and a dark blue sweater, with her hair drooping from a knot on top of her head, she seemed feminine and soft and she made him feel hollow inside.

He wanted to do something about the bruised

look around Molly's eyes. She'd already been far too hurt by far too many.

"You get along with my granddaughter?" Greta asked, seeing more than he should have revealed.

"Sure." He'd been lucky she hadn't joined them at the orchard. "She's been kind to my girls."

"I see."

Molly headed straight to Tamsin and looped a tentative arm around her shoulders. With a shy smile, Tamsin nodded at whatever Molly said.

"Excuse me. I have to..." He didn't finish. Watching Molly and Tamsin, he crossed to the opposite side of the room to cruise the laden tables. This family believed in plenty of food and celebration.

He searched for Nina and found her. Through the windows he watched her chase Evan and Lily through Eliza's garden. Tamsin's laughter drew his gaze back to her and Molly. If she'd seemed upset, he'd have an excuse to interrupt. Listening to her laugh, his only excuse for joining her and Molly was that he wanted to be with them.

"Morning, Molly," he said.

"It's almost afternoon." She checked her watch, briefly meeting his gaze. "Does Tamsin have to call me *Aunt* Molly?"

"That's between you and her."

"Then I say just plain Molly will do, and Tamsin, I'm glad you're one of us now." Molly hugged her and then let go. "Where's Nina? I'd like to invite you two on a beauty day."

"With you?" Sam asked, curious about a beauty day.

She nodded. "Manicures. Pedicures. You know, girl things."

She didn't have to drop an anvil on his head. She wanted to spend time with his girls, but he wasn't welcome.

Tamsin looked a little doubtful, maybe not ready to commit to time alone with her new aunt yet. "Nina's outside, playing chase with Evan and Lily." She pointed.

"Does she understand what's happened?" Concern for Nina made Molly meet Sam's gaze at last.

He shook his head, trying to tell her silently how sorry he was for upsetting her. Not just yesterday, but today, when he couldn't avoid invading her territory. "But she knows you all want her to be part of the family."

Molly glanced at Tamsin as if aware that her invitation had floundered. "We might be overwhelming in full force."

Color touched Tamsin's face. "I've never—I'm sure we'll…"

Sam laughed gently. "We still have a couple of weeks," he said. "I warned my office I might be away a while, and we arranged for Tamsin to do her schoolwork."

"Nothing like being homeschooled by your science-oriented dad."

Molly laughed with Tamsin, and Sam suspected they'd be sharing that girl day before he took his daughters home.

"I'm not sure how you Calverts all manage to be so generous," he said. But he was grateful.

"We've had a lot of practice." Molly nodded toward Sophie, who was cradling her baby and deep in conversation with Greta. "A cousin marries. She expects us to accept her husband. Before that, I became Mom and Dad's foster child. I was immediately a Calvert, though I'd lived in this town in someone else's family for eight years."

"That must have been weird," Tamsin said. Sam agreed, but watched Molly, anxious that he and his daughter not overstep boundaries.

"It was strange for me," Molly said. She looked at Tamsin with wisdom in her eyes. "I tested them. I thought I might be here on sufferance, but they outlasted all the awkward situations I put them in."

"They loved you," Tamsin said.

"They wanted to love me. That's key. We Calverts understand family, no matter how it comes to us."

Sam forced himself to breathe as Molly suggested Tamsin stop pushing people away. Nodding, Tamsin evaluated Molly's advice, finally managing a smile. "I get what you're saying."

"I thought we'd understand each other."

Sam wanted to wrap his arms around Molly. If only someone had reached her as she had his child.

"It's still pretty weird to a newcomer." Tamsin eased toward the door. "I'm gonna look for Nina."

Alarm filled Molly's eyes, and she turned away from Sam. "Mind if I come with you, Tamsin? I haven't seen her yet."

"Sure." Tamsin wrinkled her face at Sam. She wasn't actively against this whole family thing, but it didn't make complete sense to her yet, either.

Thank goodness she didn't understand that the aunt so eager to care for her was also trying to evade her father. He had to defuse the tension between himself and Molly before Tamsin or anyone else noticed it.

"I'LL DRIVE YOU HOME, Molly."

After successfully avoiding Sam all afternoon, she hardly welcomed his offer. She'd cruised the brunch table and taken a position across the room from Sam and her parents. After a decent interval, she'd said goodbye to everyone except him. Apparently, he hadn't comprehended her subtle message.

"I have my car," she said.

"I know." He looked annoyed.

"What's wrong?" By now she'd used up her entire quota of diplomacy.

"You've avoided me all day. Don't you think someone will notice?"

His expression, taut and waiting, would also be obvious to anyone who bothered to walk out of the dining room.

"I'm uncomfortable because of what happened in the orchard yesterday. Give me a little time and I'll be fine." She might be lying. She didn't care. She didn't want to deal with him, and in reality, he'd barely touched her. It shouldn't matter.

"I can't give you time. I don't have it, and the girls are going to notice even if your mother doesn't."

"Speaking of which, you can't leave them here. Even Tamsin's not ready."

"That was true when today started." He nodded to her mother, playing cards with her granddaughters. "I already spoke to Eliza. She'll call if they need me."

Anger tempted Molly to drag him out and have a few words with him herself. "What did you say to my mom?"

"That I wanted to talk to you. Why wouldn't I? You need to know I'm not trying to take your place."

That remained one of her problems, but not the major one. Still, having an argument in front of her family and his daughters wouldn't be wise. "You can follow me. We'll talk. You'll come back here."

"Sounds good."

"It sounds anything but." Her shoulder brushed

his arm as she passed him on her way to pluck her fleece jacket from the closet. Instantly aware, she lowered her voice. "You're old enough to know we don't need this conversation."

"That's part of the point I planned to make."

"What?" How could she even consider getting involved with a man who made no sense?

With an impatient mutter, he reached for her arm. She stepped back, not trusting her own responses. She might have overdramatized the whole situation, but Sam was a mistake she didn't plan to make.

"Let's go." His voice echoed his grim expression.

Outside, relief at being out of her family's sight flooded her, but she hesitated. "You've left your coat." She pointed at his open-necked white shirt.

He shook his head. "It doesn't matter. Let's go."

Oh. Then she must be imagining the cold that spiraled up and down her spine. She went to her car. Without looking back, she drove toward the square. She let no man push her around.

Her familiar friend, hunger, returned.

As she neared Canon's Convenience Store, she pictured one of their golden-brown pretzels. A smear of mustard. She might die if she didn't stop for one.

She pulled into the small store's gravel lot. As she reached the front door, she saw Sam park next to her car. He caught up with her as she paid for her pretzel.

"You're hungry?"

Did he have to sound so incredulous? She took a bite and chewed, savoring the treat. Damn Sam.

"Do you want some?" She offered him the other side. "They're great."

"I just ate," he said, his gaze on her mouth. "But I admire your stamina."

She froze. This was his fault. He reminded her of feelings and passion she didn't know how to handle responsibly. Her mother wanted this man to be her sibling.

Forget it.

But he couldn't be her lover, either.

"Can we go now?" he asked.

She nodded, but waited for him to lead the way down the narrow aisle to the door. She eased in three deep breaths, staring at Sam's broad back. When had she lost all control?

Sam turned and backed into the door, looking down at her. His expression…completely unreadable.

Annoying, but that was just as well. With her wallet in one hand and her pretzel in the other, she had to accept assistance.

"We'll talk here." Instead of returning to her car, she went around the corner of the building. "The Canons have picnic tables." Glancing back, she eyed his shirt, flattened against his chest by the breeze. "Except you'll be cold."

"I'm fine."

He followed her, taking the bench on the other side of the table she chose. His eyes were wary. Mistrust shaped his mouth into a hard thin line. With her heart rapping in her ears, she longed for a glimpse of the confused, aroused man who'd been unable to resist touching her yesterday.

"Now that we're here," Sam said, "I don't know how to start."

Molly tore off a piece of her pretzel and offered it again. Sam stared at the cooling bread between her index finger and thumb. Surely its aroma tempted him, too. After a second, he took it, but he didn't eat.

"Tell me what's on your mind," she said.

"I shouldn't have done that yesterday."

The confession felt like rejection. She must be losing what mind she'd managed to salvage from the long-ago, scary days of her youth.

"We don't have to dwell on it."

"Don't you wonder why a few moments—the simplest touch—matter so much to both of us?"

"No." Her unthinking lie suddenly became the truth. "You've been alone since your wife…" But she couldn't force him to remember and miss Fiona all over again. "I made a lot of mistakes when I was a teenager, but I stopped because I didn't want to hurt Mom." She looked at him and ceased being afraid. "Your mom, too," she said, though the words pricked at a wound. "We can't forget Eliza is your mom."

"I won't."

"Uh-huh." Something must be in that pretzel. Or maybe brand-new, forbidden attraction made a woman a little drunk. "Well, not that this is any of your business, but I haven't been with anyone in ten years—"

"Ten years?" The question exploded from his mouth. "You were fifteen ten years ago. What the hell were you—"

He stopped. Realization dawned in his eyes and drew his mouth tighter. "I keep forgetting I'm too old for you. I don't even know why a fifteen-year-old would consider sex."

"I was afraid no one would love me." Shock might be good medicine for the doctor. He wouldn't want her if he knew the truth, and if she didn't get involved with Sam, she wouldn't ruin her family.

"Who was the guy?"

"Which one?" Self-flagellation might be taking the treatment too far, but no amount of suffering would erase her horrifying memories.

"Molly…"

Before she realized he'd moved, he'd joined her on her bench—facing the other way, but that didn't stop him from pulling her into his arms.

"I hate to think of you like that," he said against her hair.

"See? You're fine. I'm the bad news." His scent, a disturbing mixture of male and sunny outdoors, seduced her. "I'm not proud, but I'm explaining why I won't hurt my parents. They must have been appalled every time the phone rang back then."

"No." He rested his chin against her hair.

His heat surrounded her. His voice, low and deep, flowed over her like loving hands. Using her last ounce of willpower, she remained impassive.

"Come on, Molly. I'm not inhuman. I'm only comforting you."

Sucking in cold, fresh air, she shook her head. "Someone will see us."

"I don't care. I am sorry for yesterday," he said. "I don't usually grab at… Even if you weren't my mother's daughter, you're too young for me to look at the way I—"

"I know how you looked at me." Molly slid her hand beneath her jacket, flattening her palm against her stomach.

He watched, his breath deepening. He slid his fingers down her forearm, reaching her wrist before she jerked her hand into the open. "Don't," she said.

"I'm trying." His rueful smile would have interested her if they were allowed to see each other as man and woman.

She eased away from him.

"You don't have to run," he said. "I won't ever touch you like that again."

"You're lying."

"Maybe I am." He studied her face, but her whole body responded by flushing.

"You aren't too old," she said.

"Huh?"

She shrugged. "You're the wrong guy because of my mom, not because of your age. She wants us to be a blended family, a brother and sister."

"I'm not *your* family," he said with emphasis.

"No." She laughed in sheer relief because he shared her need to keep that straight.

"But you don't have to worry I'll embarrass you every time I see you. I mean, don't avoid me the way you did today." His voice trailed off, but then he cleared his throat. "I'm attracted to you, but I'm not an animal."

She scooted away from him, the rough wooden bench pulling at her jeans. "Let's face facts. Your birth mother adopted me and your daughters need a family. Unfortunately, I liked having your hands on me and you wanted to touch me."

Dragging another breath into his lungs, he reached for her. She tried to push him away, but he managed to twine his fingers with hers. "You liked it?"

"I'm not a polite woman when a guy does something I don't want," she said. "If I'd wanted you to stop, you'd have known. But now—when I'm thinking sort of clearly—I have to make sure we both stop doing anything that could hurt my mom."

"You're right." He pulled back, but then leaned toward her again, and his scent wrapped her in an embrace she couldn't resist. His arms came halfway around her before he stopped himself again. "You're right." He stood, his feet crunching on the gravel, his voice rough. "But please don't be afraid of me next time I see you."

"I'm not afraid." She was terrified, but not the way he meant. He wouldn't force her to do anything. Her eagerness was the problem.

Sam rocked on his feet. His urge to comfort her was so clear in his eyes that she almost sensed him touching her. But he seemed to reach the same conclusions that frustrated her. Making a guttural sound deep in his throat, he spun away and left without looking back.

As the slam of his car door echoed in the cold Tennessee air, she slumped against the edge of the table. She should have handled her problems years ago. She'd never chosen to stop having sex as treatment for her loneliness. She'd simply stopped.

And now was not the time to discover a man who tempted her to handle such feelings as an adult. A man couldn't make her life right. Sam couldn't fill the empty spaces inside her.

# CHAPTER SEVEN

A KEENING SCREAM ripped Sam from sleep. He shot to his feet and ran across the dark room, shoving open Nina's door.

"Daddy?" She didn't sound like herself; her voice was high and thin. Breathlessly, she called to him, begging him to keep her from the "bad man" who kept coming for her mom. It was a recurring nightmare. Nina didn't understand about car accidents. People walked away from them on TV and in the movies. In her little girl logic, she figured a bad man must have stolen her mother.

"Don't take my mommy." She pushed at Sam with desperate hands.

"Nina, it's Daddy." He sat on her bed and caught her arms, his chest tight and aching. "Nina," he said, evading her thrashing hands, "you're all right. You're with Daddy and Tamsin."

"The bad man wants Mommy. He's looking for her."

"I'm sorry, baby." Sam wanted to cry, too. No five-year-old should experience the type of fear that dogged Nina. "No one's taking anyone else around here. I promise."

"Daddy?"

Waking at last, she stood and shoved down the twisted bedding. Then, with her arms straight out, she lunged toward him, almost knocking the wind out of him as she dropped against his chest.

"Daddy." Her sobs shook him, but he couldn't help her. He could only hold her until she realized he was real and the dream wasn't, and that he'd do anything to keep her safe.

"Dad?" Tamsin startled him, appearing in the doorway half-asleep but concerned for Nina.

"She's okay."

"She doesn't sound okay." She dropped onto the bed at Nina's back. "It's just a dream," she said, her voice zombielike. They'd both repeated the same words too many times. Patting Nina with one hand as she turned to reach for the lamp, Tamsin managed to poke Sam in the face. She turned back. "Oh, sorry, Dad."

"Doesn't matter."

She found the light switch, and Sam blinked in the sudden brightness. Nina buried her face in his chest and shielded the sides of her face with her hands.

"Hurt my eyes." She sounded more like herself. An irritable whine pushed the fear out of her voice.

"I'll turn it off in a minute." Tamsin planted both hands on Nina's bed and pushed herself to her feet. "I have to find the thermostat. It's too hot in here. No wonder you're having bad dreams." She looked down at Sam. "I always have bad dreams when I have to sleep in a room that's too hot."

"Well, don't turn it down so low you freeze her."

"Dad…!" Her condescension was music to his ears. He could take contempt for his fatherly concern. Panic he couldn't resolve was almost too much to stand.

"I'm sorry we woke you."

"I kind of expected it."

He stared at her as she groped along the wall. "What do you mean? I thought you were certain the heat caused her nightmare."

"The heat and today." She stopped at the door again. "Your thermostat must control the heat in this room."

"I guess. Tamsin, are you saying you expected Nina to have a nightmare even though Eliza seems happy to have us? Is being part of this family so horrible?"

"No."

At least she sounded firm on that. He was beginning to think he didn't understand the female mind well enough to raise two daughters properly.

"It's a huge change, though." Tamsin stepped into his room. "Dad, where's your thermostat?"

"Beside the hall door. Are you unhappy about Eliza?"

"Grandma," Nina said, sleep already returning to her voice.

"Yes, Grandma." He stroked her hair. Like a cat, she grew drowsy at the first touch. "Tamsin?"

"I like her. And Patrick and Molly, but they come with a crowd. We don't know them."

"But do you want to?" Surely he'd asked before. He tried to remember.

"Yeah." Tamsin came back. "But they're a lot to take at once, and I feel disloyal to our real grandpa and grandma."

"I miss them more than ever tonight, too," Sam admitted. "I lay awake for a long time thinking about them."

"And Mom."

"And Mom." Memories of his gentle wife filled his head. She'd loved their daughters, resisted the precautions he'd forced on her. The nanny he'd hired, for instance, who was supposed to save Fiona's strength. Sam had annoyed his wife because she'd wanted a "normal" life. How would she feel about a normal existence for their girls that included tree climbing and running wildly up and down Bardill's Ridge, Tennessee?

"Eliza and the others won't take our real family's place for you, will they, Dad? You're not going to move us up here?"

"Tamsin…" He stopped stroking Nina's hair to

reach for her sister's shoulder. Nina complained a bit, her voice muffled in his T-shirt. "I promised I wouldn't pull you out of your school or away from your friends, and you know I won't stop loving your mom and my parents. But I do have room for Eliza and her family."

She sat down so hard she bounced. "I was thinking." She glanced at him for a second, then looked away. "You're going to meet another woman one day. You'll get married again."

The image of Molly flitted through his mind, her scent, her determination to do the right thing. Her love for family. Molly had her whole life ahead of her. A husband. Children.

"You don't need to worry, Tamsin. Just get used to Eliza. Try to love her back, because I think she already loves you."

"How can she?" But Tamsin was a smart girl, and she felt Eliza's affection the same as he did. Pleasure deepened her voice. "She doesn't even know us, but she made them all accept us as if we've been here forever."

"You're okay with staying another two weeks?" he asked.

"I miss my friends."

A tiny snore from Nina surprised them both. Sam laughed but tried to keep it quiet so as not to wake her. Tamsin's grin comforted him.

"We would have gone home today if Eliza hadn't wanted us," he said.

"But she does." Tamsin sounded stunned, but also pleased.

Tamsin wasn't the only one who felt ambivalent about leaving or staying. He did, too. Desiring Molly couldn't be more wrong. Finding the family he'd sought for sixteen months added pressure instead of relieving it.

"I didn't give anyone a choice," he said. "I should have made sure you were okay with all this."

"I am okay. I just feel torn."

"You won't run off again?"

"Dad…"

He'd gone too far. She launched herself to her feet, and Sam could barely refrain from dragging her back to him and Nina.

"I don't know how to convince you shopping is not running away."

"Did you take any money with you?"

"What would I buy in a store like that?"

Nina rolled her head on his chest, disturbed at the tension in their voices. Sam took a breath before he answered. "That's why I'm concerned. I'm clueless." Might as well admit it. "But even I know you have no interest in antique glassware."

"I was bored, Dad. You don't have to drag me back to Dr. Brandon."

She'd hated going to the therapist, but her grief had terrified him. "Dr. Brandon helped you?"

"I don't need help now."

"Okay. I'll try to believe you."

"You're the one hiring detectives and chasing Eliza down. I was happy with you and Nina."

Sam stared at his daughter as if she'd turned into a stranger. "That's more than I've managed to extract from you for almost a year and a half. Were you really happy with your sister and me?"

She stood, half smiling, half embarrassed. "Yeah, Dad. But I'm sleepy now. I'm going back to bed."

"Tamsin, let me point out one thing."

"What?" She'd perfected teenage boredom, and it sounded so good to him. So normal.

Relief widened his smile until his cheeks hurt. "Today Eliza showed you how much she wanted to be your grandmother, and tonight you can admit you actually love your family. Can't be coincidence."

Tamsin smirked, but light returned to her eyes, reminding him how he'd missed it in the apathy of her grief. "Right, Dad. Whatever you say. Nina's drooling on you."

At her languid exit, he looked down. A puddle had pooled on his T-shirt. What did he care? He clasped his little girl against his heart. He loved these two more than he'd ever thought possible.

Finally, he understood what Fiona had meant when she'd talked about a mother's savage love. Such talk from his wife had always confused him, for she seemed anything but savage.

Now he got it. He hadn't learned to love their girls more, but his urge to protect them had doubled, tripled—who knew how much deeper it went? Having sole care of them scared him half out of his wits.

He tucked Nina back into her bed, laughing when she wrapped her arms around his neck, then let them plummet to her sides. Straightening, he peeled his T-shirt away from his chest, but he didn't change.

Baby drool. A badge of honor.

MONDAY AFTERNOON Molly told herself she was going straight home from school. Even kindergarten and first grade students produced plenty of papers to mark, and her lesson plans seemed to be a little sketchy this week. She'd tried to prepare, but her new family kept getting between her and her work. Going straight home, without passing the Dogwood, was her only option.

Fine and dandy, except she should have avoided the square, too. Movement and color caught her eye as she waited at a red light. The fall wind had picked up enough to make kite-flying irresistible. And not just for children.

Molly recognized Sam hauling Nina and a fluorescent-lime kite from the courthouse side of the square to the church side. Every time the kite lifted, Nina yanked the string and forced it back down.

Molly laughed, but the impatient driver behind her played a rude song on his car horn. She jumped and hit the gas and stalled her engine. It started again as the driver veered around her, but she glanced, embarrassed, toward the square and met Sam's gaze just in time to see the kite nose-dive into the grass.

Sam and Nina both ran to save it. Molly eased her foot down on the gas pedal.

A smart woman would drive home according to plan. That's right. Hide inside her little house. Make sure she steered clear of Sam until she could face him without seeing how he abandoned all dignity to be a father to his children.

He'd altered Molly's family, ruined her slight sense of security and filled her with doubt. And she admired him for it, because she would have been afraid to ask her own birth mother to love her. She'd never searched for the woman who'd vanished the day Molly had told her she was pregnant. And her father had moved away years before.

Suddenly, the bright kite jagged through the air above the square's fence. It darted into an oak, lodging itself on the end of a pointed branch, showering the sidewalk and grass with orange and red leaves.

At a glimpse of Nina's distraught expression, Molly pulled into the nearest parking space, sighing at her own weakness. Sam would need help retrieving the kite before her cousin Zach, the sheriff, arrested him for trespassing in the town's trees.

"Sam," she called as soon as she locked her car door. He looked up from comforting Nina, and his smile seemed to reach inside Molly. He shouldn't seem so happy to see her.

"Hey," he said. "Nina, look, it's your tree-climbing friend. We're saved."

Molly laughed, and Nina managed a watery smile. "Will you help my daddy, big girl?"

"Big girl" sounded so much nicer than "Aunt Molly." "I'll help, but I feel duty-bound to mention it's a plastic kite and easily replaceable."

Nina started crying again. "I want Dorothy. I don't want a new kite." A small mass of melodrama as she grabbed her father's shirt. "We can't leave her in the tree, Daddy."

He eyed Molly over her head.

"She named it," Molly said.

"Yeah." His gaze faltered, and he turned toward the kite, drawing Nina with him. Loss of composure only made him more attractive.

"We'd better move." Molly strode to the tree. "Someone's going to see and call Zach to arrest us. Bardill's Ridge is full of busybodies." She'd accepted that fact about her hometown from the first time she remembered walking down the street with Bonnie and felt that everyone expected her to be like her birth mother.

"Why would he arrest us?" Sam was beneath

her as she grabbed the lowest branch and swung into the tree.

"Didn't you see the signs? It's probably because of the liability, but the law disapproves of tree climbing in the square." She scrabbled for purchase in a cradle of twisted branch and trunk but her flats, so perfect for walking up and down classroom aisles, lacked traction for climbing.

Sam caught her and gave her butt a shove. Car horns and whispering leaves, the cloudy sky and the crisp air faded as shocks shot through her body. She dragged herself into the tree, determined to escape Sam's broad hands.

"Sorry," he said, wiping his palms on his thighs when she finally reached her perch and glared down at him.

His chagrined smile made her shiver. "This is starting to be a habit with us."

"You'd better be underneath me if I fall." She climbed to the next branch, testing it before she trusted it to hold her full weight.

"Be careful," Nina said with emphasis. "Don't tear my kite."

"Nina, you may be the cutest little girl ever born, but you're a rat, too." Smiling at Nina's giggles, Molly edged toward the kite, reaching with her fingertips.

"You need longer arms," Sam said.

So her charms were overwhelming him. She

spared him a scowl and scooted a few inches farther. "I'm going to push it off," she said.

"Good idea."

"But gently." Nina pressed her hands together. "Don't hurt Dorothy."

"Why did you call it Dorothy?" Using the tip of her index finger, Molly nudged the kite's closest wooden brace. The kite rocked but didn't budge.

"She flies." Sam's deep voice distracted her. "Like in *The Wizard of Oz.*"

"That Dorothy had a house." Molly risked a quick look down to find him watching her closely.

Dizzy, she wrapped one arm around a tree limb. The ground looked too far away; her sudden weakness had nothing to do with Sam.

"My Dorothy doesn't need a house to fly." Nina sounded proud, and Molly gave one last try. Stretching, she pushed the kite as hard as she could, managing to send it fluttering earthward in the wind. Nina immediately ran after it.

"Let me help you down, Molly."

"I don't think that's a good idea." She pointed toward Nina. "Better get her."

The little girl had gotten hold of the kite string and was bolting across the grass, trying to get the kite flying again. Molly didn't fear for her as much as for the innocent passersby who had to duck as she ran them down.

"Good idea." Sam loped after her as an older woman raced, squeaking, out of Nina's path.

Molly inched back toward the trunk and finally swung down out of the tree. She brushed bark and dirt off her khakis and gave up her white shirt as a lost cause.

"Miss…big girl…Aunt Molly!"

Nina had reversed course, but her shout alerted the citizens in her path. They scattered. Molly laughed when Nina bounced into her, with her father hot on her trail.

"Thanks, Aunt Molly." Her eyes wide, she patted Molly's shirt. "Eww. You're dirty. Look how dirty she is, Daddy."

"I think we owe you a shirt," Sam said.

"No, you don't. I chose to climb the tree in my work clothes."

"I should have done it."

She felt unaccountably petite as she eyed the breadth of his shoulders. "You'd crack that branch."

He lifted both eyebrows, a hint of offense in his eyes as he patted his flat stomach.

"Well, I'd better head home," she said. "I'm painting the booths for the fall festival." And babbling.

"Fall festival?" he asked, his interest intensified. "What's that?"

"For the school. It's only a small schoolhouse. We put on a festival every year to raise funds."

"Eliza says you teach two grades?"

She nodded. "As do the other three teachers,

and the principal takes the eighth-grade students. Some local parents choose to bus their children out to larger county schools, so Bardill's Ridge doesn't support a middle school or junior high. The job's more interesting because I get to switch back and forth between the two grades, and the children learn early to occupy themselves while I'm busy with the other class.''

''I didn't realize schools like that still existed.'' He nodded. ''But I wish Tamsin and Nina had the kind of concentrated attention they'd get in such small classes.''

Molly smiled. ''I shouldn't give the wrong impression. Most of the kids browbeat their parents to send them to larger schools.'' She warmed to the subject. She loved her job. ''I can see why they want a taste of life outside town, and maybe it's good to be exposed to a more sophisticated setting. But when I was a child I felt safer here.''

His eyes narrowed, and she wondered exactly how much of her past he had uncovered.

''That was a long time ago,'' she said.

Without comment, he ran his hand through his wind-tousled hair. ''Where are the booths?''

''In pieces at my house.'' She turned on her much-the-worse-for-wear heel and started for her car.

Sam curved his hand around her wrist. ''Don't you need help?''

"I have until Halloween weekend, so I have plenty of time."

"But do you want help?"

Molly resisted the heat of his touch. He was just a man, and she should have found a better way to deal with men. Total abstention seemed to have set her up for a big, ungainly crush on the least appropriate male she'd ever know. "I…"

"I'll bring Tamsin and Nina." He grinned, obviously enjoying her unease. "And Eliza."

"You're already bored here?"

"*I* am. I'm gonna fly my kite." Nina sprinted away from them.

"Nina," Sam called, "only straight in front of me, along the fence. And don't run over anyone else."

"Aw, Dad."

He laughed. "She likes to copy Tamsin."

Even Molly had to laugh. Nina perfectly parroted the tone of a bored teenager.

"So we'll see you later?" Sam asked.

Molly tried not to choke. She'd dealt with more frightening characters. Handling Sam's games shouldn't be so tough.

He leaned closer, ramming his hands into his pockets. "The more time we spend together, the sooner we'll learn to act natural."

Such frankness from a man who'd professed to want her was a whole new and confusing tack. Bewilderment put her at a disadvantage.

"You touched my stomach. It meant nothing."

Bleakness tainted his smile. "It's still on both our minds."

Molly found too much honesty could smother a woman. Silence on the subject would have felt more civilized.

Sam went on. "You're fifteen years younger than I am. You deserve a future I've already lived—marriage, children. You're the daughter Eliza chose. Most of all, you're part of the family Eliza's allowing my daughters and me to embrace." He rocked back on his heels. "I'd just as soon learn to embrace you in a way that won't make my birth mother run screaming from my life."

Molly's mouth worked, but shock still robbed her of speech. Sam had no idea how Eliza had rescued her. And fifteen years mattered to him, but Molly had probably been older at eight years of age than he was now.

Illogically, she wanted to laugh. Then she fought the sting of tears. She never cried. And he might be wrong about the facts, but he was right about them having to learn to behave normally.

"I guess you've covered everything." She gestured at his fists in his pockets and donned her best who-gives-a-damn tone. "I hope those surgeon's hands are also good at painting."

# CHAPTER EIGHT

SAM LEFT NINA with Patrick and Eliza because he couldn't find Tamsin. This time, instead of launching a search party, he decided to find her by himself. She might be falling into the habit of disappearing, but he didn't want to embarrass her in front of the family.

He strolled the square, feeling no particular sense of urgency. She seemed to enjoy spending time alone in Bardill's Ridge. Tamsin would be sixteen soon, and Sam was trying to give her space. He just had to convince her she should communicate details about where she was going and how long she planned to stay.

He stopped in front of the glass shop, but Tamsin wasn't there this time. Sam still didn't worry, but after a couple of circuits around the square, he began to scrutinize the people roaming in and out of the stores more closely. He ventured along the side streets, and fear grabbed him by the throat.

"What's with this girl?" His question drew the wary gaze of a woman barely older than Molly, pushing a stroller that carried two babies. He nodded, then his attention slipped to a girl in black who eased out of the bagel shop.

Not Tamsin.

How much longer should he search before he called Zach?

Sam glanced at his watch. Common sense told him Tamsin was most likely safe in an insulated, everyone-knows-everyone-else town like Bardill's Ridge. Certainly, the people who lived here scrutinized him every time he set foot out of the bed and breakfast. He'd gotten used to the curious glances, even if he wondered how long the rumors would circulate before people accepted him and his girls as Eliza's family.

He turned onto the last street he intended to search before he called the police. A pool hall and a pub stood side by side; she couldn't be in either of those. How did they survive in such a quiet little town?

Well, everyone had a secret.

Sam barely glanced through the windows of the Wild Thing Tattoo Parlor. But his daughter's terrified face, staring back at him, made him stop.

"Tamsin. Damn it."

She might not have heard the words, but she grasped the sentiment. She hurried to the door, steering him back when he tried to move inside.

"I need to talk with the guy who owns this place," he said.

"Woman." Tamsin latched on to his arm, prepared to drag him back to the B and B. "And don't embarrass me, Dad."

"Embarrass you? I'm going to have her arrested for even considering giving you a tattoo."

"I wanted a piercing, and she wouldn't do it without permission."

"Thank God for her fear of the law, since my daughter no longer seems to have good sense." He took her arm and turned her away, noticing the faint scent of pot floating out of a nearby doorway. "I can't believe this place is so close to the courthouse."

"I can't believe you."

He stared down at her, frustration gnawing at his control. "I'm coming to the end of my rope with you."

"I wanted a ring for my navel, Dad, not a spike through my head. Why do you always have to make a drama out of the littlest thing?"

Every word slapped him. "I'm trying not to treat you as if you were Nina's age, but if you have to act immature, I can change my tactics."

"Ooh!" She pursed her lips in stubborn disdain.

"You'd better rethink your approach, little girl."

"A navel piercing. That's all."

How to get realities through a fifteen-year-old girl's skull? "What about hepatitis, Tamsin?"

"Dad, those places sterilize their instruments

these days." She lifted her hands as if begging someone—anyone at all—to hear her plight. Then she faced him. "Life is not a hospital."

"Maybe it should be." She'd lost him, but then he was trying hard not to shake his beloved child.

"So you'd be in charge." At her raised voice, several men paused on their way into the pool hall.

"That's not such a bad idea, either." Sam took her arm again and led her around the corner to the relative safety of less adult-oriented establishments. "I'd keep young girls out of tattoo parlors."

"You'd lock me in a safe little bubble. You thought someday, if you tried hard enough, you'd save Mom. That didn't happen. Now you're trying to force us down Eliza Calvert's throat—but she's actually going along with you."

"And that's why you wanted your navel pierced?" Tamsin mystified him.

She stopped on the other side of the post box that squatted on the sidewalk. "I saw you with Molly and Nina."

Sam shook his head slightly. "What?"

Her stare became a weapon. "I can tell by the way you look at her. I noticed before, but now I know I'm right."

He felt like the kid caught in the wrong. "You're right about what? We were flying a kite."

"You're interested in Molly."

He had to lie. He couldn't admit to feelings that

had made her want to rebel. "Molly is my mother's daughter. I want her to like you and your sister. I want her to love you."

"I *saw* the way you looked at her." The pain of betrayal laced his daughter's voice. He reached for her again, but she arched away from him. "She's hardly older than I am."

"And you're imagining things." He squirmed inside, but Tamsin's response only reinforced the fact that he'd made the right decision.

"Thanks a lot, but I'm not a baby. I know how a guy looks at a girl."

"I don't look at Molly Calvert any way at all." A door behind Tamsin opened. The bell hanging above it tinkled, and Sam moved his daughter out of the way as a man in a dark jacket came out. Suddenly, Sam noticed Tamsin wore only a T-shirt. He took off his own coat and, ignoring her protests, wrapped it around her shoulders. "Are you looking for a reason not to like Eliza and her family?"

"Trying to blame me because you can't date Molly?"

"I'm not."

"Eliza's not my grandma."

"You saw Molly and me in the square with Nina, and you felt so bad you have to reject Eliza and find a way to punish me?"

"Punish you?" Her look reminded him of Fiona, protesting against his concern. She'd learned to live with her faulty heart muscle and the possibility it might take her from him and their daughters. Sam never had. He'd begged her to take precautions. She'd laughed at him with the same mocking look he could see on Tamsin's face.

"But why punish yourself?" He hated the idea of her turning her anger toward him at herself.

"Everyone gets a belly button piercing."

"Not to get back at their dad."

She looped strands of hair behind one ear, but doubt replaced her mockery. "You dragged us here. You forced Eliza to think of us as family, and now you're dying to put the moves on Molly. How am I supposed to love someone who might try to take my mother's place?"

He nearly staggered. The accusation in his little girl's gaze made him want to close his eyes, but he resisted. He had one chance to save this situation. He wouldn't screw up his daughters' opportunity to have a family.

"No one will take your mother's place. She'll be with you and Nina and me forever. Tamsin, I loved her from the time I was ten years old." He wouldn't think of Molly, of the passion she barely managed to bank and how it seduced him after Fiona's gentleness. He'd always been half afraid of his love for his fragile wife.

Now he felt devious, both for wanting Molly and for trying to hide his feelings. Here he was, demanding his daughter be straight with him, while he lied like crazy.

"I'm not convinced." Tamsin pushed her arms through his jacket sleeves. "You're not even convinced."

"I don't know where you get your ideas."

"I saw, Dad. I'm not Nina. I'm not gullible." She started to turn away, but Sam curled his fingers into the hem of his flapping jacket.

"Despite what you think of me, Tamsin, you're fifteen years old, not an adult. You will let me know where you're going and when you plan to come back. I'm not wandering any more streets thinking you might have been grabbed or run away." Her outraged expression usually silenced him, but he'd had enough. No matter what he had done, she had to respect rules that kept her safe. "If you can't check in as you know you're supposed to do, I'll be glad to follow you like a shadow."

"As if you don't anyway."

"Wrong attitude, Tamsin, but you're making it easier for me. I don't like giving you room to grow up." Admitting it should have felt better.

"Like I don't know?" She snorted. "You can't control everyone's life."

"I'm still in charge of yours."

They stared at each other, two opponents squared off on the sidewalk, forcing other pedestrians to go around them. Sam backed down first. He felt in the wrong, lying to her.

"Why don't we go home to Savannah for a while, Tamsin? I have work to do. You could catch up in your own school."

She breathed deeply. "Are you trying to punish me now?"

"Why do you see me as the enemy? I'm trying to give you a break."

She hesitated, and Sam shivered in air that seemed to grow colder. "What do you want, Tamsin?"

"I want to go home."

MOLLY COULDN'T DECIDE whether to dance or drag her feet. Sam and the girls had been gone for three weeks, but they were due at her mother's for dinner, and Nina had asked Molly to go trick-or-treating with her after.

Molly didn't know about Sam's plans. She didn't care. She'd missed both girls. Worry for Tamsin had dogged her since the day the girl had gone missing, and then they'd returned to Savannah.

Molly had shown up for breakfast in time to watch Sam and Tamsin maintain their distance from each other, a simple feat amid the noisy family members who'd come by en masse.

Knowing Sam and the girls had planned to stay, Molly had stared at him in surprise when he'd announced their departure. He'd slid his gaze away from her, and when Molly couldn't resist looking at Tamsin, the teenager had also averted her eyes.

Unease had trickled down Molly's spine, but Nina, waving an English muffin in one hand and Judy in the other, had distracted her with a shout of "Big girl."

Molly hadn't heard from them since they'd gone, though Sam had kept in touch with her mother. The girls had left school at noon today to catch a flight with their father to Knoxville. Only her memory of Tamsin's watchful glance had prevented Molly from volunteering to drive down the mountains and pick them up at the airport.

She looked forward to this weekend with them, the fall festival tomorrow, dinner with the family on Sunday. It all felt good.

"Miss Calvert?" A small girl in a pumpkin costume tugged at her skirt with huge sad eyes. "Miss Calvert, Joey says I grew in a weed patch."

Molly held in a laugh and tried to frown at Joey. "A pumpkin patch. Everyone loves pumpkin patches. Didn't your mommy and daddy take you to one?"

The whole class started volunteering their pumpkin patch experiences, and Molly settled them on the green "story rug" in her classroom's coziest corner. Might as well give up on math this afternoon. Halloween was too exciting.

After school, Molly rushed home and dressed in

her ghostly shroud. Not much of a seamstress, she'd cut a hole in a white sheet. She considered painting her face white, but what if she frightened Nina?

Her heart pulsed in her throat as she drew up to her parents' B and B. A rental car with a Knoxville plate was parked outside. It might be another guest's, but Molly longed to dash inside to see if it was Sam's. She remained behind her steering wheel, reminding herself of the facts.

Sam was her mother's son. Tamsin missed her own mom so much she couldn't open herself to affection the Calverts yearned to shower upon her. Nina was so hungry for affection she'd gobble up Tamsin's share if she could.

A sensible woman would never endanger the family who'd loved her and taught her the world could be a safe place. Molly reached for the band on the end of her braid and pulled it off, freeing her hair for a more ethereal look.

Time to concentrate on Halloween, with its candy and fun for the children. She couldn't ruin it lusting after Tamsin and Nina's father.

She threaded her fingers through her hair, then got out of the car, turning back to lock her door. Older cars like hers tempted pranksters on Hallow-een. Bardill's Ridge teens didn't mind splattering eggs on a paint job that could already use a little assistance.

"Big girl!"

Molly turned as Nina rushed through the B and B's front door and down the sidewalk. Tamsin showed up on the threshold, but lingered there as Molly scooped Nina into her arms.

"Hey, you." Nina smelled of fresh-baked cookies and children's shampoo.

"I wanna be a ghost, too." Nina cupped her hands around Molly's face. "You're very scary, big girl."

Molly laughed into her eyes. "Did your daddy bring a costume for you?"

"Yeah, but it's just that dinosaur guy. I wanna be a ghost like you."

"We can ask your dad."

"Tamsin." Nina wriggled to get down. "You be a ghost, too."

Tamsin planted both hands on either side of the doorway. "I'm not dressing up. I told you."

"Yes, you are. You're a kid, too." Nina grabbed Molly's hand to drag her up the sidewalk.

"I'll walk with you, but I'm as scary as I'm gonna be." Tamsin glanced at Molly, who thought she spied the hint of a blush on the girl's pale cheeks.

"No." Nina shook her head. "No one will give you candy if you don't dress up, and if they don't give you candy, I don't get none, either." She turned to Molly, a miniature adult in her serious stance. "Am I right?"

Molly only laughed. "Where did you hear that, Nina?"

"About candy? I know how Halloween works. Daddy took me last year."

"I meant you sounded awfully grown up." At Nina's pleased grin, Molly had to smile. "But I think you're wrong about the candy thing, at least around here. People love giving candy to children."

"Even big ones like Tamsin?"

"Yeah. I've handed it out for a long time, and I give it to anyone who comes to the door—even to kids a lot bigger than your sister."

"I can't believe that," Tamsin said. "Or maybe I just don't believe you were happy about it."

Molly spotted a nice trap and sprung it on Tamsin. "I'm always happier when the kids of any age dress up." She plucked at her own homemade costume. "I wanted to go out with you two, so I put this on. Ruined one of my best sheets."

Tamsin seemed unconvinced. "I'm the wrong age. You'd be okay being with a little girl, but I'd look like a pig, begging for candy."

Molly saw her point. "So hang back with me while Nina begs."

"It's not begging on Halloween." Nina looked pained with them both, but she grabbed her sister's hand. "Let's look through Grandma Eliza's sheets. She won't mind."

Molly exchanged a speculative look with Tamsin. Did that mean Eliza wasn't home? Was Sam with her somewhere? Molly wanted to ask where everyone was, but her brand-new determination to do the right thing for these girls kept her from mentioning their dad. She petitioned Tamsin with a smile. "Mom has plenty of old bedding."

"Not in black, I bet."

"She's not that cool, but maybe she'd have flowers."

Tamsin looked as if she might be sick, but Nina danced. "I want flowers," she said.

Molly turned her toward the house, smiling at her sister. "If Tamsin turns them down, you can have them, but I did offer them to her first."

"Aww." Nina broke off, annoyed, but content to allow her older sibling first pick.

Tamsin smiled as if people didn't put her first often enough. "You can have all the flowers you want, Nina. I'm looking for stripes or something a little less girly."

Laughing with joy she hadn't experienced in a few weeks, Molly hoisted her sheet and climbed the steps. "You won't be sorry, Tamsin. You'll have a good time. We'll go out to my aunt Beth's house because she always makes hot cocoa." She pushed the door open. "And besides, adults always get first shot at the best candy."

"I forgot that." Tamsin stood aside for them as Nina groaned at such unfairness.

Inside the silent house, Molly led the way upstairs to the linen closet, where they foraged for costumes. "My mom keeps saying we should throw these old sheets away. They're too used for a charity box, but they keep ending up back in here." Molly leaned out of the closet to gaze at the two young girls waiting with interested expressions. For the first time she realized they were her family. No matter what she felt about their father, these two girls were her nieces. "You're doing us a big favor." Her throat tight, she plunged back in.

Dark cloth. She grabbed for it. After a brisk tug, she climbed out again, brandishing a faded brown set of sheets. "Look, Tamsin. In the dark, no one will see that taupe ribbon."

"Let's trim around it," Tamsin said, with more revulsion than the circumstances warranted.

Taupe silk ribbon on a Halloween costume might be a crisis for a fifteen-year-old; Molly couldn't say. "I'll help. You're short enough that we might be able to cut that part off altogether."

"We're not going to hem them, are we? I sucked in apparel class."

Nina hissed in shock. "Ta-am-sin," she said in singsong horror, "you said a bad word."

"Sorry. I was really bad." She sounded a little sarcastic.

Molly ducked back inside the closet, trying not to laugh. "It'll be dark and this is a one-time garment. We don't need hems." She tried to picture a world where "sucked" was that bad a word. Ignoring Tamsin's apparent faux pas seemed like the best approach.

Picking through the rest of the sheets, Molly looked for something with flower sprigs for Nina. "I like the way it smells in here," she said. "Like when I was little and my mom had just finished the laundry."

Both girls poked their heads in and sniffed. Molly laughed in surprise and Tamsin grinned back. Then Nina spotted a flowered corner and grabbed at it, yanking a whole pile of sheets off a shelf in the process.

"Ooh, look." The sheet was covered with tiny pink roses. "Can I have this one?"

"Sure." Molly returned the other sheets to the shelf while Nina wrapped herself in the sheet and stumbled in another dance.

"Don't fall down the stairs." Tamsin grabbed her little sister and held her steady while Molly closed the closet door.

"My mom's sewing basket is in the family room," she said.

"We'd better hurry." Tamsin covered her mouth with her hand, embarrassed to be caught exhibiting enthusiasm. "I mean, it's going to get dark soon."

Molly pretended not to notice, but could hardly keep from pirouetting like Nina. The frost that covered Tamsin had begun to melt.

Molly hustled the girls into the family room. Tamsin's costume came easy. Nina's required a little more planning.

She was so tiny they had to cut more, but she had all sorts of requirements. It had to be the same length all around and almost touch the ground, but Molly insisted they cut it short enough to keep her from tripping over it.

Seeing a sneaker peeking out from under the costume, Tamsin leaned over and tied the dangling laces. "You're going to have to learn to do this."

"Why, when you and Dad always do it for me?"

"I'm telling Dad you said that."

Nina shrugged as if she didn't care. Then she turned to Molly, still wrestling with the sheet. "How many houses can we trick-or-treat at, big girl?"

"I thought you were going to call her Aunt Molly," Tamsin said.

"I wanna go to a bunch." Nina had decided to ignore Tamsin. "'Cause you guys are gonna eat my candy."

"Just some." Tamsin grinned in the wicked way of an older sister.

As the sun sank lower, Molly finished Nina's costume and helped her slide it over her head. Tamsin dressed in hers, too, but then ran from the room as Molly lit the lamps and checked the B and

B's candy supply—which seemed suspiciously sparse. They were still alone in the house.

Where was Sam? Where could he and her parents have gone?

Tamsin returned, producing ghostly white makeup. They all painted their faces, jostling for space at the bathroom mirror. Finally, deciding they looked more like clowns than ghosts, Molly urged the girls down to the reception area, sharing contagious giggles.

Molly dropped the short rations of candy at the desk as inspiration struck. "Wait here. You'll need something to carry your candy in." She ran back up and snatched a couple of tatty pillowcases from the linen cupboard.

"Oh, boy," Nina shouted when she saw them. "Where's yours, big—Aunt Molly?"

"I'm not going to carry one," she said. "But I got you one, Tamsin, just in case."

"I'm not using it, but I'll bring it in case Nina needs to lighten her load."

"Perfect." Nina grabbed Molly's hand again, straining toward the front door.

Tamsin held back, but a smile lurked at the corners of her mouth. She wasn't too old to be caught up in the excitement.

Molly eyed both girls. She'd pretended enough disinterest in their dad and her parents. "We can't go without telling someone we're leaving. Do you know where my mom is?"

"She's with Daddy and Grandpa Patrick." Nina's face flushed. "They went to buy more candy. I may have eaten a little and I took some for later. Then Aunt Olivia and Uncle Zach came over."

"And Evan and Lily sampled some?"

"Well, we all took a bunch." Nina giggled. "I have a bag in my room."

"Nina!" Tamsin exclaimed repressively. "I really didn't know. She's crazy about candy because Dad doesn't let us have much at one time."

Molly just laughed. "It's a special night. Who could resist grabbing by the handful?"

Tamsin's smile for her little sister held relief that Molly wasn't annoyed, and a lot of fondness for Nina. "Dad'll never let you eat it all."

"Will, too," Nina said. "Won't he, big girl?"

"Aunt Molly," Tamsin corrected.

"Aunt Molly, won't my daddy let me have all my candy?"

Molly hoisted her shoulders in an exaggerated shrug. "I'm staying out of this one, but I can't wait until they come back."

Just then the doorbell rang and a whole gang of goblins arrived. Molly ripped open the bags of candy she'd brought down, and Nina distributed the goodies. She wasn't quite as generous with the other children as she'd been with herself so Tamsin went behind her, adding to the outstretched sacks.

The sweet autumn scent of wood smoke filled

the room as kids clamored and parents beamed from just beyond the threshold. Molly oohed and aahed at the costumes, holding the door until the last little trick-or-treater departed. Then she noticed the two large, unlit pumpkins on the porch.

"Girls, what say we light the candles in the pumpkins?"

"Yeah." Nina crowed with delight. She bolted toward the hall to the kitchen, but then stopped, grabbing her sheet in her excitement. "But I'm not supposed to play with fire."

"Trust me," Tamsin said. "That's a good rule."

Molly produced suitable shock. "What did Nina do?"

"Our mom left the lighter on the bricks in front of our fireplace when Nina was first learning to walk, and she picked it up. The magazine rack was ruined before Dad got back from the kitchen with the fire extinguisher."

Ouch. "Tamsin and I had better light the candles, Nina."

She nodded, clenching her costume in her hands. "Are they big candles? How will we see them? The punkins are huge."

"They're monster candles a lady in town makes."

"Wow." Nina grabbed Molly's hand. "Let's hurry."

They took the fire starter from the kitchen drawer, and Tamsin pulled the top off the first pumpkin beside the front door. "They are huge," she said. "Look at those candles."

"They're supposed to smell like cooking pumpkin." As Molly spoke, a cool breeze swirled her hair around her face, blinding her.

"Hold your sheet, Nina." Tamsin gripped her own to keep it from flapping into the flame, while Molly raked her hair away from her eyes and followed their example before she lit the candle.

It blew out three times before she managed to shield it enough to give it a good start. She looked up at clouds sailing in front of the moon. "Rain's coming."

"Maybe Nina should take a jacket," Tamsin said.

"You both should." Down the street, movement and colors surged in the pale light of glow sticks the children used to light their way. "I wonder if they're all wearing coats."

"I'm fine," Tamsin said. "But Nina's little."

"Am not." Nina rushed across the porch to the other impossibly large pumpkin. She struggled with the top, then allowed Tamsin to help her remove it.

Headlights shone on them as the wind blew out Molly's lighter. They all turned. Molly's parents and Sam disembarked from the B and B's boat-size SUV.

"Good! You're lighting the pumpkins," Eliza

called. ''Wait. Let me get a picture of all my girls together.''

Wariness stalled Molly as Sam came around the front of the car. She'd been so eager to make the girls happy, to show them they were a vital part of her family.

But the minute Sam appeared, she remembered she didn't want to be any relation of his. Her heart bounced like a rubber ball as she searched his expression. He looked from Tamsin to her, obviously concerned.

Or so she thought, just before her hair whipped around her face again. Feeling silly in her getup, she was grateful for the cover, but if she didn't redo her braid, she'd look more like Frankenstein's bride than a ghost. And besides, she was bound to look much more conservative in a braid and her big old sheet.

She was making the right decisions here. Men came and went, but how often did a woman stumble upon the gift of two brand-new, lovable nieces?

## CHAPTER NINE

"I'LL GO WITH YOU," Sam offered, after Eliza had used all her film.

"Let me see if I can find more," she said.

Molly, twisting her hair into the craziest wind-whipped braid he'd ever seen, put the kibosh on Eliza's plan. "Nina's going to pass out if we don't start soon, and I promised the girls we'd go to Aunt Beth's for hot chocolate."

"Not to worry. She brought her cocoa into town tonight. Zach's been rounding up families all day, persuading them to bring their stuff to the square."

"Oh, but going to everyone's house is half the fun," Molly said, and Tamsin looked disappointed, too.

Nina shook her bag, clearly not caring how she got her candy. She just wanted it now.

"Where'd you get the costume, Nina?"

"From the big girl."

He glanced at Molly, who was still bemoaning the change in plans. "I like seeing everyone's decorations."

"Not as much as candy." Nina's tone suggested

she feared for Molly's sanity. She peered up at Sam. "Can we go now, Daddy?"

Molly turned to her mom. "Are you and Dad coming?"

"You want me to join the other men with their lawn chairs and candy baskets?" Patrick grinned. "I wouldn't miss it. We don't have guests tonight, Eliza. Let's just leave a note on the door and both go."

"Ready, Tamsin?" Sam asked. "Nina?"

"Yay!" Nina squealed.

He waved over his shoulder at Patrick and Eliza, who were disappearing inside the bed and breakfast to write their note. "I like your matching costumes." He smiled at Molly in gratitude. Might as well start thinking of her as his daughters' aunt. "Nina, stick close to Tamsin or she'll get run over in the dark."

"We'll stop at the grocery store and get her a glow stick," Molly teased, startling Sam.

"I'm not carrying a glow anything." Tamsin would have resented the offer of a glow stick from him, but she accepted Molly's affectionate ribbing. Molly must have used her time with the girls wisely.

"I want one." Nina hopped, too excited to walk.

"Where do we start?" he asked, mostly to make Molly look his way.

"Here's as good as any." She nudged Nina up

the path toward a well-lit house. "Have at 'em, girl."

Nina turned shy. "Come with me, Tamsin."

Tamsin looked at Sam. "I'm too old."

"Half these kids look your age." To prove his point, a group of four boys in jeans, dirty Ts and greasy hair flew past. "See?"

"They're boys."

Molly's low-pitched laugh drew Sam's gaze. He'd better not let Tamsin catch him off guard again, but if Molly had to laugh in seductive pleasure…

"Talk, talk, talk." Nina sounded exasperated— and much older than her years.

"Have you been sneaking TV time, little girl?" he asked.

"I want candy."

"I forgot." But as he took her hand, Tamsin intervened.

"I'll go, Dad."

"Thanks, Tamsin." Nina put her hand in her sister's, and they climbed the walkway together, Nina pushing aside Tamsin's billowing costume.

"Don't they break your heart?" Molly asked. "I always wanted a sibling."

Sam gritted his teeth. Between them lay Eliza's uncomfortable wish that he play that role with Molly. He shook the thought from his head. His girls came first.

''They hold my heart in their fists. I'd do anything for them.''

''I know.'' Molly's voice, too husky, touched him.

Moonlight gilded her eyes and the moisture on her lips. Sam curled his hand at his side, trying not to imagine touching her chin, turning her face to meet the brush of his lips. The strength of his need for her made him wary. He'd had to be so careful with his delicate Fiona.

The cool breeze wrapped Molly's sheet around her body and tugged strands of hair out of that misshapen braid. She remained still, but energy simmered around her. His heart beat faster, and he wished he was young enough to have a right to feel the way he did.

They wouldn't listen to the same music or know the same slang. There were enough years between them that they'd never think the same way. She truly was closer to Tamsin's generation.

Molly pointed over his shoulder. ''Here they come.''

Nina held up her bag, a pillowcase of all things. He peered inside. ''Cool.''

Nina giggled and turned to Tamsin. ''He said cool.'' She nudged Tamsin's elbow. ''Daddy said cool.''

''I've been saying it since before any of you were born.''

"Come on." Tamsin dragged her sister along. "Next house."

Sam avoided looking at Molly as his daughters left them again. "Nina's too excited. Give a kid permission to stay up past bedtime and collect a bagful of candy, and she falls apart."

"She's cute. You take good care of them, Sam."

"I try." He looked down. "Fiona was better. I think I'm too strict—the limit on television time, no junk food, homework first for Tamsin. Fiona made sure they had fun things to do as well."

"What's missing?" Molly eyed him curiously.

"She always had homemade play-dough in the fridge." He lifted his hands in confusion. "I thought it was cookie dough the first time I noticed it. Wondered why Fiona and Tamsin—we only had her then—were making lavender cookies." He twisted his mouth. "It tasted pretty awful."

"It would." Molly laughed. "What else?"

"They'd have history day, where they'd choose a place or a person and look up information on the Internet. Tamsin was invited to take her PSAT early last year, and we've already received invites from colleges. Fiona would have made a good teacher, too."

"Look again, Daddy."

Nina hurried up with her open pillowcase. He obliged with another "cool." Even Tamsin laughed as they ran down the next sidewalk.

"Did Fiona ever want to be a teacher?"

He swallowed hard. In the last sixteen months he'd learned to accept his wife's death, but he still felt angry. He'd never expected to lose her in a car accident.

"I shouldn't pry." Molly backed off. "I'm sorry."

"You aren't prying. She had heart disease. Muscle failure that meant the heart didn't pump blood correctly. She had several surgeries, but none was ever completely successful."

"Heart disease?" Molly laid her hand on his sleeve. Though their flesh made no contact, he felt her touch throughout his body. "Is that why you're a cardiologist?"

"That's why I'm a cardiologist."

"We always try to 'fix' everyone else's pain, don't we? It's the mark of an adult who didn't have the childhood he wanted."

Sam frowned, unwilling to reveal his emotions in front of her. "I don't know what you're talking about. My parents were loving, kind. They found a way to send me to medical school." His defensive tone shamed him. It wasn't the first time he'd claimed to have a loving childhood.

"You needed my mom." Molly moved in front of him. "You missed something—maybe just affection. It shouldn't matter after you're an adult, but it does."

He tried not to remember stiff congratulations for good grades, serious talks about what he'd need to contribute for college funds. He'd worked to help pay his own way, but those talks had made him feel as if he were imposing on his parents.

"I told you why I came, Molly. I've made no secret of my motives."

"Except possibly to yourself. What did you miss when you were a little boy?"

"I would have wanted to know Eliza if she were the least loving woman on earth. Just so my daughters had a place to go if something happened to me. I didn't look for her because my parents didn't love me."

Molly released him to search for Tamsin and Nina in a line of trick-or-treaters. "We've both needed more love. Maybe you never pretended you had a curfew to prove someone wanted you, but a woman who's been afraid her parents didn't love her can sense the same in another human being."

He resented her instincts even as he wanted to comfort her. "You pretended you had a curfew?"

"My birth parents were—" she steeled herself "—busy. I got in the way of all the fun they wanted to have."

Echoes of old memories hardened her eyes. He reached for her, but she absently avoided his touch.

"I always thought if I loved someone enough to get married, marriage might make it all better." Sam doubted she knew she'd spoken aloud.

There was one thing she couldn't know. He'd wanted more from his parents, but he'd also held back from Fiona, fearful that he'd hurt her with too much love, with passion that was too strong for her to bear.

He looked around for his children, uncomfortable with his own thoughts. "If my parents were so... Well, why do you think my girls miss their grandparents so much?"

Molly smiled with an older woman's wisdom. "I teach a little boy whose grandparents I knew when I was a kid. They were so stern with their daughter that she ran away even more than I did. But they smother this boy with affection. You'd be surprised how often people mellow."

Yellow light flashed across her face as the door up the sidewalk opened wider. Sam turned, waving at the woman who'd given his girls more light to see by.

He glanced back at Molly, gathering himself. All this emotional talk. Women didn't usually succeed in dissecting his feelings.

"Sometime we'll cover more of your past," he said.

"Sometime." Molly opened her hand to Nina and smiled at Tamsin.

"What do you say we skip the rest of the houses along the way and see what's happening on the square?"

"Okay," the teenager said. "We can stop on the way back if we want."

Sam chuckled, enjoying Tamsin's renewed enthusiasm. At her sharp glance he turned his laugh into a barely convincing cough. Trick-or-treating beat body piercing any day, but he'd better not push his luck.

AS SOON AS THEY reached the square, Tamsin and Nina met Olivia and Lily and Evan, and they were off. Behind them, an uncomfortable silence lingered. Molly pushed her hair over one shoulder and pretended indifference as she searched for her mom.

"That's a long note they're writing," she said.

Sam nodded.

"I thought they'd catch up with us." What had possessed her to buttonhole him about his past? What could she really know about Sam? She pointed at the paper pumpkins swinging back and forth on tree branches and quaint Victorian light poles. "Only Olivia could have organized this so quickly."

"What do you mean?"

"The twinkly lights. The white tablecloths and big plastic candy bowls. No one mentioned making a party in the square for the children. Olivia probably took over after Zach suggested it, and now it looks as if the town had been planning it for months."

"How has she fit in here?" Sam eyed her pregnant cousin-in-law with a curious glance.

Molly resisted an unsettling twinge of jealousy.

More of the old insecurity Sam had reawakened. "She loves Zach. I guess that's enough. I asked her if she misses her life in Chicago." Olivia came from one of the wealthiest families in America. Her father owned half the nation's newspapers, and his corporation produced most of the successful news programming. Olivia had run her own magazine for years, though she was only twenty-eight. "She says she never lived like normal people, until she and Evan found Zach."

"Normal people?" Sam asked, doubt in his voice. "Savannah's not a big city, but it can't rival this place for Rockwellian quaintness. I guess it's all relative."

"Yeah." Rockwellian hardly described the nights Molly had cowered under a musty, rotting bed in an empty house near the town dump. Seventeen years later the filthy scent came back to her, along with the sounds of the house literally falling apart over her head.

As if she were still eight years old, fear dried her palms and her mouth.

"There's my mom." She thanked the darkness for hiding her face. "I guess she's *our* mom."

Sam stared, his eyes catching light from a nearby streetlamp, revealing troubling thoughts. Finally, he opened his mouth, and Molly couldn't look away.

"I can't think of us being connected like that."

His rough tone seemed to wrap her in an electrical current. She searched for a safe haven. "There's my grandpa. Let's see what he's handing out."

"Aren't we too old to trick-or-treat?"

"No." Considering who they were and what her mom wanted them to be, fate was playing an excruciating trick on them both.

SETH CALVERT GREETED Molly with gratitude. "Take over. I've only been out here an hour, but these kids age me at the speed of light." A sheen of sweat filmed the older man's forehead.

Seth reached for Sam's hand to shake it. "Good to see you," he said. "Help Molly hand out my wife's chocolate milk."

Sam flinched at Seth's icy touch. "Your hands are like ice, sir."

"That's just from fishing out the bottles. My wife swears it's almost a healthy treat."

But had she noticed the way her husband tended to rub his chest at odd moments? Maybe he was trying to warm up. Maybe it was a habit. Sam glanced at Molly, who didn't seem to notice the gratitude with which her grandfather sank onto his webbed lawn chair.

"I'll sit here and scare the kids into coming by only once."

Laughing, Molly squeezed between her grandfather's table and the next one, which was piled high with chocolates in colorful foil. The woman behind it smiled, her mouth full of the goods she was handing out.

"Grandpa, what do you mean you'll scare the kids into coming by once?"

"Trick-or-treating must be thirsty work. They keep coming back." Seth turned to Sam. "Where are your daughters?"

"Olivia took Tamsin and Nina with her children."

"Good." Seth shifted in his chair, which creaked loudly enough to be heard over the sounds of happy young voices and the stiff breeze. "They need to settle into the family." He took a close look at Sam. "As do you. I'm glad you found us, Sam."

How could he be? The man didn't know Sam or his girls well enough to make such a claim. "Are you?"

"I see a change in Eliza." Molly's swift glance caught Seth's eye. "You see it, too, honey? She's more at peace with herself."

"I never knew Mom wasn't at peace."

Sam held himself still. He couldn't blame Molly if she was concerned Eliza would love him more. He'd feared most of his childhood that his adoptive mother would finally become pregnant with the child she'd longed for, and have no time or love left for him.

"You don't have to worry," he said, not caring

that her grandfather was watching. "Eliza's never going to love you less."

Seth pushed himself forward in his chair. "Did I say something wrong? Molly, I only meant your mother is even happier with her whole family."

"Grandpa, you said nothing wrong, but I'm still getting used to all this family. In fact, I think I'll go find the girls." She turned with military precision. "See ya, Grandpa. Sam."

They both watched her go. Seth spoke first. "She says your name as if she doesn't like the way it sounds."

"I've noticed." But she didn't say it that way all the time. Sam took the chair beside Seth, enjoying conversation with another honest Calvert. He and Molly seemed to be the only ones still keeping secrets. As Seth and he took turns handing out plastic milk bottles, Sam positioned himself to see the older man's torso in the streetlight.

"I can't deal with little kids as well as I used to." Seth smiled awkwardly at Sam's sharp, surprised glance. "I love my family—don't get me wrong. But other people's kids...I don't know. They just get noisier and pushier."

Sam adopted his best bedside manner. "Do you know how long you've felt this way?"

"You're not a psychologist, are you?" Seth shifted, trying for a more comfortable position.

"I'm always interested in stress levels."

Seth smiled. "I know your type. I'm married to

one. My granddaughter, Sophie, is another, though she appears to be reformed. She appreciates family time.''

''Greta hasn't reformed?'' Sam grew more concerned as lines of strain pinched the older man's mouth.

Finally, Seth answered. ''She tries.''

His raspy voice forced Sam to come clean. ''I'm going to ask you a question, and I need you to answer honestly.''

''The thing I dislike about most of you medical types is your arrogance. You all seem to think we mere mortals must tote your robes and answer your questions and—'' Seth stopped, lifting his hand to his throat. ''I'm sorry, Sam. I've begged my wife to retire for the past year, but she always finds reasons to put it off. She sticks to a plan for a few weeks, and then she starts working overtime again, or she has to visit the community center to see how it's coming along.''

Sam would rather not alienate Seth or Greta by taking sides, but concern for Seth came out of family feeling—however new it was to him. ''I've noticed that the more people resist medical questions, the more frightened they are that something's wrong.'' He offered Molly's grandfather a look of empathy. ''Especially men. We tend to view illness as weakness, but Seth, I just want to make sure you're okay.''

''You'll fit in here just fine.'' He rubbed his

chest. "I won't be surprised if my wife and Sophie don't have you volunteering at the community center. What's on your mind?"

The change felt too abrupt, but Molly would return soon and Sam didn't want to worry her. "You breathe hard for no obvious reason, and you're pale. You look uncomfortable."

"You're thinking heart attack?" Seth refused to meet his eyes. "You're like Sophie and Greta, too attached to your job."

"Great defense, Seth, but if you won't discuss what you're feeling with me, talk to your regular doctor. Do you have chest pains? Any tightness in your left arm?"

"I don't want to offend you, Sam, but you're diagnosing me in the dark with no tests."

"I like you. I'm grateful to all of you for being so kind to my daughters and me. I don't want anything to happen to you."

"Don't worry."

Sam could have let it go. He'd made an effort and managed to annoy a man whose respect he wanted. "I'm going to tell you something I've only told Molly. My wife had heart disease. I can't help noticing physical signs that might be symptoms, because I lived with someone who was ill. Her health mattered to me so much that I spent my life looking for ways to help her get better."

"Sam, I'm sorry." Seth braced his hands on the

chair arms. "I wouldn't have said any of what I did if I'd known."

"I'm not offended, but take me seriously. See a doctor. Even if you're just making sure you're don't need one."

"Sam?"

He turned, bumping the table. "Molly."

Concern narrowed her eyes. She peered from him to her grandfather. "What's wrong?" she asked.

"Nothing."

Before she could open her mouth again, Sam nodded at Seth and took her arm. "Did you find the girls?" He steered her into the crowd.

Staring over her shoulder, she tried to shake him off. It was the first time he'd touched her without wanting to drag her to some out-of-the-way corner and make love to her, but noticing he could be objective simply awakened the desire he didn't want to feel. He released her.

"Don't try to distract me as if I'm Nina. What's wrong with my grandfather?" She rubbed her arms as if she were trying to remove all traces of his touch. "Did you say he needed an exam?"

"He says he feels fine."

Molly stepped in front of Sam, so close that he swayed. "What's wrong with Grandpa?" she asked.

"I didn't like his color when I was here last. He breathes as if he can't get enough oxygen, and he moves as if he's hurting and can't get comfortable.''

Her grimace made her even more beautiful. Family mattered more than anything else in the world to her.

''He's stubborn. If we force him, he'll refuse to see anyone. So we can't leave it up to him.''

Despite being mesmerized by her and anxious that he'd made things worse for Seth, Sam laughed. ''What's your plan?''

''We start with Sophie.'' She raised herself on tiptoe, peering over his shoulder. ''She's around here somewhere. Look for a stroller. She and Ian won't be carrying Chloe when it's this cold. They'll have her bundled up.'' She sank onto her heels again. ''Sam?''

If she repeated his name fifty times a minute, he wouldn't protest. The way she said it made him feel as if he mattered to her, too. ''Huh?''

''How certain are you?''

''I'm not, but I risked annoying Seth when I want him on my side.'' The family might close ranks against Sam, or side with a beloved grandpa.

''He'd never be that upset by something like a doctor's appointment. If Sophie can't talk him into having a checkup, we'll turn to Gran.''

Sam threaded his fingers through Molly's. For once, she let him. ''Seth could be suffering stress,'' he said. ''When I brought it up, he talked about your grandmother working too hard.''

Molly nodded. "It's a battle they keep fighting. She promised to retire last year on their anniversary, but she's still working almost regular hours, and the community health center gives her another excuse to be busy."

Sam tugged on her hand. Molly tightened her grip, and he resisted an urge to pull her against him. "Don't panic," he said. "I could be wrong."

"Unlike Grandpa, I listen to physicians." She lowered her head. Strands of hair poking out of her braid caught the meager light. Sam barely stopped himself from stroking the curve of her neck as her spicy, womanly scent rose to seduce him. "Panic is my natural state when I think I might lose anyone in my family," she said.

Family. He let go of her in case one of the sharp-eyed Calverts spotted them. "Let's find Sophie."

# CHAPTER TEN

SATURDAY MORNING ARRIVED, hurling cold rain at Molly's bedroom window. As she tucked the bedding beneath her chin, enjoying the drama, the phone rang.

"Molly?" It was Beryl Parks, her principal and fellow teacher. "We're going to have to move the festival inside the school. Can you round up your family to help transport everything?"

Molly rose on one elbow, trying to wake up. "Sure. Good thing we put all the booths in the fire station." The tiny school couldn't afford an actual gymnasium, so they'd stacked everything in the fire station's open bay at the threat of bad weather.

"We have to get a move on." Beryl laughed. "Or if people show up early, we'll put them to work."

"Good call." Molly tried to hide a yawn.

"I know. I've phoned you early, but you have the largest family. I've already browbeaten my brother and father-in-law. Hey, doesn't Peggy have twin brothers?"

"Teenagers, too. All energy," Molly said. "I'll see you as soon as I can get there."

"Thanks."

Molly called around, harassing her relatives to help move and set up. Being naturally civic-minded, they didn't require too much nagging.

She dressed in jeans and a bright green sweater, and added a fleece jacket. As she braided her hair, a touch of mortification heated her skin. Seeing last night's malformed do in the bathroom mirror startled her.

She'd certainly looked ghoulish for Halloween. She laughed out loud at the idea of wandering the square all night in front of her students and their parents.

The idea of Sam seeing her like that made her wince, but she put it out of her mind. His opinion on her looks didn't matter.

By the time she reached the fire station, cars already lined the streets, and a steady stream of parents, teachers and relatives had begun to move the festival booths from the fire station to the school, two wide squat buildings and a field away.

Molly parked and stepped out into unkind weather. She'd enjoyed it more from the warmth of her bed, but she pushed through wind and rain to the fire station.

A clown whose open mouth was the target for the beanbag toss had been left too close to the door. Molly tried to hide her childhood fear of leering clowns, but the lashing rain had turned this one into a horror-movie prop, and she lurched to a halt.

"Hey, Molly." Her grandfather turned, a big, painted bowl in his arms. "Better move, girl."

"Grandpa, should you be..."

His eyes darkened. "I like that Sam. In fact, I like him more because he knows I carry weight with the rest of the family, and he was still willing to badger me." He gestured with the bowl, so she would move out of his way. "But you don't need to worry about me."

"I forced Sam to spill his guts, and I am worried. Can't you find something less physically demanding to do? We have to set up these things in the school, you know. Someone could hand you the pieces."

"I'm not an invalid. I just got tired last night."

Aware of the people milling about them, Molly leaned closer. "Will you make an appointment?"

Grandpa gave their neighbors a scowl that was probably meant for her. "You have too much of your grandmother in you."

Tears stung her eyes. "That's the nicest thing you could have said, Grandpa."

Smirking, he hoisted his bowl higher and stepped out into the rain. Molly almost dashed after him.

"You distracted me!" She ignored other people's interest in her raised voice. Her grandfather pretended not to hear, or else the wind muffled her protest.

"What's going on?"

With a start, Molly turned. "Hi, Tamsin. I'm glad you have a coat."

"I'm from Savannah. This is like Alaska to me." She stared out at the huddled figures scurrying down the driveway. "Who are you yelling at?"

"Did I yell?" Molly grabbed the nearest stack of booth parts. "I didn't mean to."

Tamsin took an armload, too. "Someone in your family bugging you? I know that feeling. Dad will have to tie a rope around Nina to make her keep her coat on."

"I've noticed she can be headstrong."

"That's a nice way to put it."

Molly glanced down. "I wish you had a hood."

"I'm fine. Your hair looks better today, by the way."

A laugh escaped her. "You could have mentioned that last night. I was going for a ghostly flow, but then the wind kept blowing it in my face so I braided it back without looking. You let me appear like that in front of my students and their parents."

Tamsin giggled—an odd but extremely sweet sound from a girl who'd held her emotions in check so long. "I thought it was part of your costume."

"I may not be everyone's ideal of femininity, but no one chooses to weave tree branches in her hair."

Tamsin laughed as they carried their awkward loads through the wide school doors. Beryl, chic in black trousers and a matching raincoat, directed them to the farthest end of the hall that ran the building's width.

Molly and Tamsin set down their loads and ran back to the fire station. Molly had kept an eye on her grandpa's stubborn face, turned away from her as they passed on their way to and from the two buildings. He looked all right to her, but she didn't trust her own diagnostic instincts.

Finally, one of his friends talked him into taking a spot on the assembly line inside the school. By the time Molly's parents and Sam appeared with Nina and breakfast rolls, many of the booths were dried off and dressed in white cloths that hid the rain damage.

Molly saw Sam eyeing her grandfather, who was trying to tidy up the clown. "What do you think?" she asked in a low voice.

His gaze swept over her, and she wished she looked as sophisticated as Beryl. But Sam didn't seem to mind wet jeans and fleece. In his eyes, she read the same hunger she felt each time she saw him. She focused on Grandpa.

"I can't tell," Sam said. "I'd feel better if he'd let me take a closer look. What's he so scared of?"

"I don't know." She stared longingly at the table her mother had set up with hot cocoa, Danishes and doughnuts. "That he really is sick? The fact he's so determined not to pay attention scares me most of all. He seems defensive."

Sam nodded. "That's what I told him."

"You've seen it before?"

He looked at her without speaking. She guessed he had experienced reluctance like her grandfather's, and it didn't mean good news to come.

"I'm starving," she exclaimed abruptly. But instead of feeding herself, she turned her back on the ladened table and headed for the still-open doors. "I'm supposed to make sure we brought everything for the festival down here from the fire station. Save me a piece of Mom's coffee cake?"

"I'll come with you."

She should have said no, but she wanted him to come. And what could it hurt? She was frightened for her grandfather. Sam's presence comforted her. She turned and almost bumped into him.

He looked down with a smile she could barely resist. She closed her eyes for the briefest second. If only this man was not off-limits to her.

"What?"

She halted her wandering thoughts and eyed the edge of the T-shirt beneath the V of his sweater. "Grandpa," she said. "I'm worried about him. If you thought he was in immediate danger, you wouldn't wait until he chose to see a doctor, would you?''

His silence forced her to meet his gaze, but his distracted look implied they were equally bad for each other's thought processes.

''Sam?''

''You're only twenty-five, aren't you?''

''You're reminding yourself because you still think I'm inexperienced. But I'm as old as anyone you know in ways you won't ever hear about.''

''Why don't you tell me?'' He looked troubled and protective at the same time. ''I've heard rumors, but I want to know the whole truth.''

She shook her head, taking a judicious step away from him. ''You're my mother's son.''

''Come on.'' He took her arm and towed her out into rain that blew even harder into her face, soaking her instantly. ''And, no, I wouldn't leave your grandpa in danger.'' Sam had to shout to be heard.

Molly glanced back to see if any of the others were close enough to hear him. But the two of them were alone in the storm.

''Where's your coat?'' she asked, eyeing his dripping hair and wet skin. He worried about Tamsin and Nina, but who cared for him?

With disdain, he plucked at her jacket sleeve. ''Like that fleece is any warmer than my sweater.''

''You always think you know best,'' she said, then wished she hadn't. She appreciated his concern for Grandpa, but Sam was wrong about her.

Twenty-five wasn't too young for forty. "I'm sorry."

"No, I am. I don't know how to say thank-you when someone worries about me."

Hunching her shoulders, she hid a blush.

Steve Caldwell, the fire chief, had his men parking the trucks inside again. He lifted a hand in greeting as Molly skidded on the smooth cement floor.

"Trying to get dry?" He laughed as she shook herself, sending drops flying. "It's a lost cause." He moved past Molly to shake hands with Sam. "Morning. You must be Eliza's boy."

"I am."

Bemused by the level of curiosity a Bardill's Ridge visitor could incite, Molly wondered how Sam felt about his fifteen minutes in the small-town public eye.

"Glad to know you." Chief Caldwell turned, showcasing the wet, red truck at his back. "I haven't heard if you're planning to move up here, but we can always use a new volunteer. You think about that."

"I will, but my daughters are settled in Savannah. They'd fight a move."

The disappointment she felt startled Molly; she hadn't even been aware of harboring a faint hope that Sam and the girls would move to town. At the same time she was relieved. Seeing Sam every day would be an impossible task. Someone would soon glimpse her lovesick longing.

"You're from Savannah? I heard you'd come from somewhere down South, but I wasn't sure where." At last Chief Caldwell seemed to remember Molly. "You've carried everything over to the school. I had the men check before we moved the trucks back inside."

"Thanks." She lifted a soaked eyebrow at the rain blowing in. "We'd better get back."

"You could have called." The chief grinned at Sam, as if offering to share a joke at the short-sighted little woman's expense. Molly contemplated dragging the man down the street for festival duty. The kids could be brutal with a beanbag.

"I guess I should have." She bolted back into the rain, expending nervous energy by jogging all the way back to the school.

Sam reached the hall right behind her. "Let's find a towel." Amusement threaded his husky voice. "Or at least a hand dryer."

"I have towels in my classroom."

"I thought the classrooms were all locked." Sam followed her. "They told us we had to set up the booths in the hall and the lunchroom."

"I have a key," she said.

"Oh, yeah."

She felt as if she were sneaking in a boyfriend as she unlocked her door and slipped inside, Sam literally on her heels. A deeper sense of the forbidden with Sam was the last thing she needed.

"Why did they lock everyone out of the classrooms anyway?" He shut the door.

"Last year one of the kids caught the music teacher—former music teacher—and one of the city councilmen in the second-and-third-grade room." She felt foolish as her skin warmed because she was now alone with him. "The gossip flew. Mrs. Brody quit, but she might have been asked to leave if she hadn't."

"Mrs. Brody? She's married?"

"Widowed, but it didn't matter. She misbehaved in front of a student." Molly crossed to the cupboard and pulled out two towels. Behind her she heard a door click.

She whirled. "What are you doing?"

"Locking the door." His expression reminded her of Chief Caldwell's opinion of her common sense. "I don't want you fired for being in here with me."

"Locking the door won't make us look less guilty." She tossed him one of the towels.

"We won't be doing anything to feel guilty about." His grim smile almost challenged her.

Fortunately, she'd learned the hard way to resist. As soon as she found time, she was going to start dating again. Anything to make Sam look less attractive.

The towel sure didn't help. His head emerged,

and his face was rough and ruddy, as if he were just waking from a deep sleep. His curls sprang loose as he dried them, making him look younger.

Molly searched for a different subject. "Back to Grandpa. Did you talk to Sophie?" They hadn't found her on the square before Nina had grown tired and wanted to go home.

Sam disappeared under the towel again. She wished he'd stop doing that. His fingers splayed against the white terry cloth, long and articulate, dark and capable.

"She promised to speak to Seth. According to Eliza, Sophie has some pull with him."

"You told Mom?"

He nodded, but he hesitated before speaking again. "We're leaving tomorrow night so I can get Tamsin back to school. I had to make sure someone would take action if Seth puts it off."

"She didn't say a word to me." Irrationally, Molly felt left out, as if Sam and Eliza were sharing secrets. Did he consider her incapable of warning the family? "You really do think I'm young, don't you?"

"I didn't include you in the conversation because you weren't sitting at Eliza's kitchen table last night."

Eliza's table. Not the family table that had also belonged to Molly for the past seventeen years. She buried her face in a towel this time. "You don't have to use that overly patient tone."

"I don't have a clue what you're talking about."

She lowered the towel and hoped she'd managed to avoid smearing her mascara. "I'm sorry." She tossed the towel toward the sink at the back of the room and put a desk between them. Admitting her own insecurities required a little cover. "You're my mother's natural child—the one thing I've never been, the one thing I cannot possibly ever be, no matter how hard I try. Maybe you'll mean more to her than I do. I'm twenty-five years old, and no matter how you see me, I'm far too mature to feel this way, but I don't want you to push me out of my mom's life. Though I keep fighting it, the fact remains that that worries me."

"Molly, I don't want that, either." He circled the desk, but she backed behind another. "Wait," he said. "We're both worried about problems that don't exist. You've lived with my birth mother for most of your life. You're her child in ways I can never match. She'll see your wedding, the birth of your first child." She flinched, but he didn't notice. He reached for her hand and pulled her as close as the desk allowed. "You're afraid I'll steal your parents, but I'm more concerned about my feelings for you. You have a future, a family of your own to make. I've already done those things, and they're milestones that I don't want to steal from you."

"We're both determined to do the right thing

and we're so noble we're starting to make me sick.''

His reminding her of the baby she would never have sparked the recklessness she'd evaded so long. She turned her hand and locked it around Sam's wrist. Then she stepped around the desk and looped her free arm around his neck.

''You can't steal what a woman is willing to give.'' Though he strained away from her, she rose on tiptoe to reach his mouth with hers.

His hand tightened, but his body remained unyielding. She softened her lips, wanting him even more because he held back. She pressed her mouth against his, then raised her gaze to read his urgent denial. ''Please, Sam.''

He hesitated, his face taut, then groaned, opening his mouth.

Just as she imagined pushing him onto the nearest desk, he lifted his head to kiss her forehead, the bridge of her nose, her cheekbones. His mouth was tender, his movements reluctant, as if he were memorizing her.

''You think this is the only time you'll ever kiss me, right?'' she said.

''Um-hmm.''

She ached. He might be correct. As his lips possessed hers once more, Molly tasted her own tears of gratitude. She'd never thought to feel desire again, and she'd never suspected it could be so pure, so plainly good.

When Sam pulled away, she stumbled. But he marched to the front of the classroom.

"This is all wrong." He bunched his fists in his pockets. His eyes, hollow with pain, burned into her, despite the twenty feet between them.

She grabbed at the nearest desk to avoid running to him.

A strange feeling of relief made her light-headed. "You talk about stealing from me, but you're a decent person. I don't know much about men, but I believe you won't hurt me any more than you'd hurt my parents or your daughters."

"Molly…" His soft gaze begged her not to go on.

"Mom wants to think of you and me as brother and sister. I can't see you like that, but I'll try to ignore any other possibilities." She wiped her mouth.

"Don't." He stared at her hand as if he'd like to stop her from rubbing his kiss away.

"It's not completely a lost cause." Despite his obvious feelings for her, he was willing to push her away. Anger surprised her with a thirst for revenge. In pain, she wanted him to regret missing his chance with her. "I'm grateful. You made me remember what feeling whole is like, but you can't be the one I feel this way with."

"One kiss convinced you?" His eyes became flat, and she instantly regretted trying to hurt him. "Why did you kiss me, Molly?"

"I don't know." How could she explain her old habit of doing the wrong thing just to test people who cared for her? "I wanted to know how you'd feel. How I'd feel kissing you."

"And now?" His voice trembled. With anger or desire? She couldn't tell which, and he shook his head in denial. "Don't answer." He turned to the door, as impatient with himself as with her. "You only made our lives more difficult."

Nodding, she watched him leave. "Maybe," she said to the closing door. "But it was worth finding out I could love again."

## CHAPTER ELEVEN

MANY OF THE festivalgoers had taken advantage of slowing rain to run for their cars. The smaller crowd gave Eliza a perfect view of Molly, juggling beanbags with Tamsin and Nina.

Laughing, Molly scooped up all the beanbags Nina hadn't managed to toss through the clown's mouth. Tamsin grabbed the last one, just beyond Molly's reach.

"You own the world, don't you?" Patrick wrapped his arms around Eliza's waist from behind, his voice washing over her with love. "Feels like it, doesn't it, seeing those girls together?"

"I'm so relieved Molly's been able to make friends with Nina and Tamsin."

"Why would you even worry? No one could understand how a little girl needs family better than Molly."

"I'm talking about more than that. I keep wondering if she can accept Sam's daughters as her own family. Maybe she'll give up her crazy attitude about not adopting."

"She's still young." Patrick dropped his arms, sounding disturbed. "Don't push our daughter."

"Push her? Haven't you noticed she doesn't let anyone get close? She doesn't risk growing attached."

"She's careful since the miscarriage. She'll make a good mom someday—if she wants to be. But Eliza, don't go pointing out this happy family is the reason she should start thinking about filling her house with children."

His sarcasm stung. "What do you mean by 'happy family'?"

"Nothing." He looked away from her.

"You're trying to hide the remains of a grudge."

"I just want Molly to find her own way."

"You're still upset about Sam and the girls?" Eliza had done her penance. "We agreed to start over."

"And I've made Sam comfortable. Those girls feel as if they belong to us now, but I still don't see the world the way I used to."

"You mean because of me?"

Patrick blew out a breath as if holding back an answer. Finally, he met her gaze. "I believed I knew the way you thought before. Now I wonder."

"I'd never hurt you or Molly."

"Not on purpose," he agreed. "But you think you did me a favor, keeping quiet about Sam all those years?"

"No." The word exploded from her. "I wish I'd told you the truth years ago. Apart from the agony of keeping a secret from you, we've all lost time with Sam and Tamsin and Nina."

"You're still talking about what's important to you." He stepped around her, kissed her swiftly, and then stepped back. "Before we go any further, I want to say I love you, and I want our life to go on. But I've faced the facts. You didn't trust me. Now, how do I know you trust Molly enough to let her decide for herself what she wants?"

"What are you talking about?" What he'd said hurt, but the kiss gave her faith in the future. "One minute you blame me for something I thought you'd forgiven, and the next, you accuse me of meddling."

"We have a ways to go before we find out what's normal between us. But I'm talking about Molly. She's my daughter, too, and she matters just as much to me as she does to you."

"All I'm hoping is that her feelings for *our* new granddaughters might mean she'll be willing to adopt one day. She'll never be happy without her own child."

"You mean you weren't," he said quietly. "That doesn't necessarily hold true for Molly."

What was he saying? Had their whole life been a lie? "Patrick, you wanted Molly, didn't you?"

Anger sparked in his gaze and heat rose between

them—not a pleasant heat. "Don't ever suggest that I didn't."

She dragged his hand close to her heart, despite his reluctance to be touched. "I'm relieved. I'd hate to think I hid Sam from you and then forced Molly on you."

"Molly is my daughter," he said again, moody but proud, as his gaze rested on her.

"It's the family I've dreamed of all my life, Patrick. Since the day I gave up Sam."

"I can't imagine what you went through." He tugged his hand free and curved his arm around her shoulder. "I don't want you to be hurt like that again."

"Patrick, are you and I going to be happy?"

"It's work, Eliza. More work than we're used to."

"But do you want to try?"

He nodded, resting his chin on her shoulder. "Especially when I watch our girls playing together."

Eliza let herself not just hope, but believe. "Molly and Sam and the girls really are our big, happy family." She leaned into his body. "And we can destroy that hideous clown in a bonfire as soon as the rain stops. What more could we ask?"

SAM TOOK THE GIRLS home to Savannah on Sunday night. Grateful that no one—most of all Tamsin—had seen how much a single kiss with Molly had affected him, he managed to stay away for ten full days and planned on a much longer separation.

According to his caller ID, Molly phoned several times, but he managed to clear her name and number before either of the girls saw it. Startling him during the second week, Sophie called one night just after Tamsin had printed a class project in his office and headed for bed.

"Sam? I know it's late, but we had an unexpected delivery up at the baby farm, and I couldn't call until now."

"Is something wrong?" He couldn't help assuming the worst. Disaster often reached a man through unexpected phone calls.

"We're all fine here." She brushed his concern aside. Images of life at Bardill's Ridge went through his mind—Eliza setting up the dining room for the guests' breakfast; Molly, her mind on papers she had to mark before morning, stopping by to ease her mother's workload. "I'm glad I caught you at home," Sophie continued. "Do you have any free time—say, next Friday?"

"What do you need?"

"We're deciding on a property for the health center, and I thought you might view the possibilities with us."

"Me?" He had no say. He wouldn't be moving to Bardill's Ridge. He'd promised the girls.

"Even if you aren't joining us, we want to offer as much care as possible up here. We've talked to a few specialists in the larger towns nearby, and they'll visit the clinic, but I thought you could help us choose the proper space and equipment.''

He'd like to do something for his birth mother's hometown. ''Thanks for asking, Sophie. What time do you need me on Friday?''

''I'm sure you have patients. So do some of us. Uncle Patrick and Grandpa are also coming along to discuss the legal stuff. We've agreed to meet at Dr. Fedderson's office at about eight. I know you'll still have to leave work early, but what do you think?''

''Eight is fine.'' He wrote down Dr. Fedderson's name and address. ''Eight o'clock. I'll get directions from Eliza.''

''Great.'' Sophie sounded as if she'd ticked off an item on her to-do list. ''I'll see you on Friday, around eight o'clock. Thanks for helping out.''

''My pleasure.'' Trite, but painfully true. This tie to Bardill's Ridge wouldn't change his daughters' lives, but it made him feel as if he belonged.

They got a flight to Knoxville, where Sam rented a car, reaching the Dogwood on Friday in time to drop off his daughters and get directions from Eliza. She steered the girls toward the kitchen, and all but shoved him back out the door.

''I've got dinner for Tamsin and Nina, but I thought Patrick and Molly and you and I could share something later,'' she said. ''Don't forget to bring Molly back.''

"Is she going along?" He ignored the hammering of his heart. He wasn't ready to face Molly, or Tamsin's radar where he and Molly were concerned.

"She's meeting you after you finish. Go," Eliza said. "The others are waiting."

Laughing, he started toward the front door, but came back to hug her. "Thanks," he said.

"For?"

"For pushing us around as if we really are family. You're not wearing your kid gloves tonight."

Blushing, she looked pleased. "You've been my family since the moment you told me who you were." Tears wet her eyes. "Now get out of here before Greta sends a posse." She gave him another gentle shove, and this time he went. He wouldn't put a posse past anyone in this family.

Eliza's directions were easy to follow. After he greeted the others and met the physicians, whose faces were blurs in Dr. Fedderson's dark parking lot, Sam got back into his car and followed the convoy. Their first stop was a former supermarket converted to a flea market that couldn't keep up with the stalls on the square. According to Patrick and Seth, the building had been empty for eight months.

"And we have permission to do construction," Seth added.

"Have you looked at the heating and AC?" Sophie sniffed, clearly offended by the stale air.

"It's musty because it's been empty," Greta said.

"I'm hot, though." Sophie circled her finger around her collar. "And it can't be hormones from nursing Chloe."

"No, it's hot," Dr. Fedderson agreed. "And I think we'd have to do a ton of renovations to turn this wide-open space into medical offices."

"That's why they're offering such a good price," Patrick said. "Don't forget that."

"You keep it in mind for us," Greta said, "when we fall in love with something more suitable and more expensive."

"Leave the boy alone." Seth defended their son, ignoring the smirking expressions of the physicians who'd joined them on this jaunt. "We have to weigh the cost, and that's Patrick's job."

"I know." Greta looped an arm through his and pressed close to him. "You're hot, too. You're sweating."

Both Sam and Sophie turned. Seth noticed and rolled his eyes. Not the most reassuring response. He broke away from his wife and leaned over Patrick's shoulder to consult his son's clipboard. "Next, we have a vet's office. Larger than your place, Tom," he said to Dr. Fedderson, "because this town has more animals showing up for treatment than humans."

Tom nodded. "I believe it. Folks around here take more precautions with their livelihood than with their own health. I sometimes wish I'd gone into cows rather than people.''

Sam followed Sophie and Greta and Seth through the supermarket doors. Behind them, Dr. Fedderson talked with three of his colleagues. Sam still wasn't sure why Sophie had invited him rather than the specialists who'd agreed to work up here when needed.

Sam was the last to enter the vet's office. According to the sign outside, four veterinarians shared the space. ''They're building something larger out by Henderson's Seed and Feed,'' Seth said. ''They can afford a brand-new building.''

Sam grinned at the irony of life in Bardill's Ridge, but his mind was on his sort-of-grandfather's health. ''Seth.'' Putting a hand on the other man's arm, he held him back. ''Did you have an exam?''

''I promised, didn't I?''

''Have you scheduled it?'' In the waiting room lights, Seth's face looked pale.

''I saw Tom Fedderson. I'm in the pink. Now drop it before you scare my wife.''

''You're part of my family now. Part of my daughters' family. You matter to me. Why didn't you tell Greta that everything's all right?''

''I didn't want to worry her before and now it doesn't matter.''

Sam released him. ''I guess that's true.'' He took a relieved breath. ''I'm glad you were right.''

"Thanks, son." His smile held genuine warmth. "Now let's catch up."

Loud murmurs told Sam they'd walked into the winner before he could discern actual conversation.

"We'll have to scour the place with bleach, but then we'll have ready-made treatment rooms." The ENT specialist opened a couple of doors before he paused at the reception desk.

"Herb," said the orthopedic surgeon, her exasperated tone boding ill for their future alliance, "vets are just as sanitary as we are. The place just needs a moving-in cleaning."

"And we'll have space for a small outpatient OR when we remove the animal crates out back," Sophie said.

"What do you think, Sam?" Greta looked from him to Seth as if she'd just noticed them hanging back.

If Seth wanted to keep his good health a secret, Sam would go along with the plan. He stepped away from the man who really had begun to feel like his grandfather. "I doubt we'll find anything comparable."

"I agree," Tom said. "We'll face the least construction here."

"Don't you think you should view the other buildings?" Seth pointed at the list. "We found good choices for the money."

"Seth, we all know this town," Greta said. "And we're familiar with the buildings. Nothing else will compare. Let's just find out when the present group is moving out and then start making plans.''

Instead of answering, Seth ran his right hand down his left arm. Sam started toward him as the older man's face changed, going dull at first and then crumpling with pain. Without a word, Seth slid to the floor.

Sam followed. "Seth?" He turned him over. Unconscious. Pale. Sweat as cold as ice sheened his skin.

"Seth!" Greta screamed his name, dropping to her knees beside him.

Sophie's voice lifted in fear as well. Other exclamations faded while he focused on Seth.

Sam checked for a pulse and found none. He pinched Seth's nose and covered his mouth and breathed twice for him. Seth's chest rose and fell. Sam checked for a pulse again. None.

"Does anyone have an aspirin?" Sam yanked the front of Seth's shirt open. Buttons bounced off the floor and onto Greta's skirt.

Sophie eased her grandmother out of the way. "I'll breathe," she said. "You do the compressions, Sam. Someone dial 9-1-1."

"Tom, what did Seth's ECG look like?"

Tom Fedderson, on his cell phone, stopped speaking to the emergency services operator. "His what?"

In the nonprofessional side of Sam's brain, rage

at Seth's senseless behavior boiled over. But he'd deal with that after the man was healthy again. "Ask for the ambulance." Sam finished the first cycle of fifteen pumps.

Sophie gave her grandfather two breaths. Sam checked for a pulse. He shook his head at Sophie and did another set of fifteen compressions. Then she breathed again.

"Hold up, Sophie." He checked once more for a pulse, his own heart pounding as he sensed Greta's gaze focused directly on him. "Don't worry. I'm not letting him go."

"That sounds good, but you may not have the last word." Greta rested her cheek against her husband's. "Don't leave me, Seth Calvert. Don't you dare leave me!"

"Gran, I have to…" Tears clogged Sophie's voice.

"Move, Sophie." She couldn't cry and breathe at the same time, and Sam certainly understood the need for tears. "Someone else take over."

The ENT specialist slid into Sophie's place. As Tom tucked his phone away, Sam checked again.

"Ahh. There it is. You keep fighting, Seth." Tachycardia—far too rapid, but undeniably a beating pulse. "We've got him. Tom, you haven't seen an electrocardiogram on him?"

"No. In fact, I've been calling him for two months because his physical's overdue."

"He knew something was wrong."

Seth groaned, his eyes fluttering open. "I'm sorry, Greta."

"You *did* know." His wife's traumatized voice accused. She fumbled in her purse, brought out an old-fashioned pill case and offered an aspirin to Sam.

"It's full strength?" he asked, and Greta nodded. "Someone get water," he said.

"Give it to me." Sophie took the aspirin. "Grandpa, I'm going to crush it. You'll find it easier to swallow."

Greta fell across Seth's chest and then sprang back as if wary of doing more damage.

Sam checked his pulse again and took a look at his own watch. Patients who received clot-busting thrombolytics within ninety minutes of an infraction were one-seventh as likely to die.

Seth fumbled for Greta's hand, and she clenched it in both of hers. "You knew, too, Sam?"

"He said Tom had given him a clean bill of health. I'd pushed him because I didn't like his color or the way he breathed heavily under exertion."

"I noticed, too, Gran." Sophie brought the aspirin back in a spoon, along with a glass of water. "I found the break room." She and Sam eased Seth up so he could chew the aspirin and then drink the water.

He sighed, his mouth still twisted by the aspirin's bitterness as they eased him back down.

Sophie wrapped her arms around her grandmother. "And he seemed to be sweating for no reason. I tried to talk to you about it last summer."

"I don't remember." Greta's tears flowed freely now. "Seth, we have to make changes."

He nodded slightly. A siren whined in the distance.

"I hear the ambulance," Tom said. "Thank God for small towns."

The paramedics arrived, and Sam explained what had happened. As they loaded Seth onto a gurney, Sam pulled Greta from Sophie's arms. "I'd like to ride with you," he said. "I want to watch the ECG on the way to the hospital."

"We're so close it's not worth starting," the first paramedic warned.

"You're starting it."

Greta took Sam's arm. "Do come."

He nodded, knowing how she felt. Physicians might be arrogant, but they were as vulnerable as any "civilian" when a loved one was in danger. He searched for Patrick. "Someone needs to tell Eliza and Beth and Zach." His head spun. "And Molly." He needed to see her face. He craved the reassurance she gave him.

"I'll make the calls." Patrick broke his death

grip on the clipboard and approached his father. "Dad, I could kill you myself for letting this happen."

"Son, you're nearly sixty years old. Too long in the tooth to make childish threats." Seth patted his son's face with his open palm. "Come see me tonight if they let you, okay?"

Patrick nodded, clutching his father's wrist.

"Patrick, can you make sure someone stays with my daughters?" Sam didn't wait for a response. He followed Seth to the ambulance and the all-too-unreliable guarantees medical technology offered.

MOLLY SENT HER MOTHER with her dad, but they'd barely left when James Kendall called.

"I'm in town to see Olivia, and I'm watching Lily and Evan while she and Zach go to the hospital. Sophie mentioned Sam had accompanied Seth in the ambulance. I know Tamsin's old enough to look after herself, but I thought he might need me to watch Nina."

Tamsin could probably look after Nina just fine, but no one wanted to leave a teenager, still grieving for her own mom, in charge of a little girl during a health scare.

Molly sagged against the table in her mother's kitchen. "Thanks, James, but Nina's asleep."

"Evan and Lily are still awake. I'll bundle them

into the car and we'll do a sleepover at the Dogwood.''

"You've got the hang of this grandfather
thing.''

He cleared his throat. "I've been Evan's grandfather for seven years.''

Despite his gruff tone, she could tell he was
pleased. "Sorry," she said, her concentration and
hope with her own grandpa. "I'll get rooms ready
for you all.''

"Thanks. See you in a few minutes.''

Molly arranged accommodations for James and
Lily and Evan. Then she hurried back downstairs
to find Tamsin sprawled sideways in an armchair,
worry etched on her face.

"You're going to the hospital, too?''

"Not if you don't want to hang around here with
James.'' Molly reached for the phone. "I can call
him back.''

"No.'' Tamsin had forgotten her black makeup
this trip, and her face looked incredibly young.
"I'm just worried about Seth. Did you talk to my
dad?''

Was that an extra layer of wariness in her gaze?
"No, but I wish I had," Molly said. "I'll call as
soon as I know anything.''

"Thanks.'' Startling the daylights out of Molly,
Tamsin quickly closed the distance between them

and clasped her in a hug. "And make sure Eliza and Patrick are all right."

Wanting to cry, Molly couldn't speak. She managed a nod, but then the doorbell rang, and she bolted. James offered a reassuring smile as Evan and Lily wrapped themselves around Molly.

"Is Grampa Seth going to die?" Lily asked.

"No, honey." She might be lying, but she'd take the heat later if she was wrong. She refused to consider the worst.

"Let Aunt Molly go now, kidlets." James Kendall had certainly unbent in the past year. He'd made the transition from international media emperor to Tennessean grandfather with ease. "Your aunt will let us all know what happens."

"I left the doors to your rooms open. Try to settle in for the night." Molly hugged both children and then turned to Tamsin. "You're okay?"

The girl nodded, showing a defenselessness that Molly had never seen in her.

"Do you want to come with me?" Molly asked.

Tamsin hesitated, but shook her head. "Nina might be afraid if she woke up and one of us wasn't here."

"You're probably right, but Tamsin, don't think you aren't just as important to this family because you're staying here. Grandpa needs all our hope no matter where it's coming from."

A slow smile curved Tamsin's mouth. "I'll be hoping from here."

After hugging her again, Molly thanked James once more and rushed to her car. She gave brief consideration to the traffic laws as she drove to the hospital.

She was the last Calvert to enter the CICU waiting room, where Gran sat wringing her hands.

"Any news yet?" Molly asked.

Sophie made space beside her on a hard vinyl bench. "They're testing myoglobin and enzyme markers, the MB isoform, and troponin T."

"Myoglobin is a protein. MB isoform and troponin are chemicals. They're all released into the blood after the heart muscle is damaged. The levels indicate how damaged the muscle is," Greta explained dully.

"Having a family full of doctors can be worse than knowing nothing at all—which is why I'm asking," Molly said.

"Thanks for saying that, Molly." Eliza crossed the room to hug both her and Sophie. "I didn't have the nerve."

"They'll test and decide how they need to treat him next." Greta twisted her head as if her neck was tight with stress. "How can this be Seth we're talking about? I've wasted so much time. He asked me to quit working a year ago. You all know by now how close we came to splitting up, and still I've dragged my feet. What kind of fool puts off being with her husband because she's afraid she'll be bored at home?''

Molly lifted her head. "Afraid?'' She understood that. Fear was a powerful motivation.

She thought of Sam, of his mouth against hers, hungry and hard, of his heart beating fast under her palms. He might be part of her family, but she hadn't chosen her feelings for him, and they weren't wrong.

Fear of losing love had made her life cold.

What kind of fool let any fear deny her a chance at love?

## CHAPTER TWELVE

MOLLY STOOD WATCH at the door while Aunt Beth, Eliza, Sophie and Olivia comforted her grandmother. Around the women, their men waited, Ian with his hands in his pockets, Uncle Ethan at his side, with his shoulder braced against a wall. Zach stared through the window at the waning sun, his gaze aggressive, angry and impotent, until he finally looked at Olivia and their eyes met in a clash of need and nurturing.

Molly turned away. She empathized most with Zach. How the hell were they supposed to stand around here and do nothing but wait while Grandpa's life rested in someone else's hands? Thank God for Sam, who was at least allowed to observe at Grandpa's side.

"Sam is one of the best cardiologists in the country." Sophie searched for Ian, clearly looking for an emotional reassurance that made Molly feel more alone. "He'll know what to do."

"He doesn't have privileges in this hospital." Gran's already red eyes filled with new tears.

"Grandpa was conscious. He's going to be all right."

"Why didn't I just give in and retire? I may have caused this." Gran's voice rose hysterically. "I quit, Sophie. Consider this my resignation from the Mom's Place and the clinic—from everything that ever takes me away from Seth for more than five minutes again."

Once more, wives and husbands turned to each other, and the silent connections formed a web of love that seemed just out of Molly's reach.

Sam. She felt his absence like an ache only he could ease. She turned her back on her family and stared through the glass door. When would he come tell them about Grandpa's condition? "I'm going to find a nurse who'll talk to us."

"Wait, Molly." Sophie tried to stop her. "Sam will come straight here."

"I have to do something. I can't stand waiting. If someone comes before I get back, page me."

She shoved the door open and slipped through the gap, hoping no one would follow. Until she managed some control she couldn't stay in that room another second. She loved her family and cherished their support, but she wanted what so many of them had.

A love all her own. Someone she could turn to when no one else would do. Someone who would turn to her because only she filled his needs.

She loved Sam. Not someone. Sam.

Avoiding the nurses' station, she reached for her cell phone to call home. Her pockets were empty. She'd left the phone at home or in her car. She searched for a pay phone and dug enough change from her pocket to make the call.

She took the receiver off the hook, but froze when Sam, his tie askew, his collar open, his eyes weary, pushed through the metal door before her.

Sam stopped, too, staring at her.

"Molly." His voice, low and thick, called to her.

She didn't stop to think; she simply ran into Sam's arms. He held her as close as she'd dreamed of being held. Barely able to breathe, she clung to him.

"He's okay," Sam said against her throat. "He's okay."

"Thank God." She sought the warmth of his long, hard body. "Is Grandpa going to stay okay?"

"I think so. He'll need treatment. We're not sure of everything yet." Sam lifted his head, stroking her hair away from her face with shaking hands. He stared as if he'd never seen her before. "Are you all right?"

"I feel better now than I did three minutes ago."

He pulled her close again, and she felt his heart pounding against her cheek. "You won't lose him. Or anyone. I won't let it happen. Don't worry."

She should move. No one would be able to mistake her intentions, clinging to Sam as if to life itself.

Her breath caught in her throat like a hiccup. "We've crossed a line."

"Any man can promise a woman he won't let her grandfather die. Even you can't make rules about that."

"You ran away from the school festival."

"Because I didn't want my daughters or Eliza walking in on us. Now, I don't care. I keep seeing Greta wishing she'd spent more time with Seth. According to Sophie and Seth, she's a fine physician, but she was helpless."

"That's what I've been thinking all night, too." She tightened her arms around him, and he ran his hands down her sides, his touch possessive.

Molly, who'd believed in love but never possession, sank against him.

"We should go." But she didn't want to move. With a deep, reluctant breath, she forced herself to step out of his arms, and then tugged him down the hall. "The others are waiting."

"I don't have long. I want to go back and sit with him after your gran sees him." He stopped her, his eyes intense. Lifting one hand, he stroked her cheek with the backs of his fingers. "Have you talked to Tamsin and Nina?"

"I was with them. James brought Evan and Lily over, and they're all staying at the B and B tonight. But I promised Tamsin I'd call."

"Good."

Though they were talking about family and important matters, the inexplicable bond between them demanded attention, too. Sam pulled her close again, and Molly went to him, glad they both felt the same need.

"Sam." She wrapped her arms around his waist, anchoring herself in a make-believe world where she had the right to hold him. "Gran's scared to death. We have to go inside." She broke away and opened the waiting room door.

Gran leaped to her feet, dragging Sophie with her. "Well?"

"He'll need further treatment in a few weeks. We're watching him, but he looks good."

Sophie sank to her chair. Sighs of relief filled the room.

"He's going to live?" Gran pinned Sam with a stern look. "You promise?"

His mouth quirked up at one corner, and he sent Molly a poignant glance. Heat flooded her body as she hoped no one else noticed. Her grandmother only wanted the same promise he'd willingly given her.

"Greta, you know the odds and the possibilities," Sam said. "Seth's been through a lot, and he's fighting. That helps any patient."

Gran slipped into the chair beside Sophie, and the family crowded around her. She held out her hands. "Come tell me everything, Sam."

He looked back at Molly, silently calling her to his side. It was another foolish mistake in front of their family, but today had scared them all and everyone clustered together.

Molly reminded herself what she had to lose if she openly declared her feelings—the mother and father who'd taken her out of hell and made her safe.

She stared from her mother to Sam, and stayed where she was. She wouldn't be able to hide her feelings if she touched him or he laid a finger on her.

"I'll call the children and James."

Resentment flickered in his expression, but he nodded, and she had the feeling he'd expected her response. She might be weak and afraid, but she'd fought too long and hard for her parents' respect to risk hurting them in a moment when Grandpa's illness might have artificially heightened her and Sam's feelings.

She escaped into the hall and found her change for the phone again. James answered on the first ring. "Well?" he asked, as impatiently as if he'd been waiting for a scoop from his ace reporter.

"He's going to be fine. Sam says he'll need more treatment in a few weeks."

"Good." James sounded relieved. "You'd be surprised how familiar that story is to a guy my age."

"Your friends?" Molly asked.

"Sometimes. You want to talk to Tamsin? I hear her in the hall."

"Sure. Are the others all right? Nina? Zach and Olivia will ask me about Evan and Lily, too."

"Nina hasn't stirred since you left, and Evan and Lily are both asleep. Hold on a second." His voice changed as if he'd turned away and cupped a hand over the phone. "Tamsin's been wandering around her room, but I imagine I wasn't supposed to notice the pacing."

Molly's heart went out to the young girl who'd already lost too much. "Thanks for your help. I'd better speak to her."

"Sure, but do me a favor, okay? Will you tell Beth I talked to you?" Beth, Zach's mother, saw as much of James as Olivia did on his frequent visits to Bardill's Ridge. The entire family had started taking bets on when he'd finally speak up.

"Want me to say anything else?" Molly asked hopefully.

"No. She'll understand."

She smiled in spite of the anxiety sawing at her stomach. Aunt Beth and a media tycoon. Hard to imagine, since Aunt Beth had remained single after her husband's death, but no one could blame James Kendall for falling under her spell. She was a loving woman. Besides, who wouldn't want to be a Calvert?

"Molly?"

"Tamsin, hey."

"How's Grandpa? Is he going to be okay?"

"Your dad says he is."

"He'd know." She said it matter-of-factly. Her assurance relieved Molly's mind.

"James says you've been pacing."

"I thought he probably heard me, but he didn't bug me about it. He's cool."

Sam would be envious. She'd never called him cool in Molly's hearing. "Are you going to be okay now?"

"I guess. I don't like when people are sick."

Molly could understand why. "I trust your dad, Tamsin."

"I do, too. Do you think he'll call soon?"

On cue, the door down the hall opened again, and Sam stepped out. "Molly—"

"Here he is now, Tamsin."

"Oh, I'm glad."

Molly backed away to give them privacy, but Sam caught her hand as she passed him the phone. He only let her go when she tugged forcefully. She feared they'd already taken too many risks today.

"No," he was saying to Tamsin, "I'll stay until Seth's resting comfortably. He's alarmed, and I'm a familiar face."

"Part of the family," Molly said. He looked at her, his frown growing deeper, until she went inside the waiting room.

AFTER EACH COUSIN or son or daughter-in-law said good-night to Grandpa, they went home, one by one or couple by couple. Molly gave James's message to Aunt Beth, and barely restrained herself from calling the whole family's attention to her aunt's schoolgirl blush.

Sophie's dad left for Knoxville to pick up his former wife, Nita, who'd got on a plane the moment he'd called her with the news that his father was ill. Since Sophie's marriage, they'd tried to reconcile their own. Everyone else still doubted Nita, but Ethan consistently stood by her.

Nita's arrival reminded Molly how tender family connections might be. She couldn't allow hunger for physical comfort to overwhelm her common sense. Sam and the girls were part of the family, like everyone else around here. She couldn't create a whole new set of circumstances that would make even her mother look at Sam differently.

Molly's mom and dad waited for Gran to finish her good-nights to Grandpa, who'd smiled woozily and hugged Molly with surprising strength during her own brief visit to his monitor-laden room.

"You don't have to wait, too," Patrick said.

"I don't mind. I'll walk you to the car. If Gran changes her mind about staying with you, I'll go home with her."

"I won't let her change her mind," Eliza said. "She needs comfort, and the children will be good for her in the morning."

"If they don't worry her to death." Patrick

hugged his wife close to take the sting out of his remark.

"Greta's been my mother, too, for over thirty years. She'll find consolation in the children."

Molly regarded both her parents with surprise as their voices rose. "This is a strange argument."

Her mom sighed. "We're all on edge."

"He's my dad." Patrick pulled his arm back to rub his face with both hands. "I keep thinking he might have died."

"Now, Patrick," Gran said from the door, "let's not borrow trouble. I won't survive the night if I let myself consider that. Eliza," she continued, turning to a more pleasant subject, "I wish you'd seen Sam and Sophie. I forgot everything I ever knew about medical care and turned into a scared wife. They dropped to Seth's side and saved his life."

Eliza's smile held a mother's pride, and for once, Molly didn't fear Sam would make her mom forget her. She was too grateful for what he'd done. "I hope I never have to see him at work, but I'm glad he was there," Eliza said.

"He's going to wait with Seth until he sleeps. The nurse asked me to leave because Seth tries to stay awake when I'm near." Gran hugged Molly. "Are you coming to the B and B with us?"

"No, it'll be pretty full there once you settle in." Molly clasped her grandmother's sturdy body. "James brought Evan and Lily for the night so he could be there for Tamsin and Nina, and I could come here.''

"That was nice." She fluttered her hands nervously. "Who'd picture a man like that babysitting?"

"He loves family, like everyone else." Patrick stood, examining the area to make sure they weren't leaving anything behind. "Look how protective he was of Olivia when she first brought Evan to meet Zach."

Molly smiled at memories of the big silver RV James had driven from Chicago, fearing tiny Bardill's Ridge wouldn't offer all the necessary amenities.

"I never thought he'd be one of us, though," Gran said with a smile at Eliza. "Like Sam and the girls have become."

Molly's heartbeat became rapid and disturbing. "I need to get moving." What she needed was a few solitary minutes away from everyone who reminded her of the debt that was growing too heavy. "Early day in the morning."

"You don't have school on Saturday," her father said.

"Oh, yeah."

She led the way to the elevator, not allowing herself to look back for a glimpse of Sam. In the lobby downstairs, she wished her family goodnight again and agreed to meet them all at the Dogwood in the morning. No one seemed to consider her need to see Tamsin and Nina unusual before coming to the hospital. They were Sam's daughters. They were her nieces. Ties that bound tightly.

She split off from the others to cross the dark parking lot. In her car, she immediately started the engine, but then glanced up to the third floor where Grandpa lay, fragile and unnervingly ill, as Sam waited, lending him strength.

She couldn't force herself to leave. She looked away from the exit as her parents' car disappeared. Making a slow revolution around the edges of the lot, Molly parked again at the front in a splash of light near the hospital's entrance.

She grew as cold as the air, imagining Zach or one of his deputies driving up beside her to ask why a lone woman would wait in a car on a November night that was quickly turning into morning.

To be close to Grandpa. To be near Sam. She felt them, up in that open room with the chattering machines and blinking monitors. In that waiting room her family had comforted her, but in ways she'd never realized before, she'd remained an outsider.

Even those concerns paled.

She felt as if she belonged here, close to Sam, as Grandpa fought for life and Sam refused to end his vigil. She zipped her fleece jacket all the way to her chin and wrapped her arms around herself as she sank into the little warmth her seat provided.

An hour, maybe more, passed. Time kept ticking as memories paraded through her mind—family apple picking, Grandpa manning the barbecue in the orchard. Her grandparents dancing as they'd celebrated their anniversary last year. Her grandfather spilling an unwilling tear over Chloe, Sophie's baby, as he'd also become her godfather at her christening.

Her final memory—Sam trying to diagnose her grandfather in the dark on Halloween—made her sit up straight in the car. Who was she trying to fool?

Her heart hurt tonight because she might have lost her grandfather. She longed for comfort from the man she loved. Sam. Molly might ruin her mother's ideal vision of a blended family, but tonight she needed Sam, and no one else would do.

She reached into the back seat, scrambling for paper from the canvas bag she carried to school each day. On a torn sheet, she scribbled, "I'm waiting for you. M."

Without giving herself time to think, she ran into the hospital and rode the elevator back to her grandfather's floor.

The nurse at CICU, a guy who'd graduated from high school with Molly, came around the desk to meet her. "Sorry, Molly," he said. "You can't go in this late."

"Hi, Chad. Is Sa—Dr. Lockwood still with Grandpa?"

The nurse pointed through the window, and she saw Sam slumped in a chair beside her grandfather's bed. Grandpa's mouth moved slowly. They were still talking.

"Shouldn't he be asleep?" she asked, concerned all over again.

"He's fine. Who knows what they're saying to each other? Sometimes a guy who comes that close to death needs to talk, but you can tell he's getting sleepy."

"Okay." She gnawed the inside of her cheek. "I hate this."

"Families do."

With a reluctant smile, she held up her note. "Will you hand this to Sam when he leaves?"

"Sure." Chad caught her fingertips as he took the note. "Try not to worry. Your brother's a good man."

"He's not my—" That argument seemed fairly pointless just now. "Thanks. Night, Chad."

Outside again, she found the car colder than ever. But Chad had been right—her grandfather must have been tired, because Sam suddenly pushed through the glass doors to stop beneath the entrance sign, scanning the parking lot.

Feeling so afraid she was almost sick, Molly opened her car door. The sound drew Sam's gaze. She heard a groan, half sexual, half sheer relief, as he found her in the darkness.

The sound had come from her own throat.

Sam's face seemed to drain of color as Molly ran across the street. She stopped just beyond his reach. His eyes were two perfect circles filled with turbulent longing. He opened his arms, and she fell into them—a perfect fit.

He buried his face in her hair. His fingers trembled against her back. "I hoped you'd stay. I had no reason to hope, but I did."

"I couldn't leave without you. I'm afraid for Grandpa and worried about my family, but I stayed because of you."

"Let me be with you tonight, Molly."

"I need you." She lifted her face, which was humiliatingly wet with tears. Sam had caused most of her out-of-control emotions since he'd come to town with Tamsin and Nina.

He caught her cheeks in his hands and brushed his lips across hers. He held her too gently. In frustration, she locked her arms around his neck and opened her mouth, inviting him to take all she could offer, all the yearning and the comfort, all the passion she'd put entirely out of her mind until he'd brought desire back into her life.

Sam pushed her against a sign post, his body hard against hers, heedless of the harsh light that suddenly had her opening her eyes. She blinked, imagining curious gazes at the windows above them.

"I should be ashamed," she said, half lost in the past.

"No." He traced the column of her throat with his mouth. "Don't leave me now, Molly."

"Come to my house." She leaned back in his arms. "We can't stay here. Someone will see."

"You like to hide?" His husky tone seduced her as he traced her rib cage with his fingers. His restless touch robbed her of breath.

"Sam, I don't think we should make love in front of the hospital. Come with me." Resolutely, she turned toward her car.

Without another word, Sam followed. He opened the passenger door and got in, leaning his head against the back of the seat.

"Are you tired?" she asked.

"I felt better the minute I saw your note."

Her heart skipped a beat or three. "Nothing happened to Grandpa?"

Sam looked her way. "No. He's fine."

At Canon's store, he touched her sleeve. "Stop. Are they open?"

"What do you need?"

He stared at her. "Molly…"

In silence he waited. She realized neither of them had planned for tonight, and understood what he wanted to buy. "Oh. Sam, do you think we could stop at the gas station instead? Mr. Canon and everyone else who works here know me."

"The gas station is fine." He leaned back again, closing his eyes. "You aren't going to back down because this is an unromantic purchase?"

"We'd be less romantic without it." Not that she needed birth control, but that part of her history would not become his business tonight.

His soft laugh reached all the way to the pit of her stomach.

She drove around the lighted square, empty of stalls, even of fall leaves this close to Thanksgiving. Taking a left just after the library, she headed for her house. When she reached the gas station, Sam seemed to be dozing.

Leaving him in the car, she prayed she wouldn't know the person behind the counter. She nearly sang as she paid a stranger, who barely looked away from the all-night news to take her money.

Sam woke as she opened the door again. He stared at the box. "Why didn't you wake me?"

"It's fine."

At her house, she opened the garage and drove inside. She took her time turning off the headlights, pulling out the keys. Sam stroked her arm, his heart in his eyes. Unless she dreamed the longing that pulled her across the console.

He kissed her without his earlier restraint. He released her only to kiss each corner of her mouth. "Let's go inside." His disturbing eyes pushed her out of the car. He met her in front of the hood, turning her with his hands at her hips.

Love was too intense, the urge to be closer too imperative—a dream made real in Sam's arms.

Grasping her shoulders, he urged her toward the

door that led to her kitchen. At the last second he jabbed the remote control to shut the garage door. Molly flipped on the kitchen light, but Sam was already bending. His mouth delighted her, and she kissed him, letting him lift her onto the counter. The box of condoms hit the surface behind her as he reached for the hem of her jacket. Both fleece and blouse were removed by his impatient hands.

"Not here." She opened the buttons on his shirt. "If it's one night, I want it to be more than fumbling on the Formica."

Sam lifted his head bemused, but laughed a little. God, how she loved a man who laughed. "It's butcher block," he said, unknotting his tie.

"I have a bed."

"Show me."

"I'm scared."

His face, sharp with desire, looked unfamiliar but then he smiled again, and she sighed in relief. He pulled her off the counter and held her in front of him as he headed toward the hallway.

"I'm strong, and I won't let anyone hurt you," he said.

"You could hurt me." The bitter confession slipped out of her mouth before she could swallow it. She'd let boys hurt her when she'd been a little girl, pretending to be a woman.

"You'll always be safe with me," Sam said, "and I'd pretty much kill anyone else who tried to harm you, so you can let down your guard."

She tried to face him. He wasn't talking one night, and they couldn't risk more. Understanding her too well, he tightened his arms around her waist and propelled her forward.

"We could hurt Mom, Sam."

"I'm not going to argue about Eliza's expectations now, and I refuse to remember you deserve a man your own age. All I know is that I need you, and you want me. I'm grateful."

Grateful? Had anyone ever been grateful for her before? Molly's heart melted as if she'd never been afraid. She held on to Sam's hands. The corners of the box he'd picked up again dug into her, but she didn't let go, afraid that if she relaxed her grip he might disappear. "What are you doing to my life?"

"You're talking too much, Molly."

Climbing the stairs proved difficult in tandem. Especially with Sam's mouth pressed to her throat, finding pulse points that drove her insane. At last they reached the bedroom no man had ever shared with her.

. She edged away from him to turn on a lamp. She felt too warm as she stared at Sam, at his chest, brown and broad through the opening of his shirt. Now or never. Could she spend one night with this man and never be with him like that again?

She sighed, coming back to reach for his tie. His smile, as knowing as if he'd already made love to her, sent blood rushing through her ears. He hadn't touched her intimately yet, but the bond tugging them closer and closer had nothing to do with family affection.

UNTIL THE MOMENT she slipped his tie from his open collar, Sam had expected Molly to send him away. Before the tie hit the floor, she was back in his arms. Where she belonged. He'd leave no doubt about that.

Together, they might be his birth mother's worst nightmare, but he needed this woman who deserved so much more than a forty-year-old father of two.

Indecision glittered in her eyes until he took her mouth again. Dizzy with lust, he tried to hold back, used to being careful because of Fiona. Molly pushed his shirt off his shoulders, desperation sharpening her movements.

Her silk bra rubbed pleasurably against his skin, but he wanted more—the silk of her flesh. He wrestled with the bra's front catch, smiling against her mouth when she helped him with shaking fingers.

He tugged the straps off, hungry to see her. She lifted her hands and the wisp of lace fell to the floor. His own breath stopped as the sweet curves of her breasts seduced him. Unaccountably shy, Molly covered herself.

Need overcame patience.

Sam eased her hands away, bending to cover a

hardening nipple with his mouth. Her groan nearly dropped him to the floor. She tasted so good as she bent over him, chasing goose bumps across his skin with the tips of her nails.

"Sam." She sang his name, her voice low, husky.

Starving for her as he was, he required no encouragement. An irresistible compulsion to taste every inch of her soft skin drove him to his knees.

He unfastened the button at her waistband and slowly drew back her jeans. Her waist curved inward, inviting him to caress the hipbones that had so fascinated him in the orchard. He kissed the right one, delighting in her deep, stuttering breath. She lifted her leg as if she wanted it around him. He stroked her thigh, but planted her foot back on the ground.

The zipper. He dragged it the rest of the way down, looking into Molly's troubled blue gaze.

"You want me to do this faster?" he asked.

"I..." She licked dry lips, and he wanted to do that for her, too. "I don't know."

"Lie down."

She remained standing, incredibly sexy with bare breasts and unzipped jeans.

"You just can't take an order, can you?" He straightened, grinning as he cupped her chin in his hand. Any excuse to explore the warmth of her mouth. She might believe tonight was the only one they'd have together, but Sam had already lost one woman he'd loved to the whims of fate. He didn't intend to let Molly choose to give him up.

He followed the curve of her chin with his mouth, blowing gently on her skin. Arching against him, she slid her fingers down his arms, tracing his muscles, filling him with a ridiculous sense of his own strength. Smiling at his ego, he welcomed her seeking hands and kissed his way down her breastbone. The thudding of her heart beneath his lips erased his smile.

"Molly." He said her name in surprise, but on his lips it felt like a charm. Her name spelled hope for the future. He eased her onto the bed.

She inhaled, flattening her stomach.

"Molly," he said again. He pulled her jeans down her legs, reveling in the curves he uncovered. Each flutter of her muscles beneath his palms intensified his arousal. Her hands slid over the sheets, before she clenched them into fists. The action startled him.

She seemed to regard lovemaking as a sacrifice rather than the gift her need felt to him. He pressed his lips to her thigh, desperate to return the pleasure he received in simply touching her.

After he rid her of shoes and socks and jeans, he stood over her and began to take off his own clothes. She watched, her breathing shallow. When he stopped, gripping his waistband, Molly opened her hands. "Sam, please come back here. I'm getting scared without you."

"It isn't just tonight."

She lifted herself on her elbows. "Huh?"

"You think we're sharing one night out of our lifetimes, but you're wrong. I thought you should know."

Eyes wide, she nodded, but not with understanding. "You don't have to promise."

"What?" Her statement made no sense. Why wouldn't she demand a commitment from a man who was about to make love to her?

"I'm responsible for myself."

"Molly." He stared, trying to understand. "I'm not an immature boy from your past. You should ask whatever you want from me."

Tears pooled in her eyes, and he forgot about his jeans. He covered her body, offering her comfort, kissing away the tears that hurt him as much as her. "You're worth everything to me."

Her laughter barely covered a sob. He kissed her over and over again, longing only to erase her past. But somewhere in the middle of comfort, passion overtook them. They both pushed his jeans down his legs, and he kicked them off. She reached for the box behind her head, and he took it from her. His hands shook as he opened the lid. He felt self-conscious in his boxers when she was nude and so beautiful.

She stared at the wrappers inside the box. "I'm glad I bought more than one."

He laughed and she slid the band off her braid.

As she began to thread her fingers through her hair, he caught her hand.

"Let me." He separated the strands. "Your hair…I love the way it smells, the way it feels." He pressed the strands to his chest, and she joined her hand to his. The silky texture teased his skin. Listening to his own harsh breathing, he met Molly's eyes. Bathed in the heat of her gaze, he forgot the reasons they shouldn't be together.

She slid her thumb over his nipple and it tightened, and he could only see her as the woman who'd taken his heart. Molly pushed her hair out of the way and replaced her fingers with her mouth, teasing him with her tongue until he had to press her head against him.

She had other ideas. She pushed him onto his back and straddled his hips, staring down at him with a hint of acquisitiveness in her gaze. She gave him a new smile, a secret he had yet to unlock. She drew his hands to her full breasts, cupping the hardened tips with his palms.

While he caressed her, she explored his muscles with her fingertips, from his shoulders to his waist—over and over again, pausing only to lick the path her hands had blazed. Her tongue lit fires he had to quench. She made him forget to be gentle.

When he locked one hand in her hair, she raised her head, seducing him with a siren's glance. He arched beneath her, wanting to be inside. Now. Quickly.

She stroked his legs with the balls of her feet, sliding her body over his. Cradling him against her pelvis, she rose and fell with each swell of passion that gripped her.

He restrained an urge to take her, to remind her she was with him and would be again and again. But then she whispered his name against his shoulder, with a scrape of her teeth. Her lips found a pulse, and his throat constricted. She suckled the point of his chin, and her kisses felt like the most intimate touch. Finally, she opened his mouth with her thumb and then replaced it with her tongue.

After one sweet stroke, he abandoned all pretense of restraint. He rolled her beneath him and parted her knees, pausing only to sheathe himself. As Molly rose with him, he moaned against her slender neck and sank inside her.

Love made tonight right. Love made him right for Molly and Molly perfect for him. She felt like heaven. Loving her felt like heaven.

He'd never before forgotten himself in his longing for another human being. He'd never before lost sight of where his body ended and where a woman's took him. Tonight he craved a connection with Molly that nothing and no one could possibly break.

As he savored these first delicious moments and Molly's touch—her fingers, tight and desperate, clutching his hips—time rolled on, faster and faster.

His own need spun out of control, until the inevitable became imperative. Molly tightened around him with a sweet cry of triumph and pleasure.

He buried his face in her throat, muffling his own guttural sigh, along with the need to swear he would love her forever. He would, but telling her might scare her right out of his arms.

# CHAPTER THIRTEEN

MUCH LATER, Molly opened her eyes and saw Sam's face bathed in moonlight. She hadn't dreamed these hours in his arms. She pushed her elbow beneath the pillow, lifting her head to see him clearly.

Heavy cotton sheeting rubbed against her bare skin. She glanced down with a vague memory of Sam pulling the bedding over them before he'd turned off the light. Aware of the cloth, aware of Sam's hard bones and resilient muscle pressed against her, she felt odd—as if her body, unexpectedly sore and yet totally satiated, had belonged to someone else, but tonight she'd reclaimed it.

"Hey," Sam said.

She looked into his eyes. Awake, he seemed wary. Second thoughts tightened his face. "Did I wake you?" she asked,

"No." He said nothing more.

"Time to go, Sam?" She knew that expression. She'd seen it on every boy she'd turned to for comfort, for intimacy no human being could provide.

The morning-after urge to escape. She lifted the corner of the sheet. "Go ahead."

Inexorably, his gaze traveled down her body and heated up. Physical response. Provoking a physical response was her specialty. Emotions were another question. Who knew how to hold another human being?

She dropped the sheet. "Better get out on your side."

"Don't misunderstand me, Molly."

"You're too honest. I can see exactly what you're thinking. I'm some Snow White who's been frozen up here in the mountains." She couldn't disabuse him with the whole truth, despite a longing to hurt him as his reluctance cut her. "Let's leave it at this. I've handled this situation once or twice before."

"What happened to you?" He caught the hand she'd lifted toward her face. "I have a right to know after last night."

"You don't want rights." She tugged her hand free.

"Let me explain."

"Why bother? I look for something no one can give."

"Not this time, Molly. And you were too young to know what you wanted before. I know Eliza and Patrick took you in as a foster child when you were eight. You had problems, and then you went in the hospital at fifteen. I don't know what happened, but you came out a different person. My detective actually said 'a different young woman,' as if you were no longer a child after that.''

"I don't want to discuss it, Sam.'' She pulled the sheet up to her chin, sliding it off his nude, beautiful chest. "You already seem desperate. I don't want to make it worse.''

The look he gave her turned her uncertainty into a lead weight.

"I'll tell you my secrets.'' He pulled her hand to his chest. The swift, steady thud of his heartbeat frightened her.

"Don't panic. I told you I didn't require commitment.''

"Cut it out, Molly. I feel guilty. Not guilty— disloyal.'' His mouth twisted as if he hated admitting it. "I haven't been with anyone since Fiona. I couldn't have stopped myself from making love to you last night, but I think I still had to say goodbye to her. She was always sick, Molly. She had a heart condition, and I had to be careful with her.'' He shook his head, his hair brushing over the pale green pillowcase. "Even…at times like last night. Molly, I feel guilty telling you how it was with her. But you don't want caution. You want to be torn apart.''

Molly blushed. Who the hell knew she could blush in bed?

He took her other hand and pressed them both

against his skin. "I was nearly dead without you, Molly, but I felt a little disloyal to Fiona."

She froze. "You're not talking about leaving."

"No." He sucked the pad of her index finger between his lips, and she couldn't help shifting her legs beneath the sheets. "I'm forty years old," he said. "And jaded. In a single moment I lost everything I ever worked for, and I'm guilty because I want more than I had, and I want it with you."

"Our family..."

"Tamsin will be upset at first. She already accused me of trying to replace Fiona with you, but she's wrong. You make your own place, and I love you in a way that Fiona has nothing to do with."

Molly sat up, not caring that she'd dragged the sheet off him and that it had fallen to her waist. "No."

"How much time can we count on? Sickness dogged Fiona all her life, but she died in a car accident as if her heart condition never existed. Your grandfather hovered on the edge of death last night without a chance to settle things. Our time can end no matter what we do to keep safe." He held her with such desire and yearning it unlocked an overwhelming measure of love in her well-guarded heart. "I don't want Eliza to be upset when we tell her. She's my mom. I'm as attached to this family as if I'd always known them, but I can't give you up. I'll blackmail you with the knowledge that you could lose me in a moment, too.''

"My mother thinks of you as my brother.''

"I've never been your brother—in your eyes or mine. You are my lover, and I have to hope Eliza loves us both enough to adjust her thinking. She wants us both to be happy, and I don't believe she'll think we set out to make this happen. What do you or I or Eliza want more than family?''

He knew her mom well already, but he hadn't heard the full list of his lover's sins. "Everyone knows how often I've screwed up. They'll think this is one more bad-girl escapade.''

"We'll talk to Eliza. I don't care how often we have to explain. Our family will realize we love each other.''

"I never said so.''

"You're afraid. You need love you think no one can give you. I'm dying to give it. You only have to take the chance.''

He was right, and she tried to push her fear away without acknowledging it. "Do you think I'd risk losing my family—the only safety I've ever known—for a few nights with you?''

"Forever is more than a few nights, Molly.''

"Forever?'' She shook her head, unable to believe. "I can't see a hint of forever. My mom and dad—my cousins and my grandparents and aunts and uncles—are the only forever I think about. You're a distraction, maybe even a return to bad habits, but I'm not throwing away my future on a man who's finally recovering from grief for his wife.''

''Try to hurt me, Molly. It won't work. You won't push me away.'' His smile held incredible tenderness—the kind a man offered only in his bed with a woman who meant something to him. ''Remember, I've been Tamsin's only parent for sixteen months.''

Drowning in his compassion, Molly had to smile. ''I'm not fifteen anymore. I'm making adult decisions, and you're under the influence of the first sex you've had since your wife…''

''I'm not fooling myself. I'll wait as long as it takes to convince you and everyone we both love that I'm serious. Just don't make me wait too long. I want babies and grandchildren and a life with you.''

Without warning, pain cut into her heart. ''Babies.'' She choked on the word. ''You don't want me. I can't have babies.''

His gaze went wide. ''What?''

She felt as if she were falling. A last, minuscule flicker of hope died with his shock. ''I had a miscarriage at fifteen—and not with the first boy I slept with. This guy was twenty-one. I'm not the woman for you. I'm a girl who was hungry for love and pretty sure I was unlovable. My parents dumped me, and I did everything I could to make sure Patrick and Eliza Calvert would also abandon me before I loved them too much to survive another rejection.'' She gasped for air. ''I'm still paying, but I made a bargain as I lay in that hospital bed, knowing I'd ruined my life. If my parents could look me in the eye and not hate me, I promised myself I'd never hurt them again.'' She felt like glass on the point of shattering. ''Do you think the news that I slept with my mother's son won't hurt her?''

''Don't try to make us into something dirty, Molly. I'm a man who found my birth mother. You're the woman I love. I want you and I'm willing to claim you in front of my children and *our* family. I believe in Eliza. You just have to claim me, too.''

She spied a chink in his armor. ''You need to be claimed because you think Mom abandoned you. Maybe you need to hurt her. But I won't help.''

''I thought I was jaded, but you beat me all to heck.'' He shook his head, and the lines that fanned out from his eyes endeared him to her.

She wanted to kiss them away. She wanted to lend him some of the fifteen years between them that he'd considered a problem. She'd have loved him no matter what age he was, and maybe her old, old soul needed an older man. But he had no idea how conservative her mother was, how carefully she'd lived her life to avoid doing anything more wrong than giving up the only child she'd ever given birth to.

"I'm right, Sam." Molly gave him the sheet and reached for a robe she'd tossed on the floor some night in the past week. "You'll see it with time, and Tamsin never has to know about us."

Sam's laugh startled her. "Are you kidding me? She'll have to see us in the same room eventually. I'm furious right now, but what I feel most is a need to bury myself in you again."

Molly shivered. "Your mother disapproves of crude talk. You'll want to be careful of that around her."

She marched out of the room, prepared to hide in her bathroom until he finally took the hint and departed.

SAM WAITED IN MOLLY'S BED for about half an hour before he came to terms with her plan. Then he knocked at her bathroom door. She ignored him. The house might have been empty.

"Whatever you do won't change the way I feel. That may be your habit, to alienate the people who love you best, but it won't work with me, Molly. I'm smart enough to value love."

"No real man would say that," she said through the door.

"The fact that I'm saying it should show you how much I love you."

He showered and dressed in another bathroom

and left, because it was pointless to argue anymore. Until Molly was willing to listen, nothing he said would convince her they'd be good together.

Sam stopped by the hospital to study Seth's test results with his physicians, including the specialist who'd come from Knoxville. Seth was resting, but Sam arranged to return later that day to help the others explain he'd need a bypass in a few weeks.

From the hospital, he returned to the Dogwood, reaching the B and B in time to bump into James Kendall taking Lily and Evan home. The other man left, brushing off Sam's gratitude as if it made him uncomfortable.

Eliza hurried out of the kitchen with Patrick close on her heels. "How's Seth?" she asked.

"Sleeping." Sam shifted his gaze to Patrick. "He's going to need a bypass in about three weeks. I can't do it because he's my family." Molly might be serious about rejecting him, but nothing would change his growing attachment to Seth and all the other Calverts who'd so generously accepted him and his girls. "I'll come back to observe the operation, though."

"Good. Mother will feel better if you're here." Patrick opened the door beside the reception desk, beckoning Sam through.

"Are Tamsin and Nina awake yet?"

"Haven't stirred a peep," Eliza said. "But you must be tired and hungry."

"I am. Both." And he felt incredibly dishonest.

He couldn't take advantage of her hospitality and keep her in the dark. And he couldn't bring his children back here for a while. He felt incapable of being near Molly under the circumstances. Crossing into the family side of the Dogwood, he caught his mother's arm in the narrow hallway. "Eliza? Patrick?"

They turned. The loving smile on Eliza's face twisted his gut.

"I need to talk to you and the girls later."

"Okay." Worry creased her forehead. "About Seth?"

"No, no. He's going to be fine. Bypasses are common enough these days, and he's strong. I don't expect any problems."

Patrick nodded. "Fine. After you all get some food in your stomachs then."

Sam's reluctance about their coming talk must have communicated itself to his mother and her husband. After breakfast, Patrick looked the part of a judge as he sat on a love seat in the living room. Eliza took the sofa to his right. Tamsin and Nina sat together, flanking his left. Sam doubted his chances with the jury.

"What's your news?" Patrick asked. "Has the health center seduced you?"

"Dad?" Tamsin faced him. "You want to move?"

"No, it's worse. I'm in love with Molly." He allowed Tamsin and Eliza time for their collective gasps to subside. Patrick heaved himself off the love seat. Nina eyed her dad with a funny look on her little face. He sat and scooped her onto his knee as he went on. "Tamsin, I'm not trying to replace your mom. I loved Fiona. You know how much I loved her. If she were still with us, I'd never have looked at anyone else, but she's gone now, and I— I fell in love with Molly."

"You're in love with my daughter?" Patrick's furious look grazed Eliza as if this were partially her fault. "That's the damnedest thing. Eliza, are you hearing this?"

"I feel dizzy," she said. "Molly? Our Molly, Sam?"

"Dad." Tamsin closed her mouth, then tried again. "Is she okay? Why isn't she here?"

"She doesn't want me."

Tamsin missed what he'd said this time. "I know I was mad after I saw you in the square, but I've had time to get used to the idea that she's not really Eliza's daughter."

"Oh, yes, she is." Shock made Eliza's tone strident. "In every way that matters most."

"Where is my child?" Patrick asked. "What have you done to her?"

"She's not a child, Patrick." Sam couldn't help pointing it out, as her age was a sore point with him, too. "Molly's fine. I asked her for a chance, and she turned me down. She's as angry as you, Patrick."

"What did you think? You come to town, her adoptive mother's birth son, and now you're *in love?* You're fifteen years older than Molly. You have a half-grown daughter and a baby."

"Who's a baby?" Nina took immediate offense. "Tamsin's as big as me."

Tamsin laughed. Her humor provided the most bizarre moment Sam had yet experienced in this conversation, but it gave him hope. Tamsin was finally recovering from her mother's death. "You're the baby," she said to her sister. "I'm the half-grown one."

"And you, Sam, are the perv—" Patrick broke off, cautious about finishing the thought in front of the children.

"I know," Sam said. "I've screwed this up."

"Uh-oh, Daddy."

"Sorry, Nina." He kissed her tiny nose, and she hugged him.

"Bad word, Daddy."

"I know." He faced his accusers. "As I said, Molly turned me down. So, Patrick, Eliza, you have nothing to worry about. Tamsin, I just needed to make sure you knew that I can't help loving Molly, but it doesn't change the way I felt about your mom." He hugged Nina again. "And I have to explain we're not going to visit Grandma for a little while until Molly feels better about seeing me."

"Oh, no. I want to see Grandma." Nina shot

into Eliza's lap. "Grandma, you want us to come back, don't you?"

"I'll always want you, Nina." She carried her to Tamsin's side, gathering them both in her arms. "You're my girls, too."

Tamsin peered at Sam through weepy eyes. "I don't see why we have to stay away."

"Molly's upset with me, and she's worried about her mom." Sam took a deep breath. "I'm not giving up on her, and I want to be honest, or I wouldn't be telling you both. I've grown—" He broke off, then took a deep breath. "I love you, Mom."

He met her gaze and smiled in relief at her gasp of joy. She dragged the girls to him and they all embraced. Only Patrick stood aloof.

"I'd never hurt you." Sam caught his mother's tearful face in his hands and then hugged his daughters close to him. "Or Patrick or anyone else in this family. You're all important to me, but love—the kind I feel for Molly—is too rare to throw away on a technicality."

"You don't mind ruining Molly's family?" Patrick asked.

"Am I doing that? If I make her happy and keep her safe, would you be unhappy?"

"Molly allows no one to protect her. You obviously don't know her."

"Maybe," Sam said, "but this is my fault, not

hers, and you shouldn't blame her. My feelings don't have to ruin anything for her.''

"Then why bring it up?" Patrick asked.

"I feel dishonest, taking advantage of your house and your affection. And, most of all, I had to explain to my daughters why we won't be back." He met Tamsin's wounded gaze. "For a while."

"I'll talk to Molly," Eliza said, looking at her husband for a moment. "You're right, Sam, about love being worth overcoming a few difficulties. And when the rest of the family knows we accept you, they'll be happy for you, too."

"You have no problem with this?" Patrick's question exploded from him, startling Tamsin and Nina. He pressed an awkward hand to Tamsin's shoulder. "It's not that I don't want you or your sister here." He eyed Sam with some hostility. "Or even your father. But, Sam, the thought of you and Molly…"

"I'm shocked," Eliza admitted. "But Sam's not Molly's brother. I'd be more upset if one of them remained uncomfortable with us. Sam, I really will talk to her."

He shook his head, sinking into his own chair with relief. At least she hadn't called him a pervert. Molly had pegged their mother all wrong. Thank God. No matter what came of this for him, Eliza and Molly would be all right together. "I don't want her to accept me to please you." He looked at his girls uncomfortably. "So, no. Thanks, Eliza."

"I preferred 'Mom.'" She glanced at each of the girls' upturned faces, too. "But okay. Have you considered that you really don't understand Molly?"

"Hey—" Patrick clearly wasn't through with him yet "—you leave her alone." He spared the briefest look for his new granddaughters, whom he obviously loved. "Leave her alone before you cause more problems."

"You're right, Patrick. And please, try not to say too much to her, either. She's afraid you'll be disappointed in her."

"Not in her. I don't get you, though."

Sam tried to picture his response if a guy talked to him like this about Tamsin in a few years. The man would go home without his head—and various other vital parts.

Sam forced himself to his feet, still tired, but no longer pleasurably so. "Girls, what say we pack? We have to catch that afternoon flight to Savannah."

"But Sam, what about Thanksgiving?" Eliza asked.

He shrugged. "I can't come back here and make Molly unhappy."

Eliza looked torn. Their breakup had put her in the position Molly had feared. Sam gathered his girls in his arms.

"We'll all look forward to Christmas." By then, with a little distance, Molly might find life stretched ahead, empty without him, too.

SAM HAD TOLD HER PARENTS about them. A few days of her mother's anxious glances and her father's worried avoidance told her more than outright accusations would have. Furious with Sam, Molly followed their example and said nothing.

Her mother's lack of a nervous breakdown relieved her, but Molly couldn't talk about Sam yet. She devoted herself to work and then told her family a friend had invited her to visit for Thanksgiving.

It was a lie, and Eliza obviously guessed that when Molly told her she'd be away. She never missed a family gathering.

"He's not coming," Eliza said.

"Who?" Choosing to misunderstand, Molly traced a scar on the reception desk. It was the week before Thanksgiving and she'd stopped on the way to school.

"Molly, I love you. I love Sam. I thought of you one way, but you feel another."

Molly stared at her mother. "You know?"

"Sam told us. I'm glad he realized he had nothing to hide."

"It was my secret to tell." She pushed her fists against her eyes to keep from bawling like a baby.

"And his. He loves you. He wanted us to understand why he had to stay away."

Molly opened her mouth and closed it. "You're not upset?" Of course, Sam hadn't admitted he'd spent the night in her house.

"I was surprised because I thought I'd notice if you were falling in love with a man, even my son."

Molly pulled away from her mother's hands. "Falling in love? What are you talking about?" She seemed to be more upset than her mother. And more rational.

"Maybe you're the one with the problem. Why would you reject Sam, knowing I understand?"

Good question. Molly had no answer. "I'm late for school."

"Molly, wait." Her mother held her the way she had when Molly had woken with nightmares as a child. Holding her so close she couldn't escape if she wanted to, Eliza had always promised none of her bad dreams would come to life again. "You mean more to me than my own ideas of a family. We can all change the pictures we create in our heads."

Molly thought she might suffocate. For the first time in her life, she broke free of Eliza's arms and fled.

She didn't want to see Sam, couldn't face Tamsin. Her mother's tolerance destroyed almost all her reasons for not committing to Sam. And where her mother led, the rest of the family would follow. Gladly. They all owed Sam for Grandpa's good health.

Molly needed time to breathe, to find the real reasons for her fear. She wouldn't be able to avoid Sam or the girls when he came back for her grandfather's operation.

THAT MORNING FINALLY came. Molly dropped by the hospital early and snuck in to wish her grandfather luck. He cast a wary eye toward the door of his room, as Gran blocked Molly from the nurse's view.

"You fight now, you hear?" Molly hugged Grandpa with all her might.

"I'm fine, girl. That Sam drove me half out of my mind nagging me to get a checkup, but I feel better knowing he'll be in there with me. If something goes wrong, I don't see him worrying about a little thing like the right to operate here before he takes over."

Molly could laugh at that. "That's true. He's promised you're going to be fine."

"I trust him," Gran said, "and you know I don't think anyone's a better physician than I."

"Now, Greta, if you take up heart surgery…" her husband began in a cranky voice.

Molly and Gran laughed, hugging each other for support. "I wouldn't put it past her, either, Grandpa." Molly glimpsed a frowning nurse over her grandmother's shoulder. "I'd better get out of here. I thought I'd hang around with Tamsin and Nina today." She'd missed them like crazy in the past three weeks, and she wasn't as wary of seeing them without Sam there. "I'll be back as soon as they let us visit, Grandpa."

"I love you, little girl."

She hugged him again, grateful he'd already made it this far.

Gran walked her to the door, where the nurse waited with a stiff expression. Molly smiled at the woman, another long-ago classmate.

"I thought you'd outgrown sneaking in and out of inappropriate places, Molly."

"Except when they hold my grandfather." Molly looked back. "You'll take extra special care of him, Tina?"

The other woman tugged Molly into the hall, but a smile softened her stern visage. "That's the way we feel about all our patients, but Mr. Calvert is unique."

On her way to the B and B, Molly passed Sam driving toward the hospital. He was frowning, his mind clearly on Grandpa's surgery. Molly turned to watch him pass, her heart an aching bruise. Only the thought of Tamsin and Nina got her mind on the road again.

As she pulled up at the house, her mom and dad were heading to their car. They waited for her to get out.

"Did you want to ride with us?" Eliza asked. "We've just put up a sign on the registration desk."

"I'm staying with the girls." She smiled at her mom. "I'm a little nervous, but they must be worried, too, and I already stopped to see Grandpa."

"They let you in?" her dad asked.

"Not exactly, but they let me talk to him before they tossed me out."

"Good enough." Her father peered at the house and then frowned at Molly. "You have to sort this out, honey."

"How do you feel about it, Dad?"

"Like any father who doesn't want his daughter mixed up with a guy who's older and should have known better." He took both her arms in his hands. "But I love you. Nothing could ever change my loving you, Molly. Get that through your head."

She kissed his cheek. She felt isolated, forced to make this decision alone.

"They're our family, too," he said, earning a hand on his back from her mother. "And we need you all. Figure it out and stop hurting yourself." He cleared his throat, as if finished with the subject. "Tamsin says she's looked after Nina before."

"I want to see them. We'll be fine. Just call when you have news."

"We will." Eliza linked her hand with Patrick's

and pulled him toward the car. "Come on. If Molly can sneak in, so can we."

Molly laughed at the idea of her mother and father creeping around the hospital halls, and they muttered at her as they went on their way. She walked up the path and opened the Dogwood's door.

Immediately, a small body jumped into her arms. "Big girl!"

Molly bit back tears as she hugged tiny Nina. Her warmth and unstinting affection were a gift Molly hadn't cherished enough until this very moment.

Tamsin walked out of the dining room, her finger marking her place in a book at her side. "Hi." In jeans and a sweater and the lightest brush of "normal" makeup, she looked like a completely different girl.

"What happened to you?" Molly asked with a grin.

"Dad has enough to think about right now." She put her shoulders back and took a deep breath, as if she were about to dive into deep water. "And I'm feeling better. Dad was right about finding family here."

Molly held out an arm to her as well. When Tamsin walked into her embrace, Molly's heart melted right through the floor. "You won't forget what's happened to you," she said softly, "but we love you and Nina as if you'd always been ours."

"I got that when you made me have Mr. Kendall as a baby-sitter. This is the only family on earth who thinks fifteen-year-olds need sitting."

Molly laughed. "We do seem to attract the overprotective, but it's all meant with affection."

Tamsin moved back to neutral ground again. "You don't have to stay with us today, though."

"Yes you do." Nina locked her arm around Molly's throat.

"I'm siding with the little sister," Molly said. "I took a day off work so I could see you both."

"Dad's really good. You don't have to worry about something bad happening to Grandpa," Tamsin assured her.

Fear slapped Molly hard. "I didn't think of that."

"Oh." Tamsin pressed her hand to her mouth. "I wish I hadn't mentioned it."

"Big girl," Nina said, leaning back to get a good look at Molly, "if Daddy loves you, why can't you live with us?"

Fortunately, panic tightened every muscle in Molly's body or she might have dropped Nina, and little girls didn't bounce as well as big girls' hearts.

## CHAPTER FOURTEEN

"YOUR DAD CAN'T KEEP a secret," Molly said.

"He thought we should know why he was keeping us away from here."

"He could have made something up." She blushed thinking of Sam declaring to his children and her parents that he loved her.

"Dad's honest." Tamsin sounded older than her years. Grief did that to a teenager. "He may not make the smartest decisions, but he stands by them."

"Tamsin..." Molly studied the clothing that had turned her into a more "normal-looking" teenager. "You haven't made these changes because you expect me to..."

"No one takes my mom's place." Tamsin reached for her little sister and Nina went, though she clung to Molly, too. "But Dad deserves to be happy. We all do."

"Big girl, are you going to live with us?"

"No, honey, I can't." Even if she could reconcile her feelings for Sam, which incredibly seemed to bother no one but her, she couldn't leave Bardill's Ridge. "Let's not talk about it today when Grandpa's on our minds. Did you two bring homework?"

"We're staying the whole weekend," Tamsin said. "I have plenty of time."

"I wanna do homework." Nina bounced so hard in her sister's arms, Tamsin had to put her down. "I never get to do homework. We just play house and read stories and swing upside down when Miss Jana's not looking."

Molly laughed. "Poor Miss Jana, the day she finds out. Why don't we go swing upside down at the playground on the square?"

"I'm not up for the actual swinging," Tamsin said.

"Let me check my cell phone." As Tamsin checked hers, too, Molly retrieved it from her purse, examined the power level and tucked it into her pocket.

"It makes your pants bulge."

"Thanks, Nina. We'll hope I don't split a seam."

Even Tamsin giggled as they tumbled out the front door. "Don't be too smug," Molly said. "As soon as the blood rushes to our heads on the swings, we're coming back here and you're starting homework."

Tamsin looked crestfallen, and Nina grabbed Molly's hand to swing on her until they reached the playground. "Will you make me do homework, too?"

"I can't wait till the day she has to do it," Tamsin said in a sisterly spirit of vengeance.

SETH'S SURGERY WENT WELL. Sam had entered the room with an unusual sense of dread, but finally, he went on to recovery, and Sam was able to accompany the cardiologist to the waiting room. The family sagged with a collective sigh of relief the moment they saw his face.

Seth's specialist, Dr. Myer, scrutinized Sam. "I guess you already told them everything they need to know. We completed a perfectly routine double bypass. He's going to recover well. He'll need to make some changes—diet, exercise. I'd like to discuss the way he handles stress."

Greta reached them first, shaking Dr. Myer's hand. "Thank you so much." Turning from him, she took Sam in her arms. "And thank you for going in there with him. He told me how much better he felt about the surgery knowing you'd be there." She switched to the other doctor again. "Not that he doubted your ability, but Sam's our grandson. You know how that is."

Sam's throat tightened. What a strange time to find the acceptance he'd longed for all his life. He kissed the top of Greta's head. "Thanks, Gran."

She elbowed him. "About time you learned what to call me."

Dr. Myer turned away from the family display. "Any questions, anyone?" He consulted the clock on the far wall. "I'm staying overnight, but I need to return to Knoxville tomorrow. Tom Fedderson has asked me to meet with a couple of his patients today, so I'll be around." He touched Greta's arm. "You have my pager number, and so do the nurses. I'll check on Seth all day."

He disappeared and the family closed in, all pounding Sam's back and shoulders as if he'd saved Grandpa's life. "I didn't do anything," he said. "In fact, I would have been a bad choice of surgeons. Terror is no way to face an operation."

"It's the only way to feel when your grandfather's in danger," Patrick said. "Thank you, son." He held out his hand, but the moment Sam took his, the older man pulled him into a hug. "Whatever happens," he said in a low voice, "you're welcome here with us. Your family." He was referring to Molly, of course.

"Sam, Sam." Eliza nudged her husband out of the way. "I'm so glad everyone's okay, and I'm glad you came to us."

"I didn't do the surgery," Sam said again, uncomfortable with the unearned shower of gratitude. "Someone should call Molly. I'll call Tamsin."

He sensed his mother's concerned gaze but avoided it. He'd hoped Molly would have missed him or the girls enough to call during their three-week absence from Bardill's Ridge.

Late in the afternoon, after Sam had been able to assure them Seth was progressing well and Dr. Myer had visited a couple more times, the Calverts began to fade away. Eventually, Greta stationed herself as close to Seth as the nursing staff allowed, and Sam waited alone with Sophie and Ian and Tom Fedderson.

"Have you noticed how much we need a cardiologist in town?" Sophie asked out of the blue.

"My thoughts, exactly," Tom said. "Part of many of my patients' reluctance has to do with the trip down to Knoxville to see a specialist. We have a community of farmers up here, and they too easily put off until the end of planting season a drive that turns into an all-day event."

Sam stared at them, but laughed as Ian looked on in commiseration. "I have to consider my girls," Sam said. "They're settled in Savannah."

"They have family here now," Sophie said. "If the lack of facilities stops you, you've come at the perfect time. Tell us what you want at the health center, and we'll make it happen. We have Olivia Kendall Calvert's fund-raising abilities on our side."

"Sophie, Bardill's Ridge may not be everyone's little slice of heaven," Ian said with a rueful grin. "She forced me down here, too."

"But it's your slice of heaven now." Affection filled her glance.

"Yeah, but I was never based in one place for

long before. Sam has a home and a practice and a history.''

''What's all that without family?''

Sam stared at his new cousin. He had no answer. If the girls agreed, and if he stood some chance of living here without driving Molly away, he'd move tomorrow. He'd devoted his life to his work before because of his family.

At forty, it was time for him to switch priorities. And if Tom was right, he had something to offer this community that would make up for what he relinquished in access to medical facilities.

''See?'' Sophie said. ''You can't argue.''

''I brought two good arguments with me,'' he said. ''Tamsin and Nina.''

Sophie looked frustrated. Ian and Tom both laughed at her. And Sam massaged his temples, ignoring the pain of his true argument. He loved Molly, and he couldn't live in the same town if it made her miserable.

MOLLY TRIED TO KEEP Nina's noise level down as Tamsin did her homework, but the five-year-old was too excited about doing one-plus-ones on a whiteboard in the living room. And Tamsin could have left at any time, as Nina felt obliged to point out.

After Tamsin put her books away, she drew animals on the whiteboard, infuriating her ''at-school'' little sister until they all agreed to start supper. Molly breathed a sigh of relief when her parents came in through the kitchen door.

"Grandpa must be okay or you wouldn't have come home."

"We'd have called if he'd taken a turn for the worse. He's doing well. Still groggy." Eliza scooped Nina up as the little girl danced around her. She hugged Tamsin at the same time. "But we all got to say good-night, and we thought we'd take you out to dinner to celebrate."

"I sense we don't have to." Patrick sniffed appreciatively. "What's cooking?"

"I'm showing Molly how to make real Southern fried chicken," Tamsin said.

"She doesn't realize cooking isn't my strong point."

"She'll tumble to the truth any minute now." Patrick offered the unflattering statement as helpful reassurance.

"Grandma, come look at my homework." Hanging from Eliza's arms, Nina pointed toward the living room with her hands and her feet. "But you have to ignore the puppies. Tamsin drew 'em 'cause she doesn't know how school works."

Tamsin snickered as they left the room. "She makes me nuts about school. And Dad expects me to be excited because she is."

"She doesn't go every day yet. That's the difference."

"You chose a career where you go every day."

"I'm paying back," Molly said. "I made a mess of school when I was a kid, but Mom helped me despite the fact that she must have dreaded seeing my face in the doorway. She taught there so it felt natural for me to take her place when she and Dad opened the Dogwood."

Tamsin frowned. "That doesn't sound like Grandma."

"What do you mean?"

"She'd never expect you to take her place at work."

Molly stared at her. "That wasn't what I meant." But it was, in a way.

A sound behind her made her turn, and she discovered her mother standing there, looking both angry and dismayed.

"Tamsin, Molly and I need to talk."

Tamsin looked unsure. "I started something."

Her grandmother smiled with the same gentle reassurance that Molly had known since she was eight. She prayed that smile retained its magic, that it would make Tamsin feel as loved and appreciated.

"Everything's fine, Tamsin," Molly said.

"I'm not a kid."

Eliza dropped an arm around her granddaughter's shoulder. "Give Molly a little break. She had a strange life before she was your age, and she assumes most fifteen-year-olds are even younger than they are, because she was a whole lot older than her years.''

"Mom," Molly said, "Tamsin doesn't need to know."

"I didn't mean to get you in trouble, Molly," Tamsin said.

Molly laughed this time. "I'm not a kid, either."

Tamsin grimaced. "We'll need to talk, too." She yelled for Nina in the passageway.

"Now, what's this about you staying in Bardill's Ridge to pay me back?"

"I didn't say that, Mom. You know I love the kids. I have a great job and a lot more freedom than I'd have in a larger school system."

Eliza's eyes became clouded. "When did you realize you had all this freedom?"

Damn. She'd dealt with Molly's former, not-so-honest bent for too long. "A couple of years ago," Molly said.

"I never asked you to chain yourself to this town."

"Do you have to sound so angry I stayed? I wanted to be close to you and Dad."

"But did you love living here?"

"I'm twenty-five, Mom. Even if I hadn't made so many mistakes, this would still be the time when I'd decide where to live."

"But why didn't you try other places?" Eliza grabbed Molly, reminding her of that other mother, who'd often tried to shake her to her senses.

"Don't, Mom."

Eliza narrowed her eyes. "When are you going to learn your old life is over? Put it behind you. You belong to us now, and you have since you were eight. Your father and I would have fought for you like...like parents, Molly. Like *your* parents, even if Bonnie had tried to take you from us."

Molly stared through her tears, unable to talk and unspeakably grateful at the same time.

"Why did you lock yourself in this town, in my school?"

"Because I was afraid." A truth Molly hadn't even recognized spilled out of her. "If I moved too far away, if I didn't remind you I was here, you might not have loved me anymore. You and Grandpa and Gran and everyone else. Even Zach and Sophie. That's why I stole from the candy rack at the gas station and tossed rocks at fire trucks and slept with strange boys and got pregnant at fifteen. Because I was afraid you wouldn't love me, and I had to find out if you would, no matter what I did."

Eliza fell against the counter. "You've never set a foot wrong since you lost the baby."

"I owe you and Dad for loving me anyway."

"Molly." Her dad said her name in a horrified voice.

She turned. "Dad?" Her first thought was that

he wouldn't love her now that he knew everything about her.

"Why didn't you trust us?" he asked. "Why didn't you just say what you felt?"

She shuddered. "What if I'd made you realize you had no reason to love me?"

"You idiot," he said in unadulterated pain. "You hurt yourself over and over again, and you hurt us, too, because you were afraid we didn't really love you?"

"You knew that." Fresh horror opened in front of her. It wasn't over.

She'd done the same thing to Sam—pushed him away because she didn't believe she was lovable. Her mom and her family had been a handy excuse. Anyone might be shocked if a girl fell in love with the son her mother had given up for adoption, but they weren't the real obstacle. Fear had stopped her from believing in Sam.

She had to find him.

"Molly, are you okay?" her dad asked worriedly, his voice coming to her through a fog.

She looked over his shoulder at the door she should be running through right now. "I know my psychologist told you the same things she said to me. I couldn't believe in myself so I kept testing you."

"She must have put it differently." Her dad wiped sweat off his forehead. "I didn't let myself picture you with those boys who hurt you. I knew you were scared when the cops picked you up, but I didn't understand until this minute what was going on."

"How could I make life harder for a judge?" she asked.

"Don't try to joke." Eliza turned her around, her grip rougher than Molly had ever known it. "You know the truth now? That nothing would ever change the way we feel about you?"

"Am I your daughter, Mom?" Molly looked into Eliza's distinctive eyes. "Since Sam's come?"

"You'll be my baby girl until the day I die. You were my baby at eight when I worried every day that Bonnie would come back for you. You were my baby when you nearly died losing your own child. You're my girl, Molly."

"Our girl." Patrick pulled her from her mom's arms. "You were never anyone else's. So forget that stuff, once and for all. Stop hurting yourself."

"And stop hurting the man who wants nothing more than to love you."

Another voice. Deeper, even thicker with emotion.

Molly rubbed tears from her face and eyed her mother with panic. Patrick pulled her behind him.

"Sam, she's not ready."

Eleven years of relatively good mental health helped bring Molly to her senses. She stepped out from behind her father, reclaiming her independence. "I'm not a kid." She laughed, and her mom looked worried. "It's all right," Molly said. "I just reminded myself of Tamsin."

"We have to talk." Sam had no time for a family chat. "Now. Alone."

"I agree." Molly nodded. Her parents turned to her in one movement, and she gathered them close. "Maybe I'll always be a little bit of the abandoned Molly," she said, "but I needed to hear I still mean as much to you."

"How could you doubt us?" Eliza's affronted tone pushed Molly's insecurities further into the past, where they belonged.

"Mother," Sam said, "can I talk to Molly now?"

"Sure, son."

Molly stared at them. Mother? Son?

Sam hugged Eliza, love gentling his face. Happiness shot through Molly, all the way to the tips of her fingers and toes and even the ends of her hair. He deserved love after the grief he'd known. After being a consolation son, he deserved a mom whose gift was unstinting love.

"Eliza," her dad said, "why don't we give these two some privacy?"

"Thanks." Sam relinquished his mother, but he watched Patrick help her from the room before he looked at Molly. "Is she all right?"

"She's emotional."

"That's unusual around here."

Molly laughed through tears that continued to cloud her vision of him. "So you heard everything?"

"The part where you're afraid of people not loving you enough. That pertains to me."

She nodded. "I guess."

"I'm not a guy who gives up. I'll love you forever."

She shivered, wanting to believe. "I'm not brave. Do you know how long forever lasts, Sam?"

He frowned, a hint of old pain in his eyes. "Sometimes it's short, but I choose to believe in a long rest-of-our-lives."

"What about those babies you wanted?"

He swallowed. His throat worked, and she remembered how his skin felt against her mouth. She needed him in that moment as she'd never needed anyone else in her life. A sharp need that cut through pain and fear and loneliness. It even made her daring.

"Sam, we were both adopted."

He curved his mouth. "I wanted to give you that gift. Fiona was never supposed to have children. Medicine is my business, but she got pregnant without my consent twice before I convinced her I'd divorce her to save her life."

Molly couldn't hide horrified surprise that seemed to please Sam.

"At least I know you won't be dishonest," he

said, "but I didn't tell you for shock value. I always expected to adopt, and I will with you if you want children."

"I'm hoping Tamsin and Nina will be mine, too."

He started toward her, but three quick steps of her own took her into his arms. She clung to his muscled shoulders. This man, real and warm, loving and true, belonged to her. "I have the right to hold you."

"You're crazy, Molly. I've got a marriage proposal going in my head, and you sound grateful to put your arms around me."

"You're mine—the man I love, the man who loves me. Do people feel like this all the time, Sam?"

"You can." He kissed her, cradling her head, and she knew she was precious to him.

Opening her eyes, she held his hands. "Sam, I love you."

"I guessed," he said against her mouth.

"I won't come to you under false pretenses. I'll probably get scared again."

"I'm afraid, too." Their eyes met, serious and intense. "I am older. Maybe I look steady and settled to you, but after you realize you can trust me, you may find trusting someone your own age is more attractive."

"When I was eight years old, I lived alone in a derelict house and begged for food when I felt too guilty to steal it. Do you think I haven't felt a lot older than forty since then?''

He tightened his arms as if to squeeze those memories out of her. His mouth, pressed to her forehead, communicated terrible fear, as if he saw those terrifying nights in his love for her.

"No," she said. "I'm not trying to shock you, either. I just want to make you understand we're the right age for each other. That won't ever be an issue.''

He nodded, his head resting against hers. "Okay." He kissed her again. "You're tired of being afraid, but what happens when something bad comes up?''

With his lips against hers, she hardly managed to focus on the present, much less anticipate a future that looked unimaginably rosy. Unimaginable before today, anyway.

"Something always comes up. That's life, but I am strong. I survived all those years ago. I wouldn't consider being with you if I didn't believe I could keep my promises. We just have to make sure Tamsin and Nina can live with me."

"That's not a problem." He edged her against the wall, cornering her with lust and love inextricably mixed in his gaze. "But let them wait a few minutes. I need to be with you. Then we'll talk to the girls.''

His seeking hands brushed the undersides of her breasts as he kissed her eyes, her cheeks, her throat. Her overworked sense of responsibility deserted her. She bent her head beneath his onslaught.

"Do you want to marry me, Sam?"

His laughter tickled her throat. "Aren't we talking marriage?"

"Let's make it soon."

"I'm ready now." He lifted his head. "You're not afraid you'll change your mind?"

"Nights look too long without you between now and a wedding day."

"Oh, that. Forget about it. I can't wait." He took her mouth, seducing her with his, making promises, making love. "We'll find a way to be together."

## EPILOGUE

"Wait—I'm supposed to walk in front of you, Molly. Bridesmaids first." Tamsin muscled past her, a delicate young woman in peach silk, nestling her own bouquet in the crook of her elbow.

Clutching her father's arm, Molly could only stare at her new daughter, who was heartstoppingly beautiful. The peach gown added veins of rich mahogany to her dark hair. Tamsin, vulnerable and happy, stunned Molly into maternal tears of tenderness.

But then something made Tamsin laugh, and she snorted, nearly doubling over. And Molly had to laugh, too, at her new-mom's vision of a girl who was just normal and human and adolescent. Glancing beyond Tamsin for the cause of her most unladylike snort, Molly spied Nina, shoving Evan out of her way to better nail people with rose petals she plucked out of her basket.

"Oh, no."

"Don't worry. Your mother and I checked for thorns," Patrick said. "We didn't find even one."

"Those three will have each other in headlocks before they get to the end of the aisle."

Lily, protecting her brother, pushed Nina away from him and then paused to fling a handful of rose petals, as per her duties. Snickers echoed in the church, and Tamsin turned back, giggling.

"This is more fun than I expected."

"Promise you'll sit on them if they start throwing punches," Molly said.

Before Tamsin could answer, "Here Comes the Bride" cued them.

"Our turn." Patrick examined them both. "Ready, Tamsin?"

With a nod, she stepped out on her left foot. At a muffled flurry from in front of the altar, her shoulders started shaking again. Molly avoided looking at her in case the giggling proved infectious.

If Nina and Lily and Evan started a riot, let the nearest adults sort them out. What else was a big family for?

Together, Molly and her father passed family and friends, including several of Sam's grateful new patients. All beamed indulgent smiles that probably meant the front of the church was a wrestling match.

They reached Zach and found Evan on his shoulder, his small face red, his eyes looking for the rest of the fight his father had interrupted. Beyond him, Olivia balanced Lily on the other side of her heavily pregnant belly. Due to pop at any moment, she'd insisted on attending, telling Sam and Molly it'd be their own fault if she delivered midservice because they'd waited until he and the girls could move.

Zach shook his head in apology for his children's part in the brawl, but something about his humiliation undid Tamsin. She exploded in a laugh that rang from rafter to rafter. All the guests joined her, including Molly, who couldn't wait to see the fight on tape later.

When Tamsin stepped aside at the head of the aisle, Molly glimpsed Nina on Sam's other side, wedged between him and his best man, Grandpa.

One rose petal protruded from Nina's braid, apparently loosened in the battle. Another petal was plastered to her sweat-moistened throat. Sam's top lip was inside his bottom one as he tried to look disapproving. Molly gladly handed her flowers to Tamsin and took his hand.

"Not yet." The minister, already exhausted by the Calvert wedding, pulled them apart.

Everyone laughed again, nervousness overwhelming solemnity.

"Daddy," Nina said, in a thunderous whisper, "I didn't start—"

Interrupting her, the minister began the service, serenely ignoring the almost uncontrollable laughter around him. Molly dared not look at anyone's faces.

"Who gives this man to this woman?"

Patrick offered her hand to Sam. "Her mother and I do." He leaned across their linked fingers to kiss Molly's cheek. "But we don't give you up easily," he said.

As quick as that, her laughter turned to tears.

"Why is Molly crying, Daddy?"

"Nina," Molly's mom said from behind her, "come sit with me."

Nina stomped across the marble. Tamsin squeaked and buried her face in both bouquets. Sam looked as if he wanted to sink into the floor, and the minister went on as if it were all normal.

Just as he reached Molly's "I take thee" part, a rustling sounded behind them.

"Oh, no." Olivia raised another echo. "Oh—sorry, Reverend."

"No problem."

"A little one," she said, and Sam and Molly turned together. "My water just broke."

Sophie immediately handed Chloe to Ian. "Go on, Reverend. I've got this covered. Delivering unexpectedly is a family tradition." She beamed at Ian, who'd brought Chloe into the world on the edge of a tornado.

"Will you stop making eyes at your husband and see what's going on here?" Olivia, naturally rattled, smiled another uncertain apology at the minister. "Sorry."

He eyed Molly and Sam. "Should we—"

"Gran, you can help if you want," Sophie said. "But don't let us disturb you all up there. Go on."

"I'm not in the biz anymore." Gran remained in her seat, pausing only to offer Grandpa a virtuous smile. "You'll be fine with Sophie, Olivia."

Seth cheered improperly, but he seemed prone to happy outbursts these days. "Get on with the wedding, Reverend. Looks like some christening business might come your way today, too."

Reverend Milford consulted Sam and Molly again. "Do you want to—"

"Big girl—Aunt Molly, I mean—is Aunt Olivia gonna get her baby now?"

"I give up," Sam said as his younger daughter's whisper shook the candles out of their holders and his older girl turned away as if she couldn't be enjoying this wedding more inappropriately.

Sam caught Molly's face in his hands, and she hugged him tightly. "I pronounce us man and wife," he said. "You don't get more man and wife and crazy family than this."

He lowered his mouth to hers, and Molly lost track of everyone except Sam. Her world began with him, and in his arms she'd learned to indulge in the joy of life finding its own unexpected, love-filled pace.

# HARLEQUIN *Super*ROMANCE®

## Ordinary people.
## Extraordinary circumstances.

CODE **RED**

**Meet the dedicated emergency service workers of Courage Bay, California. They're always ready to answer the call.**

*Father by Choice*
by M.J. Rodgers
(Harlequin Superromance
#1194 April 2004)

*Silent Witness*
by Kay David
(Harlequin Superromance
#1200 May 2004)

*The Unknown Twin*
by Kathryn Shay
(Harlequin Superromance
#1206 June 2004)

**And be sure to watch for *Heatwave*,
a Code Red single title anthology coming in July 2004.**

*Available wherever Harlequin Books are sold.*

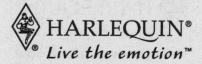

# HARLEQUIN®
## *Live the emotion*™

**Visit us at www.eHarlequin.com**

HSRCODER

# A CENTURY OF *American* DREAMS

Enjoy these uplifting
novels that explore the hopes
and dreams of changing relationships
in America over the twentieth century....

## A CENTURY OF AMERICAN DREAMS

### Written by three *USA TODAY* bestselling authors...

ANGELS WINGS
by Anne Stuart

SENTIMENTAL
JOURNEY
by Barbara Bretton

STRANGER
IN PARADISE
by Barbara Bretton

HEARTS AT RISK
by Laurie Paige

*Coming in April 2004.*

# HARLEQUIN®
*Live the emotion*™

**Visit us at www.eHarlequin.com**

RCAD2

# HARLEQUIN *Super* ROMANCE®

## What if you discovered that all you ever wanted were the things you left behind?

**GOING BACK**

### John Riley's Girl
### by Inglath Cooper
### (Superromance #1198)
### On-sale April 2004

Olivia Ashford thought she had put her hometown and John Riley behind her. But an invitation to her fifteen-year high school reunion made her realize that she needs to go back to Summerville and lay some old ghosts to rest. After leaving John without a word so many years ago, would Olivia have the courage to face him again, if only to say goodbye?

## Return to Little Hills by Janice Macdonald
### (Superromance #1201) On-sale May 2004

Edie Robinson's relationship with her mother is a precarious one. Maude is feisty and independent, and not inclined to make life easy for her daughter even though Edie's come home to help out. Edie can't wait to leave the town she'd fled years ago. But slowly a new understanding between mother and daughter begins to develop. Then Edie meets widower Peter Darling who's specifically moved to Little Hills to give his four young daughters the security of a small-town childhood. Suddenly, Edie's seeing her home through new eyes.

*Available wherever Harlequin Books are sold.*

**Visit us at www.eHarlequin.com**

HSRGBCM

# eHARLEQUIN.com

Looking for today's most popular
books at great prices?
At www.eHarlequin.com, we offer:

- An **extensive selection** of romance
  books by top authors!

- **New** releases, Themed Collections
  and hard-to-find **backlist.**

- A sneak peek at Upcoming books.

- Enticing book **excerpts** and **back
  cover copy!**

- Read recommendations from other
  readers (and post your own)!

- Find out what everybody's reading
  in **Bestsellers.**

- **Save BIG** with everyday discounts
  and exclusive online offers!

- Easy, convenient **24-hour shopping.**

- Our **Romance Legend** will help select
  reading that's *exactly* right for you!

**Your purchases are 100%
guaranteed—so shop online
at www.eHarlequin.com today!**

INTBB1

# HARLEQUIN® *Super*ROMANCE®

## Nothing Sacred
### by Tara Taylor Quinn

Shelter Valley Stories

Welcome back to Shelter Valley, Arizona. This is the kind of town everyone dreams about, the kind of place everyone wants to live. Meet your friends from previous visits—including Martha Moore, divorced mother of teenagers. And meet the new minister, David Cole Marks.

Martha's still burdened by the bitterness of a husband's betrayal. And there are secrets hidden in David's past.

Can they find in each other the shelter they seek? The happiness?

By the author of *Where the Road Ends*, *Born in the Valley* and *For the Children*.

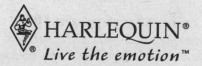

# HARLEQUIN®
*Live the emotion*™

Visit us at www.eHarlequin.com

HSRNSTTQ

## For a Baby
### by C.J. Carmichael
**(Superromance #1203)**

**On-sale May 2004**

Heather Sweeney wants to have a baby. Unfortunately, she's in love with a married man, so that's never going to happen. Then one lonely night, she turns to T. J. Collins—who always seems to stand by her when her life is at its lowest point—and a few weeks later, discovers that she's about to get her greatest wish, but with the wrong man.

## The New Baby by Brenda Mott
**(Superromance #1211) On-sale June 2004**

Amanda Kelly has made two vows to herself. She will never get involved with a man again. She will never get pregnant again. But when she finds out that Ian Bonner has lost a child, too, Amanda soon finds that the protective barrier around her heart is crumbling....

## The Toy Box by K.N. Casper
**(Superromance #1213) On-sale July 2004**

After the death of an agent, helicopter pilot Gabe Engler is sent to Tombstone, Arizona, to investigate the customs station being run by his ex-wife, Jill Manning. Gabe hasn't seen Jill since they lost their six-week-old child and their marriage fell apart. Now Gabe's hoping for a second chance. He wants Jill back—and maybe a reason to finish building the toy box he'd put away seven years ago.

*Available wherever Harlequin books are sold.*

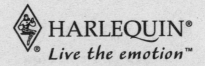

**Visit us at www.eHarlequin.com**

HSR9MLMJJ